Ashley Goldberg is an Australian writer based in Melbourne. His fiction has appeared in *New Australian Fiction 2021*, *Meanjin*, *Chiron Review*, *The Honest Ulsterman* and *Award Winning Australian Writing* among other publications. Ashley has an MA in Creative Writing from Bath Spa University and a Graduate Diploma of Professional Writing from Canberra University. His work has been shortlisted, longlisted, and anthologised in numerous competitions worldwide, including the 2017/18 Galley Beggar Press Short Story Prize and the Commonwealth Short Story Prize. In 2019, Ashley was a fellow at the Katharine Susannah Prichard Writers' Centre and a finalist for the Tasmanian Writers' Prize. *Abomination* was shortlisted for the 2020 Kill Your Darlings Unpublished Manuscript Award.

ABOMINATION

ASHLEY GOLDBERG

VINTAGE BOOKS
Australia

VINTAGE

UK | USA | Canada | Ireland | Australia
India | New Zealand | South Africa | China

Vintage is part of the Penguin Random House group of companies
whose addresses can be found at global.penguinrandomhouse.com

First published by Vintage in 2022

Cover illustrations by Ktoytor/Getty Images and Wilqkuku/Shutterstock
Cover design by Alex Ross © Penguin Random House Australia Pty Ltd
Typeset in 12.25/16.5 pt Minion Pro by Midland Typesetters, Australia

Printed and bound in Australia by Griffin Press, part of Ovato, an accredited
ISO AS/NZS 14001 Environmental Management Systems printer

A catalogue record for this book is available from the National Library of Australia

ISBN 978 1 76104 177 8

penguin.com.au

We at Penguin Random House Australia acknowledge that Aboriginal and Torres Strait Islander peoples are the Traditional Custodians and the first storytellers of the lands on which we live and work. We honour Aboriginal and Torres Strait Islander peoples' continuous connection to Country, waters, skies and communities. We celebrate Aboriginal and Torres Strait Islander stories, traditions and living cultures; and we pay our respects to Elders past and present.

For Vlad

'He who turns his ear away from hearing the Torah – even his prayer is an abomination.'

– Proverbs 28:9

Chapter 1

Ezra

Good Pho You, that's where Tegan told Ezra to meet her.

She was on her way after having visited her parents in Eltham. Her message read: *Kitsch decor, line out the door, best pho in town xx.*

Ezra turned onto Swanston Street, on his way to Chinatown. It was nearly eight o'clock and the sun was a dull glow on the edge of the horizon. His pace was slow, steps languid. He'd left their Carlton apartment twenty minutes earlier than he'd needed to, but he was too anxious to keep lying there in the dark, wishing he was someone else. There was a dull ache at the back of his head, and his stomach swam with nausea.

As he passed the entrance to Melbourne University and the modernist building he'd once had lectures in, two girls in denim shorts and tube tops overtook him. His gaze flicked to their naked shoulders, the bronze skin below their frayed cuffs. He shook his head and cursed himself. Why didn't he have a modicum of self-control?

He thought about the night before. Strobe lights and music loud enough to goosebump skin – Nineties Night.

He'd had three pints at Garden State after work with Baz and the grad, Danny. Then Baz's elderly mother was calling him, and Danny said he had mates to meet in Fitzroy – invited Ezra along, but he knew the kid was only being polite.

Walking to the tram, Ezra had seen the queue down Meyers Place and the posters outside a newsagent – pastel pinks, yellows and blues like a Fresh Prince tracksuit, white bubble writing around a cassette tape and a list of artists – Britney Spears, Backstreet Boys, Blink-182, Green Day, Boyzone, Spice Girls, New Kids on the Block, S Club 7. He checked his phone, nothing from Tegan yet. The queue was mostly men, all with short hair, in too-tight, coloured shirts with their sleeves rolled up to the elbow. But dotted throughout the line were a couple of girls in high heels, wearing short dresses and sparkly, low-cut tops stuck to their breasts by what Ezra imagined was double-sided tape. He still felt good and light from the beer, and it seemed a shame to turn in early on that feeling, so he doubled back on the line. A short brunette in a black and white striped dress smiled at him as he walked past, and that was all the encouragement he needed.

He didn't catch her name – Mary, Madeleine, Maxine. His throat hurt from shouting. What had they spoken about? What had he told her? It didn't matter, she was faceless now, but the warmth of her lower back still tingled on his fingertips. He remembered feeling as though he was falling into the curve of her neck, blissfully tumbling into darkness. He could've stayed there forever, but then a sudden and distinct sadness was on him and his chest was concrete. It took everything he had not to drop to the sticky dance floor and curl into a ball. He told her he had to use the bathroom, headed straight for the exit, didn't turn to see if she was watching, didn't care.

Fuck.

He turned down Little Bourke; his teeth chattering, though it was a twenty-five-degree evening in late February, and he could smell the damp under his shirt. He tucked his hands into his pockets to stop their shaking, but it was as though his insides were vibrating. He felt the washing-machine churn of them and was nearly sick. Only adrenaline, he told himself. 'Cause you're a guilt-ridden piece of shit.

He arrived early, as he'd expected. Kitsch might have been an understatement. Multi-coloured lanterns hung from the ceiling. The tables were made of bright green plastic and surrounded by red and blue stools. On the walls were hand drawings of a woman riding a moped, her hair trailing in the wind beneath a conical hat, a boat with ruffled orange sails and a giant *bánh mì*, shredded pork spilling out its middle. He gave Tegan's name at the door and followed a waitress inside. She directed him to the back of the restaurant where a table for two had been wedged beside a wall a few metres from the toilets. There were plenty of other tables available. Tegan would've asserted herself, asked to be seated elsewhere, but he was feeling meek, queasy and flushed.

After filling his glass with water, Ezra picked up the laminated menu, but his sight blurred and he felt as though there was a propeller in his chest. God damn hangover. He raised his glass to his mouth and water lapped over the lip, spilled onto the table. From the nearby kitchen came a chorus of clanging pans and loud voices. It was too much, all of it. Ezra lowered his forehead onto the greasy table, closed his eyes and covered his ears.

He had to end it. Two years was enough time to know. Obviously, he didn't love Tegan, and a part of him was acting out, time and time again. It would be for the best. She was too good for him, deserved better.

'I'm sorry,' he'd say. 'I'm not happy.'

She'd cry then, or get angry – throw hot tea in his face.

It was going to be difficult, but it was the right thing to do.

They'd met at a bar in Fitzroy. Tegan was sitting in a booth with a friend – auburn hair, big smile, lagoon eyes. She was the one he'd approached first, not Tegan. 'This seat taken?' he'd asked.

'Actually,' she said, glancing over at Tegan, 'I need to go to the bathroom, but mind my seat, keep my friend company?'

Tegan had a blunt dark fringe, glasses and small frowning lips. She was picking at her beer's label, dropping torn pieces into its open mouth.

'No worries,' he said.

Tegan had been having a shitty time, having recently broken up with a boyfriend she'd loved for reasons she didn't herself understand. He was a thirty-five-year-old musician who owed her five thousand dollars and kept his mattress on his bedroom floor. When the two of them flipped it over one day, they found the bottom side half-rotten with mould. Of course, Ezra didn't know any of that at the time.

'She has a boyfriend,' Tegan said as he sat down.

'Sorry?'

'My mate, she's got – a – boy – friend. Comprende?'

'Ah – okay. And you?'

'Me?' She looked up at him for the first time. Her eyes were a kind of dull grey, and Ezra couldn't tell if she was sad, or if eyes that colour always looked that way. 'Nah.' She refocused on her beer.

'Right, so – could I get you another label to destroy?'

She took her hands off the bottle, turned back to Ezra and

rolled her eyes. 'Please don't give me some shitty line about sexual frustration.'

'Wasn't planning on it,' Ezra said, sliding out of his seat. 'Was just headed to the bar.'

'All right,' she said. 'Get me the biggest label they've got.'

He hadn't intended to buy her a drink, having figured she was too terse for him. But the line at the bar was long and from the back of it he could still see Tegan in the booth.

Without him to fend off, her hands were quiet, features settled. It wasn't a serendipitously placed light that compelled him to buy her a longneck and sit back down. If anything, it was the opposite – a kind of absence surrounded her, a vacuum amid all that noise of booze and bodies. A loneliness, or at least Ezra chose to see it that way, because for as long as he could remember he'd felt as though there was something lacking in him, a puzzle piece that had fallen between the couch cushions, and he thought that perhaps Tegan, better than anyone, might understand that feeling.

Five hours later, and they were back at his share house where Tegan revealed curves that fit perfectly into his palms and a penchant for biting his chest. They'd fucked until his bed frame scratched the floorboards, till his housemates had to text him to keep it down, till dehydration. They continued like that for days, weeks – fucking like they hated each other. A visceral, desperate and raw grasping and clawing of one another as though their lives depended on them coming often and together.

And then, one day, something changed and Tegan asked Ezra to go slowly, while on top, and when he finished she shuddered, placed her hands on his back and whispered while he was still inside of her, 'I think I'm falling for you, Ezra Steinberg.'

Their relationship had been predicated on sex – maybe that's all it should have ever been? They'd tried to make it more than that, but it hadn't worked out. His feelings had never escalated like Tegan's. But they'd both had a nice time. They could reflect on that. Their lives weren't worse for having had each other in them.

A cool breeze swept through the restaurant. Ezra rolled back his shoulders, cracked his neck and took another drink of water. The thudding in his chest lessened, and he wasn't as bothered by the chaotic kitchen clanks. It was the right thing to do. He was resolute now.

His phone vibrated in his pocket.

running late, trams, sorry xx.

That was fine. It'd give him more time to prepare. A waitress came over, and he ordered a Saigon beer. 'It's not something I can put my finger on,' he practised saying the words to himself, 'it's a feeling. Sometimes you just know.'

His phone vibrated again. He assumed it was Tegan telling him to order for her, and it occurred to him that he should hold off on food, get it over and done with. But it wasn't Tegan, rather a Facebook notification of an event invitation.

BRING HIRSCH TO JUSTICE

Ezra tapped on the link. It was for a rally at Parliament House. He scrolled down.

> On Tuesday the 12th of March 2019, the Israeli Minister of Justice will be visiting the Victorian State Parliament as part of an official delegation. Disgracefully, the Israeli Government has let Rabbi Joel Hirsch, paedophile and predator, live as a free man for almost twenty years, ignoring the Australian Government's request for his extradition. Hirsch, who is wanted for numerous counts

of sexual abuse of boys at the Yahel Academy school, fled the country in 1999 and has successfully avoided justice since by feigning mental illness. Join us in pressuring the Israeli Justice Minister to extradite this monster so that his victims and their families can see him brought to justice once and for all.

'Saigon beer.'

Ezra jolted upright, knocking over his water. 'Shit.' He stood up, dabbed at the spill with some serviettes.

The waitress smiled patiently.

'Sorry.' Ezra sat back down.

The waitress placed the beer in front of him, picked up the clump of wet serviettes and left.

Ezra focused on his breathing, took a sip of beer. Rabbi Hirsch. He hadn't thought about him in years.

*

There had been rumblings on the quadrangle at recess, an undercurrent that something wasn't right; known, the way some things always are by school children. Moishe was the first to be pulled out of class, after lunch, during *Chumash*. But he had special needs, and it wasn't unusual for him and his minder to leave in the middle of a lesson. Fifteen minutes later, the Feldman twins' older brother arrived, asking for them to be excused, and five minutes after that Mrs Shulman's knuckles rapped on the classroom door, and as she escorted her son, Levi, from the room, Rabbi Horowitz's forehead bunched up the way it did when he was struggling to remember an obscure piece of Talmudic commentary.

Ezra turned to Yonatan, who gave him a bemused look and shrugged.

They both looked up, startled by the click-buzz of the loudspeaker nestled in the corner of their classroom ceiling, next to the *tav* of the Hebrew alphabet banner pinned above the blackboard. In the context of their twelve-year-old lives, that speaker boomed with the same baritone and authority as the voice of God.

'ATTENTION STUDENTS. AFTERNOON CLASSES HAVE BEEN CANCELLED. PLEASE EXIT THE SCHOOL IN AN ORDERLY FASHION. YOUR PARENTS AND GUARDIANS HAVE BEEN NOTIFIED. I REPEAT, AFTERNOON CLASSES HAVE BEEN CANCELLED. PLEASE EXIT –'

Birdsong, a car horn, a pencil hitting the floor. For a moment, it was as though the entire school was holding its breath. Then it exhaled – books slapped shut, chair legs screeched against linoleum and the thrum of chattering boys, giddy at the prospect of a half-day, drowned out their teachers' protests.

Outside, by the security gate, school bags looped over their shoulders, Ezra and Yonatan stood facing one another as students streamed by either side of them and into the street.

'What do you think's going on?' Ezra asked.

'Dunno,' Yonatan said.

'Bomb threat?' Ezra smiled, unable to hide his excitement at the thought of something of that scale happening to them.

Yonatan shook his head. His *kippah* slipped from his nest of bushy red hair, but he caught it before it could hit the ground. 'They would've moved us away from the school.'

Ezra followed his gaze to the school entrance where the prep kids remained, flanked by their teachers – arms crossed, frowning at the line of four-wheel-drives that snaked back past the gate and down the road. Could've been an attack in

Israel, Ezra thought. They might cancel school for that. A lot of students had family over there – he was pretty sure Yonatan did. Or maybe it was something bigger, more fundamental and local. At school assemblies they sang the Israeli national anthem first, Australian second. You are *Jewish Australians*, not *Australian Jews* – the message came daily. Ask your grandparents, look it up, it happened once, it could happen again. This is your community, where you belong, where you're safe.

Ezra scanned the road for dark cars with tinted windows, imagining the clap of well-shined black boots, tan uniforms, red armbands. Yonatan's fingers twirled around one of the long, curly *peyot* that hung on either side of his head. It was something he did when he was concentrating, or nervous. Ezra opened his mouth to speculate some more, when a familiar silhouette rounded the gate and quick-stepped towards them. Tall and slim, she was wearing a long-sleeved purple jumper and a black skirt that swept by her ankles. A straight-haired, dark-brown *sheitel* sat atop her head, covering what Ezra knew were curls the same red as her son's. Her lips were pursed tight, brow lumped.

As her shadow encroached on them, Yonatan turned. '*Ima*?'

Without warning, she rushed forward, knocking Ezra aside, and pressed her son's cheek tightly against her chest. Ezra didn't know where to look.

'What's going on?' Yonatan asked, edging out of her grasp.

'*Anachnu holchim habaiyita*,' Yonatan's mum said, grabbing his hand and turning to leave.

'Hello, Mrs Kaplan,' Ezra said.

'Oh.' She stopped and looked Ezra up and down. 'Hello, Ezra,' she said, shifting her focus to the line of cars. 'Is your mother on her way?'

Ezra shrugged. 'Not sure. I normally walk home, it's not far.'

She frowned and made a sound that reminded him of a vacuum cleaner. 'Okay, Ezra, get home quickly.' And then she tugged on her son's arm, telling him, in Hebrew, to hurry up.

'See ya,' Ezra said.

Yonatan waved over his shoulder, and then his mother pulled him around the gate's iron bars and out of sight.

On a normal school day, by the time Ezra reached his house in North Caulfield, he had less than an hour to himself until his mum got home from work, followed by his dad an hour or two later. But as the echo of the front door closing sounded throughout his empty house, Ezra smiled to himself, estimating that he had over two hours to luxuriate in. He headed straight for the computer.

Their boxy desktop sat on the second floor, in the corner of the landing that separated his room from his parents'. He wasn't allowed to use the Internet without permission, but sometimes, when his parents were downstairs watching the footy or a movie, he'd muffle the grind and squawk of the modem with a towel and prick up his ears for the sound of feet on the stairs – ready to press the power button, dive into his bedroom, deny everything.

But none of that was necessary now. The desktop hummed to life and Windows greeted him with its chime. While waiting for the modem to connect, he stripped off his uniform. Never truly feeling at home until he was free of it, Ezra flung each piece of clothing into the doorway of his bedroom till he was bare but for his socks and underwear.

When his parents were home, Ezra normally used the Internet under the pretext of looking up cheat codes for PlayStation games. And he did do that, but for the most part when he went online it was to go on mIRC.

Yonatan didn't have the Internet at his place – being *frum*, his family tended to avoid emerging technologies but, somehow, he still knew about the chat program before Ezra did.

At school, there had been increased chatter about the girls from Beth Chana down the road – Hannah Zeigler, Rebekah Breuer, Shlomit Zandberg. Something was happening after school, it sounded like the boys and girls were getting together and, whatever they were doing, Ezra wasn't invited.

Eventually, after weeks of sleuthing on the outskirts of conversations, his stomach sinking at the collective smiles and laughter of boys he'd considered friends, Ezra asked Yonatan if he knew what was going on, trying to seem casual, apathetic, cool.

'They're on mIRC,' Yonatan replied.

'What?' Ezra said.

'It's a chat program – on the Internet. I thought you'd have it already.'

That bugged Ezra. Things came easy to Yonatan. People were drawn to his amiable, easy-going demeanour. Teachers deferred to him in class, boys sought the desks near his and asked about his after-Shabbos weekend plans, while Ezra wasn't *frum* enough for the *frummers* nor a part of any of the more secular cliques. He didn't quite know why but by Yonatan's side seemed to be the only place he fitted in.

One day, at Glick's bakery after school, Ezra noticed two Beth Chana girls smiling at Yonatan's profile as he decided between a jam and a custard donut. They were a couple of years older than them – blue and white chequered dresses pressed outwards by burgeoning breasts. They caught Ezra staring and turned away. Yonatan chose jam and offered Ezra half, but he told him he didn't like jam and would've preferred custard.

The chat room, #YBBCG – Yahel Boys Beth Chana Girls – was almost empty. Two dozen users at best. Normally, Ezra had to scroll down the list, scrutinising the usernames to find his classmates. His was $t3inb3rg.

The first couple of times he went on mIRC he logged on as Ezra86. But there were two other Ezras in his year at Yahel, both more outgoing and athletic than him, and private chat windows flooded his screen –

SaRaXO88: Ezra!!!

Dovirules: how u Ez?

ShaZk87: hey wch 1 r u?

ShaZk87 could only be Shani Kestenberg – blonde hair, blue eyes, nub of a nose, teeth that would never need braces and skin like a Disney princess. It was rumoured that her parents were pretending to be Jewish because Beth Chana had a good reputation, that she was a *shiksa*, a *yok*, a *goy*, forbidden. And so it went without saying that she was the most popular girl in her year.

Ezra86: hey how r u? It's Steinberg.

ShaZk87 has left #YBBCG.

The next time Ezra went online, he logged on as $t3inb3rg, and no-one initiated a conversation with him. Still, Ezra returned to the chat room, again and again. After deciphering most of the usernames, he liked to watch them pop on and off screen and guess who had been talking to who. He imagined someone else doing the same, seeing him log off within seconds of ShaZk87 and then eagerly spreading gossip that there was something going on between the two of them.

But on this occasion, Ezra didn't even have the time to search for her name because someone started a chat with him – KamilToe69.

KamilToe69 was David Kamil. Taller than some grown men, he played footy for the Ajax under-15s on the weekends and boasted dark patches of hair under his armpits. Though they rarely spoke, Ezra gave David Kamil a wide berth in the corridors and on the playground, because his dark brown eyes always seemed to seek him out and linger with what felt to Ezra like some kind of ill intent.

KamilToe69: Was it u?

Was what? Ezra's throat tightened. Someone must've dobbed Kamil in for something and he was looking for the culprit. Why would Kamil think it was Ezra? Ezra wiped his hands on his bare legs, about to reply, when Kamil wrote again.

KamilToe69: Was it u Steinberg?

His pulse thumped in his ears.

$t3inb3rg: Was it me what?

KamilToe69: Hirsch

KamilToe69: did he touch you?

KamilToe69: did he fuck you?

The words were definitely there. Consonants, vowels, syllables. But Ezra couldn't make anything out of them because there was a familiar sound in his ears and, for some reason, an alarm going off in his mind – *keys*. That's what it was. Keys turning in the lock of the front door, squeaking hinges and his mum's voice calling his name.

Still half-naked, Ezra slammed his finger into the computer's power button, flung himself off his seat and scooped up his clothes, desperately pulling the wrong pant leg on and then off as he pictured his mum's footsteps on the stairs. Shirt untucked, half the buttons undone, he hurried onto his bed, having barely grabbed a book from his bedside table, as his mum's head popped around his bedroom door.

'There you are.' Her face was flushed, and her normally plaited hair had swallowed her head in a frazzled poof.

'Hi, Mum.' He made an effort to speak slowly, hoping she wouldn't notice he was out of breath. 'We got let out of school early.'

'I know. The school called.' She smiled, but it was the small, forced one she used when she was tired. 'So Dad'll be home soon, and I thought maybe we'd order pizza. What do you think?'

That was odd. They never had takeaway during the week, but he wasn't about to turn down pizza. 'Sounds great,' he said, returning her smile.

'All right, hon.' She closed her eyes, inhaled, and then exhaled slowly before opening them. 'I'm going to have a lie down for a bit, but I'll let you know when Dad's on his way.'

Ezra nodded and, taking her cue, brought the book back up to his eyeline. It was only once she left that he caught sight of the computer screen in the landing, glowing white – the cursor blinking silently in an empty box below the words *fuck you?*.

Two hours later, Ezra's dad was home, early for him, and his mum uncharacteristically ordered a meal deal that included two large pizzas, garlic bread and a bottle of Coke.

Something was up. Four slices in, Ezra pushed his plate aside, washed down a half-masticated glob with a long, fizzy swig of Coke and watched his parents pick at the pieces on their plates.

'Am I in trouble?' Ezra asked.

His parents glanced at each other, as though coming to some kind of unspoken agreement, and then his dad placed his elbows on the table and leant forward. 'Okay, son,' he said, clasping his fingers together in a way that made Ezra nervous. 'Do you know why school was cancelled today?'

Ezra shook his head.

'There was a teacher,' his dad began, but then he bit his teeth over his lower lip and sat back up.

His mum looked to his dad and took up where he left off. 'Rabbi Hirsch,' she said. 'Were you ever . . . did he ever –'

His dad interrupted. 'Talk to you – alone?'

'Talk', his dad had said. But David Kamil's words were etched into his.

'Talk' meant *touched*.

'Talk' meant *fucked*.

Something about the look in his parents' eyes made him feel guilty, embarrassed and reluctant to speak. He shook his head again. It was the truth. There was never a chance for him to be alone with Rabbi Hirsch. He'd never even had a class with him, not in all of his years at the school, but Yonatan had. Two years earlier, Rabbi Hirsch had been the *madrich* for his grade five class.

The next day was a Friday. Yahel remained closed as the school administration dealt with the fallout from the news. Ezra tried to call Yonatan, only to keep getting a busy signal. But he wasn't surprised – Yonatan's family often took their phone off the hook as Shabbat neared.

Ezra's mum called in sick to work and took him to the Blockbuster Video on Hawthorn Road, intent on keeping him occupied with rented PlayStation games. Still, he managed a few surreptitious connections to the Internet throughout the day and was able to piece together what was going on from news sites and a handful of brief mIRC conversations.

Apparently, allegations of sexual abuse had been made by a student against Rabbi Hirsch earlier in the week but, unimpressed by the responsiveness of the police, the student's family sought the attention of the media. Once the story broke, school officials acted fast, cancelling classes and announcing Rabbi Hirsch's immediate termination. Rumour had it, though, that Hirsch was connected – an upstanding and well-respected member of the community – so while some officials were working tirelessly to assure parents of their children's safety, others harboured the *frum* fugitive and arranged for him to board an Israel-bound El Al flight before the police could charge him for the alleged abuse. Needless to say, parents were outraged by his fleeing and had already begun to petition the Australian Government for his extradition.

Those were the details covered by the news. From the chat rooms Ezra learned that the complainant had been Moishe, or rather his minder, after Moishe said some concerning things to him about private lessons at Rabbi Hirsch's home. And that wasn't all – there was a byline to the story gaining momentum in the chats; no-one knew where it came from, but it carried that uneasy, back of the throat feeling of truth – Moishe wasn't the only one.

*

Who sent the invitation? Who even knew he attended Yahel at that time? Ezra looked up from his phone, scanned the restaurant. Only diners slurping their pho, adding chilli, conversing loudly. 'Stupid,' he said to himself and opened the invitation again.

Invited by Avraham Kliger

He didn't know an Avraham Kliger, so he tapped on the name. Avraham had a doughy face, thinning light brown hair, bulging dark circles beneath squinted eyes and a weary, thin-lipped smile. Middle-aged, not someone Ezra would've gone to school with. A crusader who'd got his hands on a stack of Yahel Academy yearbooks? No, that didn't feel right; like a stray eyelash, something about Avraham irked him. He studied the man's face some more – those plump cheeks if they were narrower and if his hair was darker, thicker – *Kliger*. Of course, Moishe Kliger. The special-needs boy from his class, the one who started it all. Avraham was his older brother.

Half a beer later, while Ezra was re-reading the event details, Tegan pulled out the chair opposite him and sat down. She exhaled loudly. 'I'm so sorry,' she said, placing her bag under the table. She was wearing a mustard cardigan over a buttoned-up navy dress. With one hand she swept her dark brown hair off her shoulder, tucked it behind her ear and picked up the menu. 'Have you ordered yet? I'm starving.'

She was flushed and a red stain was creeping its way up her sheet-white neck onto the low cheekbones and square jaw she'd inherited from her dad, the way it always did when they had sex. Ezra loved that, and he loved that he knew if he told her she was going red, it'd bridge across her small nose like sunburn.

And then the dry taste of beer in his mouth reminded Ezra of the night before and there was a tightening in his chest. What had he been thinking? Of course he loved her. It was a mistake. Never again. He'd make it up to her. Less drinking, more spontaneity and attention. Whatever it took, he'd do it.

'You okay?' Tegan was frowning.

Shit. She knew him too well. But he was still holding his phone, opened to the event invitation. He held it out for Tegan to read. 'You know how I went to a religious primary school?'

'Yeah –'

Ezra told Tegan about Rabbi Hirsch, recounting what he knew about Moishe's allegations, the rabbi fleeing to Israel and members of the community supposedly helping him. 'I wasn't – I'd never been in any of the rabbi's classes,' Ezra said, aware of how intently Tegan was biting her lower lip. 'It didn't happen to me, seriously.'

The waitress returned for their orders and, though Tegan maintained a stiff posture, she unblinkingly ordered a *phở bò* and a glass of Pinot Noir. Ezra followed suit, without the wine.

'Shit, Ez. I'm sorry. Why didn't you ever tell me that?'

'What? Why? Like I said, he never touched me.'

Tegan frowned again, looked down her nose at him.

'What? Don't you believe me?'

'I do, but –' Tegan paused for a moment as though she were reordering her thoughts. 'I think you're being purposefully blasé about it. You were just a kid, and he was a trusted adult, not to mention a rabbi, a leader in your community. It could've – it probably did affect your relationships with adults and authority figures.' She shook her head and reached for his hand. 'Whoever you are now . . . and I love you, but you're different to who you would've been if not for that man.'

Ezra took a long pull from his beer and nodded, though he wasn't sure he agreed with her. She wasn't objective – she couldn't be. Tegan was a Policy Officer for Australia Without Violence, a peak body for domestic violence advocacy groups. She worked with a lot of service providers as well: women's shelters, safe houses, legal aid. Ezra knew children were often involved; abuse too, though Tegan rarely went into detail. He was in awe of how balanced she seemed – how she was able to make space for him at the end of the day. In her position, he didn't know if he'd be able to support that kind of weight.

'Are you going to go?' Tegan asked, handing his phone back.

Ezra considered the event again, scrolled down and tapped on where it said '84 going 53 maybe 169 invited'. 'No, I don't really feel any need to –' Some of the names triggered something in his memory but nothing jarred until he came across a profile without a picture and the name YONI K.

Chapter 2

Yonatan

Sweating, Yonatan woke two hours before his alarm with the thread of a dream stuck to the edge of his mind as he gradually gained full consciousness – bulbous and white, a whole sky full of moon, pockmarked and brilliant. It unnerved him, its waxy shine, the sheer size of it. He'd felt uneasy beneath it, as though at any moment it might sink and crush him.

Across from him in the dark, on her own bed, Rivka turned over, murmuring in her sleep. Carefully, Yonatan extricated himself from beneath his sheets, recited *Modeh Ani* under his breath and felt for the basin of water and *natla* he'd placed by his bed the night before. After washing his hands and whispering *netilat yadayim*, Yonatan navigated his way to the door, opening and closing it with practised quiet.

In the bathroom, he noticed that the *tzitzit* he slept in was plastered to his chest. After pulling it over his head, he placed it on the cream-coloured towel rack, relieved himself, recited *asher yatzar* and walked back towards his and Rivka's bedroom.

Satisfied with the strip of darkness at the bottom of the door, Yonatan continued to his study, where he carefully closed the door behind him and sat, half-naked at his desk. The worn leather of his large office chair was cool against his bare skin. A part of him had anticipated that feeling and relished in the shiver that followed. He switched on his desktop computer, and as it whirred, he considered the walls of his study – his musty, leather-bound copies of the Babylonian Talmud, the Jerusalem Talmud, *Shulchan Aruch*, commentaries of Rashi, the Vilna Gaon, the Rashbam. It was the study of a pious man, a teacher, a man who should know which actions are *halachic* and which are in breach of Jewish law. Once the screen loaded, Yonatan clicked on his Internet browser, glanced up from the screen at the closed door and typed in the web address for Facebook.

Strictly speaking, Chief Rabbi Feiner at the Yahel *shule* had not provided an official standing on social media participation, but its use was still frowned upon in the community. Recently, some of the foremost rabbinical leaders in Israel released a newspaper article in which they referred to the advancements in modern technology as providing 'unprecedented access to immodest material' that would inevitably create a 'breach in the wall of holiness' and lead to the spiritual destruction of the Jewish people. Personally, Yonatan enjoyed engaging with technology, and on the rare occasion when pop-ups from undesirable websites infiltrated his screen, he was always quick to raise a hand to his eyes and click the cross icon in the corner of those windows. Inevitably, though, he couldn't prevent himself from seeing some of the pornographic advertisements that appeared, laden with promises and naked women.

FIND YOUR FUCKBUDDY
FREE LIVE CAMS
ASIAN GIRLS WANT TO FUCK YOU
Whenever that happened, Yonatan would immediately appeal to *Hashem* to forgive his *aveira* and keep him from future evil inclinations towards perversity and temptation.

He kept his Facebook account spare – a shortened version of his name with no other identifying information – and by following certain pages he was able to stay up to date with the works of contemporary Talmudic scholars, as well as developments in the State of Israel. Yonatan felt that the ability to access information and communicate across the world in an instant was a blessing, and, if embraced by the rest of the community, could revolutionise, without compromise, their *halachic* way of living.

Rivka, however, did not share his views. Her father, Rav Yitzchak Bloom, had been a member of the Australian Rabbinical Council and a highly regarded Talmudic scholar. He believed that, as much as possible, a *Yehudi* should live as their European ancestors did. On Shabbat, a fur-trimmed *shtreimel* on your head, your feet stockinged and a long black *bekishe* hanging past your knees. Rav Bloom shunned the advent of new technologies and never owned a car, television or computer. But it was only after the Rav's death, two years earlier, that his beliefs began to gain popularity in the community and at Yahel Academy. Concerning as this trend was, the one positive to the uptake of Rav Bloom's conservative approach was that Yonatan had little to worry about when it came to maintaining his anonymity online. Or rather, he'd thought that was the case, until two weeks ago, when he received a Facebook event invitation from Avraham Kliger.

There was a *cherem* on Avraham and the entire Kliger family, for the accusations they'd made against Rabbi Hirsch some twenty years ago. They had committed the sin of *lashon hara*, spread evil about another, and followed their accusations with *mesirah* when they reported Hirsch to the police rather than deal with the issue within the community. For their sins, Avraham and his family were ostracised, excommunicated.

Initially, when he received the notification, Yonatan assumed it was another mass-invitation from the Association of Jewish Studies in New York but, upon inspection, he saw the reference to Yahel Academy, Rabbi Hirsch, and knew he'd been found out.

He'd been brazen, foolish and led by hubris.

'*Putz*,' he'd said to himself, shaking his head.

The mouse had been slippery in Yonatan's hand. He accessed his privacy settings, deactivated his Facebook account and turned off the computer, vowing to let it alone if he should come out of it all unscathed.

*

The day after they were sent home from school, Pinchas Singer found Yonatan, after *shacharit*, and filled him in on the allegations Moishe had made against Rabbi Hirsch. A *paskudnyak*, they called him. Monster. *Chazer*. Pig. The idea was difficult for Yonatan to reconcile with the image he held of his fifth-grade teacher – a bushy brown beard, flecked with red and always split by a large white smile, his front teeth hanging over his bottom lip. He was big. Not fat or imposing, but when Reb Hirsch was in a room, he seemed to fill up most of it. He encouraged the shy, challenged the boastful and guided those who read poorly. It was rare for him to admonish anyone. His hands were large and covered in thick, black hairs from wrist to knuckle. Yonatan remembered the weight of one on his shoulder, Hirsch looking down at him, smiling with those buck teeth and asking how he'd found his homework. Could that man have done such things?

The idea plagued Yonatan all afternoon. Was it possible Moishe had been mistaken? Why would a man even want to do that to children? Could Rabbi Hirsch be both a good teacher and a monster?

An hour or so before they normally left for *mincha*, too conflicted to worry about disrupting him, Yonatan approached his father's closed study door and knocked.

'Come in,' his father said.

The study was small, or at least it appeared that way, cluttered as it was by books, a large desk and his father's hulking frame. Nearly two metres tall, Yonatan's father was referred to as a 'giant in the community and in life'.

'*Boychick*.' His father sat up and closed the *Yerushalmi* before him. 'What is it? We have time still, *nu*?'

Yonatan nodded. 'Could I ask your advice, *Abba*?'

'Of course, *boychick*. Sit down.' He gestured to the chair on the other side of his desk.

He appeared to be in an affable mood and Yonatan was glad.

Yonatan sat. Where to begin?

His father's eyes flicked to the side of his face.

Yonatan hadn't realised he was twirling one of his *peyot*. He dropped his hands to his lap.

'It's about Reb Hirsch.'

His father's lips tightened, but he didn't speak.

'The things people are saying about him . . . I cannot . . . could he have –' Yonatan took a breath. 'I did not know him like that.

He was a good teacher, but if he did those things – how am I meant to feel about him now? I thought the Talmud might –'

'Talmud.' His father's eyes sharpened. 'What is it you think the Talmud says?'

'I don't know. I thought that maybe –'

'You don't know? But you thought to interrupt my study of the Almighty's will, anyway?'

'I'm sorry. I didn't –'

'Do not speak to me of Talmud.' His father's voice shook. He stood, curled his hand into a fist and raised it as though he might strike the desk. 'And do not speak of this again. Not to me, not to anyone. *Mevin*?'

Yonatan froze. What had he done?

'*Mevin*?' his father repeated. 'You understand, Yonatan?' Wrinkles bunched up at the edges of his eyes. His cheeks were yellow, fleshy and heavy. He looked old. Yonatan knew that his parents had struggled to have children and that his arrival, somewhat late in their lives, was a surprise – a blessing from *Hashem*, his mother said. But Yonatan had never considered their age, and the sudden realisation of it only added to the disquiet that he felt.

'Yes, *Abba*,' he said.

'Good. Now go, get ready for *shule*.'

*

His Facebook account deactivated, the idle computer in Yonatan's study had taunted him. Eventually, he bargained with himself that Internet access was okay as long as he stayed off Facebook. He read everything he could find on Hirsch and the case against him – grainy newspaper articles from when the scandal first erupted, more recent headlines detailing his claims of mental illness, blog posts from advocates like Avraham Kliger.

The evidence was beyond doubt – a statement from the travel agent who had been coerced into booking Hirsch's flights, a former member of the school council who revealed that they'd voted on it and burying the truth won, and, above all, the horrific and unrelenting parallel testimonies of his victims. There was even a documentary, a few years old, that aired on SBS as part of the extradition effort. That was what did it for Yonatan – the sight of Chaim Potaznick, late twenties, short brown hair, lightly stubbled cheeks, dark, rheumy eyes and no *kippah*. Yonatan hadn't known him in school. A picture of Chaim as an awkward, large toothed pre-pubescent in his Yahel uniform flashed onto the screen as Chaim narrated what Hirsch did to him. 'He took me to the *mikvah*, told me to take off all of my clothes and get into the water, then he did the same – I thought it was okay, he was a rabbi. When he touched me, I froze – I knew it was wrong, but I thought I might get in trouble if I –' Chaim turned from the camera and wiped his eyes. 'I felt so ashamed for letting it happen, that it was somehow my fault. I knew I couldn't tell –'

Yonatan paused the video then, reactivated his Facebook account, found the Hirsch protest event and selected that he would be attending.

Sitting at his computer now, Yonatan opened the event again. Even though he'd committed the details to memory, he re-read the description. *Paedophile. Predator. Monster.* Powerful words, imbued with loathing, hate, disgust. Yonatan shook his head at the thought of his original cowardice. His concern had been unwarranted anyway. Because of the *cherem*, Avraham Kliger had no position within, or communication with, the community – he couldn't oust Yonatan any more than he could form a *minyan* on his own.

Later that morning, Yonatan met his brother-in-law, Menachem, at *mikvah.* Four years younger than Rivka, he was stout and bald but for a square patch of thin black hair on his crown. Like his sister, Menachem only came up to Yonatan's shoulders. A thick, dark beard covered his fleshy cheeks and frayed to a pointed end off his weak chin. Unruly *peyot* hung to his collarbones. Every day he wore the same long, black *rekel,* rimless glasses and a black fedora atop his round head.

Raised, as Rivka had been, with their father's militant obedience of *halacha,* Menachem's knowledge of Jewish law and the almost innumerable commentators' interpretations was second to none but, unfortunately, he lacked his late father's charisma and gained a reputation as somewhat of a zealot. He was quick to publicly denounce anyone who he believed had committed an *aveira* – a prominent community member's wife adjusting her *sheitel* in public, a neighbour's daughter dancing immodestly in her home with the blinds open. Menachem even went as far as reporting on a Yahel instructor who failed to recite *asher yatzar* on exiting the bathroom. These incidents occurred prior to his father's passing, when Yahel Academy had been trending towards more secular and liberal reform. And so it had taken significant effort from Yonatan to persuade the Yahel Principal, Rabbi Shmuel Margolis, to grant Menachem a teaching position at the school once he received his *smicha.*

In the change room, after showering, immersing themselves in the rainwater bath and saying their blessings, Yonatan asked Menachem if he wouldn't mind covering his *shiur* the next day.

Menachem stopped buttoning up his shirt. His round stomach and flabby chest were covered by swirls of dark hair. 'Tomorrow?'

Yonatan's students were part of the school's *Derech HaYashar* program – a religious studies only curriculum for students over fifteen. Menachem had never taught high school students before; rather he had been charged with taking *Chumash* classes for students in Yahel's primary school. It had only been a couple of years since Menachem's *smicha*, and though looking, he was not yet married. Yonatan thought Menachem would recognise the opportunity to impress himself on the more learned students, and he doubted his brother-in-law would be able to resist.

'It's on *Parshat Terumah*,' Yonatan said. 'Easy stuff.'

'Why can't you do it?'

'I have a dentist appointment, root canal,' Yonatan said, pointing to one of his upper canines.

Menachem frowned. 'Who's doing it – Feldman?'

'No, it's a short root – tricky. I've been referred to a *goy* specialist.' It was the truth, but the appointment wasn't for another week. He'd have to come up with another excuse then.

Menachem continued doing up his shirt. '*Terumah* . . . so the making of the *mishkan*, a discussion perhaps on the *midrash* that compares it to the creation of the universe?'

'That's right,' Yonatan smiled. 'I'll give you my notes, if you'd like.'

Menachem nodded. 'Okay, I'll do it – this time.'

Yonatan navigated through the rest of his day in a haze, through *shacharit*, his morning classes, *mincha*, and then his afternoon *shiur*. All were preoccupied with thoughts of the next day, which he planned meticulously. In the morning, before *mikvah*, he would place the purple shirt he wore last *Purim* in the car, and then following afternoon prayers, he would excuse himself for his dentist appointment. Having looked up the directions already, he would avoid the closer Ripponlea train station and drive to Elsternwick, where he would park his car, change into the coloured shirt and tuck his *peyot* into his fedora.

Because of the *cherem* it was unlikely that anyone from the community would be attending the protest, but, if he were recognised, he would be exposing himself and Rivka to the possibility of indefinite ostracisation. It was an unforgivable risk to be taking, but when he closed his eyes and recalled Chaim's tremulous words, he knew he had no choice in the matter. He would do his best to stay on the periphery of the event.

At five thirty in the afternoon, after leaving his notes on Menachem's desk, Yonatan left Yahel Academy and walked the two blocks to the home he and Rivka shared on a quiet street off Inkerman – a two-storey, two-bedroom, seventies brick veneer unit. The rent was all they could afford on Yonatan's salary, even with the owner having been a close friend of Rivka's father.

'*Shalooom*,' Yonatan called, removing his hat and jacket and hanging them up by the door.

A smoky rush of meat wafted through the house. Rivka stood by the stove, steam rising around her. She was wearing a blue blouse over a white top that ended at her elbows, and a long black skirt. A light brown kerchief covered her shorn hair, as it always did when they were alone.

'*Shalom, ahuvi*,' Rivka said.

A Tupperware container sat on the kitchen counter. Yonatan opened it, there was rugelach inside. 'Who made these?' Yonatan asked, taking one out and biting into it.

'Liat Berkowitz. She agreed to be my doula.'

The pastry dissolved on Yonatan's tongue and sweet chocolate oozed into his mouth. He brushed flakes off his beard. In their seven years of marriage, Rivka's slender frame had hardly shifted, but under that blouse there was now a discernible bump. 'Berkowitz? But she's a hundred years old. What if she gets confused about which end the baby comes out of?'

'*Oy*, don't be a *yutz*, Yoni. She's delivered half of the community.'

Yonatan laughed. 'All right, and what did she say?'

'Nothing I didn't already know. That I'm too skinny, but have good hips, so I should be okay.'

'*B'sha'a tovah*.'

Rivka placed a hand on the small mound of her belly. 'A healthy baby. A future leader of Israel.'

A valve turned in Yonatan then, and the constant hum of tension that had been running through his body all day emptied. Without it he was heavy as stone. Spots flickered in front of his eyes and he was forced to balance himself on the kitchen counter. Rivka's hand was still on her belly, her eyes far away, contemplative.

'Let me get changed,' Yonatan said, 'and then we can eat.' But the stairs were a mountain and his exhaustion only seemed to build with each step. On reaching their bedroom, he thought it would be a good idea to lie down briefly and reinvigorate himself for conversation at dinner, but as soon as he closed his eyelids, a deep oblivion took him and everything was as large and round and white as the morning.

Chapter 3

Ezra

At a quarter to four in the afternoon, Ezra shut down his computer, plucked his suit jacket off the back of his chair and picked up his bag, having told his director, Steven, that he had to take his parents to the airport and he'd make up the time tomorrow. He was halfway to the lift when Baz stopped him, because Baz, as ever, had to know everything.

'A holiday, is it? Another cruise? Where they going? Noumea is lovely this time of year. I hope they're going to Noumea.' Baz smiled wide and pushed his glasses to the back of his bulbous drinker's nose.

'They're going to London, Baz. My dad wants to visit his brother.' Ezra looked longingly at the elevators.

Baz gasped. His teeth were a haphazard crisscross of small yellow nubs. 'Blighty? Tower of London, Windsor Castle, Buckingham Palace?'

Shit, Ezra should've known better – said Germany, France, New Zealand. He'd forgotten about Baz's infatuation with the royals.

'Any chance of a souvenir? Princess Anne teacup, Prince Philip commemorative button? I saw a Duchess of York pocket-knife once.'

'I don't know, Baz. It's a quick trip they –' But Baz was practically salivating. 'All right, mate. I'll see what I can do.' Ezra took his phone out of his pocket. There were ten minutes until the rally started. 'I really gotta go, Baz. Catch you tomorrow.' He headed for the lift.

A long-serving government employee, Baz kept a calendar on his desk and crossed off the days he had left until retirement every Friday. Last time Ezra checked, it was just under two-and-a-half years.

One of Baz's favourite topics was the holiday he was going to take when his mum finally died. She was in her early nineties, a wisp of white hair atop a kind face laden with the cracks, crevices and spots of age. Dementia had set in a few years earlier, and most mornings Baz came to work laughing about his mum's misadventures with the TV remote or microwave. She'd even melted the kettle on the stove once. He didn't date and 'hadn't had a shag in years', but he liked to talk to Ezra about the men around the office – Danny the grad had a peach of an arse apparently – and what he'd get up to when he finally had the time and freedom. But there was a lack of authenticity to Baz's gallows humour, a sheen to his eyes. It seemed to Ezra that the hole his mum's eventual passing would leave wasn't going to be one that would be so easily filled.

As he rode the elevator down, Ezra made a mental note to buy one of the items Baz had mentioned from eBay.

He walked briskly down Nicholson Street, passing couples sitting in the nearby gardens, hanging off one another, unconcerned about onlookers or grass stains. A white orb of sun shone high in an otherwise blue sky. Ezra shielded his eyes with his hand, slid off his jacket and draped it over his arm.

It wasn't long before the large, columned side of Parliament House came into view. He expected to be hearing something by then – chanting, a megaphone, police sirens. But there was nothing beyond the sounds of everyday car and pedestrian traffic. He took out his phone, thinking he might have the wrong day or time, but no, he was right. To better gauge the situation, Ezra decided to cross the road to the corner of Bourke Street where he could take in the view of Parliament from outside the Imperial Hotel.

On the first landing of Parliament House, after the initial set of ten or so steps, a microphone stand had been set up. Beside it sat an equipment box of some kind, from which cables ran to two large speakers on either side of the microphone. Propped up on a suitcase in front of the microphone was a cardboard sign, the size of a coffee table, with 'BRING HIRSCH TO JUSTICE' written on it in thick black marker. Milling about at the back of the landing, by the stairs that led to the Parliament entrance, were three policemen wearing dark sunglasses, their arms folded across navy 'POLICE' vests. They didn't appear to be expecting trouble. But where were the protesters? Where was Avraham Kliger, Moishe and the rest of their family?

Feeling conspicuous on the street corner, Ezra turned to the hotel behind him. He figured he could still watch the Parliament steps at a table by the pub window, and a pint in that heat couldn't hurt either.

Inside, the bar was a spread of reddish-brown tables and bar stools with maroon seat cushions, standing on patterned, beer-encrusted carpet. Huddled beneath a flat-screen TV were a handful of heavy, bald and sheared-to-fuzz men who looked as though they'd been there for some time.

Ten minutes and half a pint later, Ezra watched as a tram pulled up outside of Parliament House and about thirty people stepped off carrying homemade placards and banners. The crowd walked towards the steps of Parliament and Ezra felt a jolt of nervous energy rumble in his gut. But once they arrived at the empty microphone stand, heads turned in circles, signs dropped to their sides and phones were pulled from pockets. It was then that Ezra saw a flash of movement out of the corner of his eye as a tall, heavy-set man in a dark suit hurried out of the pub.

His face was flushed, and though there was more weight to it and less hair than was in his profile picture, the man was clearly Avraham Kliger. Half-jogging, and failing to look both ways, Avraham jaywalked across Spring Street, narrowly avoiding an oncoming tram, whose driver dinged their bell repeatedly as he passed. Safely across the road, Avraham slowed to a walk, thrust a hand into his trouser pocket and withdrew a small black *kippah* which he placed carefully onto the back of his head.

Ezra couldn't tell if he'd said something to the crowd or not, but on Avraham's approach they picked up their signs and huddled in front of the microphone. Another tram arrived then, and the ranks of the rally swelled. Once the new members settled in, Avraham stepped in front of the microphone. Ezra sculled his beer, made for the pub's door.

Up close, the crowd was all bum fluff moustaches, backpacks and dangly op-shop earrings. They were young, too young to have been at either Yahel or Beth Chana at the same time as him. He caught sight of a Melbourne University rugby top and that felt about right. He remembered the type from his uni days, handing out flyers on the South Lawn. Arts students, Political Science majors, social justice warriors. He'd envied their passion and the sense of direction that fighting for a cause must have given them, but still scrunched up their material as soon as they were out of sight.

In the pub, he'd been slightly concerned about being recognised by old classmates, wondered if they'd assume he was one of Hirsch's victims, have to explain he wasn't and justify what he was doing there. But then, and maybe it was the beer, the sight of those wannabe kids started to piss him off. What did they know about Hirsch or Judaism for that matter? At least he'd been there at the time, had classmates who'd suffered at the hands of that bastard. He edged his way to the front of the crowd.

'Thank you, everyone, for coming here today.' Avraham spoke quietly, his eyes fixed on a point in the distance, making him seem a little disengaged. 'We're here today to bring Rabbi Hirsch to just–' A squawk of feedback shot out from the speakers and Ezra winced.

'Justice!' someone shouted, others cheered.

Avraham took a small step forward, appearing to collect himself. 'Justice,' he continued. 'A coward. A rapist. A predator.' Avraham's voice intensified with each word. 'A man who used the guise of piety to prey upon innocent children. My brother was one of Hirsch's many victims. A special, kind-hearted boy. He trusted Hirsch, my family trusted him, and Hirsch took advantage of that trust. Twenty years it's been and my brother has never recovered from the effects of Hirsch's abuse. He is a prisoner of his own mind. He suffers. My family and others suffer, while Hirsch roams free in Israel. Appeals to extradite Hirsch have been delayed and denied for years by the Israeli Government. By denying Hirsch's victims and their families justice, the Israeli Government is complicit in his crimes.'

Avraham took the microphone off its stand and placed it close to his mouth. 'Predator!' He spat the word through his teeth and it resonated throughout the crowd.

'PREDATOR!' the crowd roared in response.

'Rapist!'

'RAPIST!'

'Monster!'

'MONSTER!'

Avraham lowered the microphone for a few moments until the crowd settled. 'Five years ago, the Israeli Government tried to placate us with a home detention order for Hirsch, until he was well enough to stand trial for his extradition. For years he has claimed to be too sick to do so, but now, with the help of a private investigator, we have video footage of him in perfect health, and in breach of his home detention. In there,' Avraham pointed to the doors of Parliament, 'sits the Israeli Justice Minister, Yehudit Alon. She has the power to extradite Hirsch. Join me in presenting this new evidence to her. Join me in insisting that Hirsch be brought home and held accountable for his crimes.' He took a large breath, like he was going to speak again but lowered the microphone instead, placing a hand on a nearby speaker, as though he needed to brace himself.

The crowd began to chant. 'BRING HIRSCH TO JUSTICE! BRING HIRSCH TO JUSTICE!' They held their signs high above their heads, pumping them up and down. The air thrummed with noise and movement – a chorus of passion and rage, and Ezra could feel himself being swept up by it.

He added his voice to the others. 'BRING HIRSCH TO JUSTICE!' He raised his fist with their signs.

On the stairs behind the crowd, the police presence had increased – at least a dozen officers now. Eyes masked by sunglasses, arms held behind their backs – a line of blue holding fast between the protesters and the doors to Parliament.

'BRING HIRSCH TO JUSTICE! BRING HIRSCH TO JUSTICE!' Faster and louder the chants came, Avraham's voice booming above them all, so that it felt to Ezra as though he were somehow speaking from the heavens. The ground shifted beneath Ezra's feet and the fervor of the crowd continued to build, granting him a moment of spontaneous clarity – there was a crescendo coming.

And then it came. The front doors of Parliament House flew open. The navy line of police drew tight and Ezra was thrust forward on a wave of bodies up the steps towards it. At their approach, the policemen at the ends of the line turned inwards, forming a protective shell around a group of five or so dark-suited men and women, who exited Parliament with their heads down and hands raised in front of their faces like criminals at the Magistrates' Court, and that felt right to Ezra. That's what they were.

A voice shouted, one that Ezra hardly registered as his own, laced with vitriol, 'Criminals! Criminals!'

Tightly packed, the crowd was a swinging fist, gathering momentum, threatening to collide with the police as they made their way down the Parliament steps. The roar of their charge was deafening. But then, as suddenly as they'd appeared, the delegation was gone, rushed into waiting cars on the roadside, leaving Ezra at the bottom of the steps, unclenching his hands amongst a sea of dumbstruck students.

Seemingly reluctant to succumb to the anticlimax, the protesters milled about Parliament House. Without direction, most resorted to their phones, sat on the steps and took selfies with their signs before dissipating into the CBD. Avraham packed up the speakers, wound the microphone cord slowly over his hands. Gone was the impassioned spirit he held when rousing the crowd. His shoulders were stooped, motions listless. How many protests had he held to date in his seemingly endless twenty-year fight?

Ezra felt stupid for letting himself get worked up like that. Avraham probably fought every damn day for his family, lugged heavy audio equipment across town, likely lobbied relentlessly to foreign ministries and advocacy groups. Dropping into a protest ten minutes from work did not make you a saint. Was Ezra really any better than those tag-along kids? What an idiot he was. He should go home, bury himself in the cushion of Tegan's unconditional love and a bottle of wine. Never a better idea in the world. But before he could board a tram, Ezra caught sight of a bearded man, standing outside the Imperial, watching him intently.

Yonatan.

*

The Saturday after the scandal broke, Ezra woke early and dressed in his black suit, white dress shirt and polished school shoes. After cereal, he sat patiently at the kitchen table, waiting for his dad to wake and walk with him to *shule*. Twenty minutes later, when they were risking the embarrassment of arriving midway through the *Amidah*, Ezra went back upstairs and knocked on his parents' bedroom door.

Leaning on the frame, his dad was still in his pyjamas, bed hair sticking up in unruly cowlicks. 'Ezra –' A yawn stopped his dad mid-sentence and he squinted as though he wasn't sure of what he was seeing. 'We don't –' He shook his head. 'It's okay, we don't have to go to *shule* today.'

Ezra's family was not particularly religious. As he understood it, his parents chose Yahel Academy for its strong academic reputation and promise to never turn away any boy of Jewish faith.

Until recently, his parents had been twice-a-year Jews who only went to *shule* on Rosh Hashanah and Yom Kippur, but with Ezra's forthcoming bar mitzvah, his dad decided to make an investment in his own spirituality and now they went to *shule* every Shabbat morning.

'But – I have to.' After his parents' interrogation on Thursday night, Ezra knew he couldn't bring up Rabbi Hirsch again, but he needed to find out what the other boys knew – what Yonatan knew. 'Rabbi Horowitz said it's important for me. He said this week's *haftorah* relates to the one I'm going to have to read.'

The *shule* smelled like dust and bitter cologne. Their seats were near the back – the end of a wooden pew, stained and cracked by the sitting of countless backsides. Old men crowded into most of the seats, wearing *tallits* and breathing heavily from their mouths. Ezra figured there was a bar mitzvah that morning as, aside from holidays, that was the only time *shule* was ever packed. He leaned into the aisle. On a bench beside the *bimah* sat a boy he didn't recognise, wearing a large *tallit* over his narrow shoulders and what looked like a *Simpsons*-themed *kippah*. Not a Yahel boy. He might not even go to a Jewish school or know how to read Hebrew. He might have had to memorise the words of his *haftorah*, all gibberish and the sounds of throat-clearing to him.

When they stood for the *Amidah*, Ezra lifted onto the tips of his toes, peering over and between *kippot* until he caught sight of Yonatan, head down, *siddur* in his hands, bowing repeatedly in prayer. Flanking him were Dovid Segal, Amit Cohen and Pinchas Singer, *frum* boys from their year. Towering in the row behind them stood Yonatan's father, Reb Kaplan.

A train of younger boys ran into Ezra's row, squeezing past him and his dad without apology, to ask their fathers when the lollies would be thrown – hard candies and fruit chews that would rain upon the bar mitzvah boy from the women's section above them, once he finished his *haftorah*. Having received their answer, the younger boys shimmied back into the aisle, scurrying outside, to play handball or four square. Ezra knew this because he used to be one of them, on those two days of the year that his parents dragged him to *shule*. Yonatan had been one of those boys as well, until his father decided that he was old enough for God to hear his prayers.

Kiddush followed the service in the room adjacent to the prayer hall. Tables were loaded with drinks: wine, grape juice, vodka – paid for by the parents of the bar mitzvah boy – and enough food for the hundred or so women and men who were jockeying for serving spoons and picking flakes of herring out of their beards.

The *Kiddush* was the reason Ezra had sat and stood in pretend reverence for over three hours of *shule* service. With his dad occupied by wine and socialising, Ezra was free to seek out Yonatan and speak to him for the first time since they'd been sent home from school.

For ten minutes, he shook the hands of bearded men he didn't know and politely declined plates of cake from women, whose perfume stung his eyes, until, finally, he spotted Yonatan in a corner of the room, standing in a circle with Dovid, Pinchas and Amit. None of them were eating, but each held a cup in their hands. Ezra approached from the opposite side of the circle, hoping to catch Yonatan's eye, draw him from the others, but his head was down, focused on his drink.

'Hey,' Ezra said.

Yonatan looked up. 'Hey,' he said, without inflection, as though he'd known Ezra was there. But that was Yonatan after all – forever cool, always one step ahead.

The boys stepped back, widening the circle for Ezra. 'So –' he said, 'crazy about Rabbi Hirsch, huh?'

None of them spoke. Ezra didn't understand – weren't they talking about it? Wasn't everybody?

Yonatan drank from his cup, nodded and kept his eyes down.

'I wonder if we'll get Monday off too,' Ezra added.

Yonatan raised his head and held out his cup. 'Want some?'

'What?' Ezra took the cup, surprised to find it wasn't filled with Coke. 'What is it?'

'Vodka.'

Ezra lifted it to his nose and had to repress a gag. He shook his head, handed the cup back to Yonatan and coughed as a large hand clapped him on the shoulder.

Turning, Ezra found his face inches from a bramble of chestnut beard mottled with patches of grey. 'Ezra, my boy. Good Shabbos,' Yonatan's father said.

Ezra forced a smile. 'Good Shabbos, Reb Kaplan.'

Yonatan's father looked past him then, and Ezra's stomach sank, expecting his face to fall as he looked into his son's cup, but rather than scowl the large man held his smile. '*Boychick*, let's go,' he said, waving for Yonatan to follow him.

'See you at school,' Yonatan said. His cup had disappeared.

Ezra watched Yonatan dissolve into the crowd and wondered why he'd been acting so strangely? Why wouldn't he talk about Hirsch? Ezra supposed it could've been the vodka, or the presence of the other *frum* boys? If only he'd been able to get him alone. Resigned that he would have to wait until Monday to speak to him properly, Ezra poured himself a Coke and went in search of his dad.

'What do they expect us to do?' By the gefilte fish and cream cheese bagels, Ezra heard his dad's voice, loud and slightly slurred.

Wanting to hear more, he ducked behind a wall of black suits and pattern baldness.

'They let him go – escape to Israel. I won't support –'

'We don't know that,' a voice Ezra didn't recognise cut in. 'He was fired straight away and –'

'Bullshit.' It was nearly a shout. Though rare, Ezra recognised the threat in his dad's tone. 'They only sacked him when it hit the papers. I called Glen Eira High yesterday – next term, they'll take my son, yours too probably.'

'But that's months away. You can't take him out n–'

'Family holiday – caravan up the east coast – always wanted to do it – we've got the savings. Why not? Better than leaving my son in the hands of –'

Someone bumped into Ezra, spilling Coke onto his white shirt. 'Shit.' He went in search of a serviette, and when he returned his dad's voice was gone. After undoing his top button, Ezra raised the brown stain to his nose. He couldn't smell anything, but the chemical stench of the vodka still hung in his nostrils, mixing with the wet cat-food stink of the nearby fish, and suddenly Ezra was sure he was going to be sick.

Classes at Yahel restarted that Monday but not for Ezra. True to his word, his dad took his long-service leave and kept Ezra at home to help plan their great family adventure. Later that week, his dad went out for a few hours and returned with an unflinching grin on his face and a white pop-top caravan hitched to his Volvo.

For the eight weeks that followed, Ezra became accustomed to boredom, the use of a chemical toilet, and the clicks, cracks and gurgles of his parents' bodies. Through rain, suffocating heat and blustery winds they drove up the coast.

When he wasn't driving, Ezra's dad browsed through an old guidebook he'd bought at a secondhand bookstore and called for countless detours so they could take cheek-straining family photos in front of the Holbrook submarine, The Big Banana, The Big Pineapple, the Dog on the Tuckerbox. Moving schools wasn't mentioned on any part of their trip and Ezra didn't broach the subject with either of his parents, hoping that if he didn't remind his dad of it, he might somehow forget. But he was wrong.

On their return, at the cusp of the new school term, his parents sat him down again at the kitchen table and laid out a pamphlet with children on the front, smiling and wearing floppy sunhats and yellow uniforms. It was titled 'LEARN TO LOVE LEARNING – GLEN EIRA HIGH SCHOOL'.

'We're not *frum*,' Ezra's dad said. 'We gave Yahel a go, but it's not the life for us.'

Ezra fought it, briefly. He locked himself in his room, cried, even screamed a little. But it felt more like he was going through the motions of a tantrum rather than having one, because he'd known it was coming, and a part of him had accepted it as just one more thing he was powerless to change.

Yonatan seemed genuinely upset when Ezra told him the news. Ezra was pleased by that and by Yonatan's insistence that they see each other as much as possible in the days that remained before school restarted.

As far as Rabbi Hirsch was concerned, it was old news. After Moishe, a half-dozen additional complaints had been made, but Hirsch was still in Israel and couldn't be formally charged. The Israeli Government denied his extradition on the grounds of his poor mental health – he was depressed. And that was that – the news cycle moved on. Ezra wanted to ask Yonatan about Hirsch, but it didn't feel right while they watched TV or played basketball in his backyard. Time was short and Yonatan didn't seem any different, so what was the point of asking?

When the new term started, promises were made, plans laid out – they would call each other often, hang out on Sundays and after school, whenever they could. And Yonatan kept those promises, for a time, but as his studies intensified, Ezra became more accustomed to unanswered phone calls and having plans cancelled at the last minute, until, one day, Ezra stopped trying altogether and instead found himself wondering if their friendship hadn't been something he'd imagined all along.

*

Ezra had forgotten what had piqued his interest in the rally in the first place.

Yonatan was wearing a purple shirt, black slacks and a fedora. Though he was now a man grown, there was no mistaking him – his thick red beard and the single red sidelock, dangling by his face, were a dead giveaway.

As they stared at each other across the roadway, Ezra imagined Yonatan was tempted to turn around, pretend he hadn't recognised Ezra and walk away. At least, that was how he felt. What do you say to someone you haven't seen for twenty years? Where do you start? How much can you put in 'Hey'? If he left now, there'd be no need to face anything, to bridge a generation of time. And yet, Ezra didn't take his eyes from Yonatan. Even when crossing the road, he stayed fixed on him as though he were playing a game of Three-Card Monte.

'Ezra,' Yonatan said, nodding softly as Ezra might to a colleague in the office corridor.

Ezra meant to return the gesture, but a childish giddiness snuck up on him, and he was overcome with the need to grab this man, this ultra-Orthodox Jew, in public, and squeeze him like a near-empty shampoo bottle, but he restrained himself and smiled instead. 'Yonatan! Holy shit. What's it been? What are you doing here? I mean –'

Yonatan's lips tightened. He looked over Ezra's shoulder.

Ezra turned around. The crowd was gone, but a handful of stragglers sat on the Parliament steps, rolling cigarettes, phones in their laps. 'Right, the protest. Me too. Don't know what made me come. Can't believe Hirsch is –'

'Could we maybe,' Yonatan shifted from foot to foot, 'go somewhere else?'

'Oh, for sure, mate.' Ezra smiled again and spun to face the Imperial. 'How about a drink?'

Yonatan nodded, and looked at the bar where the after-work crowd had begun to file in. 'Maybe somewhere a little quieter.'

Ezra laughed. 'Of course. Come on, I know just the place.'

Chapter 4

Yonatan

After the conversation with his father, Yonatan felt heavy and sluggish. A man as learned as him would not have reacted so sternly without reason. Yonatan should have done some research and led with a relevant scholarly reference. Not yet bar mitzvahed, he was an ignorant child. But what about his friends? Surely, Rabbi Hirsch's name would be on everyone's lips. What would he say to them when they started talking about the rabbi? If only he could point them to the right piece of Talmudic wisdom, but where it lay only his father knew.

The following day, during the Shabbat *shacharit* service, Yonatan kept his head down and shuckled fervently, knowing none of his *frum* friends would disturb him during prayer. The issue would be afterwards, at *Kiddush* – how could he defer the inevitable then?

Across the *Kiddush* hall, he saw Amit, Pinchas and Dovid in a corner of the room, huddled together conspiratorially. Amit turned to him then, as though he sensed Yonatan watching, and waved him over. If only he had a reason to run from the room, if only a beast were to suddenly appear and chase him, as the Egyptians did the Israelites – he could burst through the congregation, out the doors and into daylight.

'Good Shabbos.' Amit lifted his cup in greeting.

'Good Shabbos,' Yonatan said.

Neither Pinchas nor Dovid turned around, but they shifted aside to make space for him.

'Over here,' Amit said, gesturing for Yonatan to come closer.

Oy. What were they gathering around? A newspaper clipping? A testimonial from one of their classmates? How should he react? Yonatan stepped into their circle.

Pinchas looked over his shoulder.

'What is it?' Yonatan asked.

Amit reached into his jacket pocket and held out a flask of vodka. 'Want some?'

Vodka, that's all it was. *Baruch Hashem*.

Yonatan had drunk wine before. His father let him share the *Kiddush* cup on Shabbat and partake in the four cups at the last Pesach seder. But he'd never tried spirits. Nonetheless, the relief he felt was enough to embolden him to do almost anything. 'Yes, *bevakasha*.'

Thankfully, none of Pinchas, Dovid or Amit mentioned Hirsch. Maybe they had been similarly told to hold their tongues. Yonatan drank to fill the silence. After forcing himself to swallow a quarter of a cup, he felt his stomach settle and limbs loosen, and he was on the cusp of forgetting about the conversation with his father, when he spotted Ezra, looking wide-eyed and eager to talk.

The Monday after that day at *shule*, school resumed at Yahel Academy and everything was the same or, at least, it nearly was. A small number of boys left the school after the incident, mostly those from more secular families. Hardly a loss as far as Yonatan's parents were concerned, but it was to him because Ezra was among them, and though he was often deferential and timid, Ezra was also the only person with whom Yonatan ever felt the burden of expectation ease.

Ezra seemed to hold some kind of unshakeable belief in Yonatan, and the times they spent at Ezra's house were some of the only ones when Yonatan felt he could relax – free from thoughts of his father, *Hashem* and the Torah. Yonatan took care to remember those moments, as though he'd known they would be fleeting – magpies warbling, a basketball bouncing on concrete, the warmth of the sun on the back of his neck, the ball splitting the clouds and sailing through the hoop, his friend's smile.

They remained in touch for a short while after Ezra moved schools, but the event precipitated the beginning of the end for them, and a part of Yonatan always wondered if Ezra's abrupt exit from Yahel was due to more than his parents' fear, if he should've noticed something, been a better friend.

*

After leaving the site of the rally, Ezra led Yonatan up the street for two blocks before abruptly turning down a narrow laneway. The ground was cobblestones. Grotesque graffiti covered the walls – monsters coloured in fluorescent pinks and purples, with tentacle arms, needle teeth and blistering tongues – demons. The foul stench of urine struck Yonatan's nostrils. He looked down, careful to avoid anything wet. At the end of the lane, beside a row of large garbage bins, was an unmarked lime green door.

Ezra approached it, turned to Yonatan and smiled. 'Trust me,' he said. 'This place is good, quiet too.'

Yonatan followed Ezra up a set of winding wooden stairs which ended at a long, dimly lit room. Iron chandeliers hung from the ceiling along with patterned pieces of Asian garments. The walls were exposed red brick, and a spicy, wooden scent pervaded the air. By a fully stocked bar a thin man, dressed in a tight navy suit, sat alone. Light shone off his glossy dark hair.

It was a *treif* restaurant. There was no question about the kitchen being kosher. Had anyone from the community seen him walk into this place, there would be no favourable judging of his actions. Yonatan could add *marit ayin* to the list of sins he was accumulating.

Ezra walked past the bar to the back corner of the room where a row of tabled booths with red leather seats were tucked away. A grating squeal emanated from the leather as they slid into either side of the booth.

Ezra placed his elbows on the table and laughed softly. 'Sorry.' He tilted his head to the side and pulled on one of his short sideburns. 'One of your *peyot* is um –'

'Oh.' Yonatan raised a hand to his cheek, and his fingers brushed the loose sidelock. Deftly he tucked it back beneath his hat. 'Thank you.' His face warmed with embarrassment.

'No worries.' Ezra shuffled out of his seat then and pushed himself up from the table. 'So, what'll it be? My shout.' He smiled.

'Vodka – Absolut if they have it, no ice.'

'Straight vodka?'

'It's . . . I know it's kosher.'

'Oh – right. Coming right up.'

The bartender was a young woman. Dyed red hair flowed onto her shoulders. She wore tight black jeans and a dark singlet that revealed more skin than Yonatan had ever seen on a woman who wasn't his wife. Ezra didn't order their drinks straight away, that much was clear. He must have said something to engage the bartender in conversation, because she laughed and Ezra, with an elbow on the bar, smiled. He looked trim and confident. The sleeves of his checked shirt were rolled up to his elbows and his forearms were dark and thick. A couple days' worth of stubble had been carefully shaped on his cheeks and neck, and though his nose was still hooked, the puffy, awkward child's face that Yonatan remembered had disappeared, replaced by sharp lines and contours that proclaimed affability when he smiled. Leaning over the bar, so close that their faces appeared to touch, the bartender said something in Ezra's ear to which he threw his head back with laughter and slapped the counter. Zealous, brazen, loud. Where did this man come from? What happened to the shy prepubescent, desperate for acceptance, who Yonatan had known?

He remembered once, when they were young, and Jarrod Freeman invited Ezra over to play *Goldeneye* on his Nintendo 64 after school.

'There's multiplayer, where you can play as this really small guy, Oddjob' – walking out of the school grounds, Ezra was a hummingbird on a sugar high – 'or this really big guy, Jaws. And there are cheat modes you can put on and –'

Ezra had played the game once before at his cousin's house, and while Yonatan believed that he liked it, he suspected Ezra had an ulterior motive in bringing him along. It was the first time in all the years they'd been friends that he'd heard of Ezra being invited to someone's house other than his, and he suspected that his friend was nervous. Also, Jarrod lived in South Caulfield, which meant a tram ride all the way down Balaclava Road, and neither of them had ever taken a tram on their own before.

To avoid being seen by their teachers or anyone in the *frum* community who might dob Yonatan in, they ignored the tram stop outside the 7-Eleven on the corner of Hotham and Balaclava and opted for one further down the road.

Only once the tram was visible in the distance did Ezra stop talking and pick up his backpack. When it was one stop away, he went pale. 'What about . . . do you think we need tickets?'

'I don't think it should take that long,' Yonatan said. 'If we see inspectors we'll just get off and walk.'

Ezra nodded, and Yonatan hailed the approaching tram. But as soon as the door closed behind them with a squeal and clunk, Yonatan felt as though they'd made a big mistake. The tram was packed with girls from a nearby school, on their way home, or to go shopping, or play with dolls – whatever it was girls did after school. They weren't Jewish either. Some of them had light skin like him, but others were black, brown or Asian. Jews didn't come in those colours or, at least, none he'd ever met.

There was no room to sit, so Ezra and Yonatan stood, holding onto a pole by the door.

Opposite them, on a seat, were two girls a little older than them wearing purple and white chequered school dresses. One had blonde hair tied into plaits that hung over her shoulders. The other was Asian and wore a pink headband atop her dazzling straight dark hair. They were staring at him and Ezra and whispering to each other. Yonatan hadn't meant to catch their eyes, but once he did, they both smiled.

'Hey,' the Asian girl said. 'Do . . . you . . . speak . . . English?' Yonatan thought that was funny coming from an Asian girl.

'Yeah, of course,' Yonatan said.

The girls giggled. 'Why do you have those?' the blonde girl asked.

'What?'

'The twirly things. It looks funny.'

'They're my *peyot* – we're not allowed to cut them. We're Jewish.'

'How come he doesn't have them then?'

Yonatan turned to Ezra and waited for him to reply. His cheeks were red, but he was facing away, looking out the tram window.

'What about those, coming out of your pants?' the Asian girl asked, pointing to the fringes of his *tzitzit*.

'There's a singlet under here.' He pulled up his school shirt a bit to show them. 'They just hang off the end. We have to wear them.'

'And why the hat?' the blonde girl asked.

Yonatan had forgotten about the large blue *kippah* on the back of his head. 'It's to remember that *Hashem* is above us – actually everywhere, that he's everywhere.'

'*Hashem?*'

'Yeah, you know –' He pointed upwards.

'Oh – is that what you call God?'

Yonatan nodded.

'Is that why the pope wears one too?'

He had no idea who the pope was. 'Maybe.'

'Can I try it on?' the Asian girl asked.

He shook his head. 'Sorry. I'm not meant to –'

'What about your friend? Can I try his?'

Ezra was still fixed on the houses running by the tram window.

'Does he speak? Hey!'

Ezra turned his head then, as though he'd just heard her. 'Sorry?'

'Hi.' She smiled, and her cheeks dimpled. 'Can I try on your hat?'

'Ah, I –' Ezra turned to Yonatan, as if he was asking for approval.

Yonatan shrugged. He didn't feel like it was his place to make the decision for Ezra.

Ezra unclipped the *kippah* from the back of his head and held it out with both hands, like he was presenting a gift, when, without warning, the tram driver slammed the brakes, and Ezra went sprawling on top of the girls.

Yonatan laughed and so did the girls but, beet red, Ezra, still clutching onto his *kippah,* flung himself off them as though they were on fire. 'I'm sorry. I didn't mean to –'

The girls laughed again, straightened their dresses over their knees and smiled. Yonatan figured they were about to tell him not to worry about it, ask if they could still see the hat, when the tram doors opened and Ezra shot out of them like a rock from David's sling.

Is that what had made this Ezra, this gregarious flirt leaning on the bar? Did life without Torah mean that he lived to prove to his younger self what he wasn't? What would he say to Ezra if he were one of his students, coming to him for guidance? Rav Alexandri perhaps: 'Every man in whom there is haughtiness of spirit will be disturbed by the slightest wind.'

Ezra paid for the drinks and returned with a pint of beer and a shot of vodka.

'Cheers,' he said, raising his glass toward Yonatan's.

'*L'chaim*,' Yonatan said, and their glasses clinked.

Ezra laughed. 'Right, of course. *L'chaim*.' He took a sip of his beer, placed it down, laughed again and shook his head, smiling.

'What?' Yonatan asked.

'It's just crazy,' Ezra said. 'Seeing you like . . . this.' He gestured at Yonatan's hat and beard. 'As an adult I mean.'

Yonatan smiled back. 'You've grown up as well.' And then there was a moment of awkward quiet, with each of them turning from the other and looking into their glasses, shy as he and Rivka on their first date.

'Sooo, how have you been?' Ezra asked.

On their walk to the bar, Yonatan had been thinking about a question like that, and how he would respond. For some reason, his instinct was to be defensive, explain that his path had been laid out for him since they were boys and it was inevitable that he should end up the man he was today. But then he realised that he was being ridiculous – he had nothing to prove to Ezra, who was the one who had gone off the *derech* and was living a secular life, flirting with barmaids he'd just met. 'After Yahel Academy, I studied to receive my *smicha*, and then attended a *kollel* for a few years, and now I actually teach the *Derech HaYashar* boys at Yahel – Talmud, *Chumash*, you know the drill.'

Ezra's eyebrows rose and he put his beer down. '*Smicha*, eh? So that means you're –'

Yonatan nodded.

'Rabbi Yoni Kaplan.' Ezra laughed again. 'Well,' he raised his beer, '*L'chaim*, Rabbi Kaplan.'

'*L'chaim*,' Yonatan repeated. 'And you?'

'Me?'

'What have you been doing?'

'Ah,' Ezra nodded and took another sip from his beer. 'I work for the government. Legal policy, nothing special – kind of fell into it.'

'How so?'

'After uni, I went backpacking, six months around Europe, trying to find myself, all that clichéd nonsense. When I got home, I meandered for a while, did some odd jobs, worked in a deli and a mailroom, eventually decided to get my act together and applied for a bunch of graduate programs. The one that stuck was for the Department of Families and Social Services.' He took a long draught of his beer. 'I'm a legal officer in the Social Services Division. Still don't know what I'm doing there half the time – don't often agree with the policies that it's my job to put into place, but most of the time general bureaucracy makes sure nothing gets done.'

'I see – work isn't what drives you.'

Ezra laughed. 'No – no it isn't.'

'Family then, are you married?'

'Me? Nah, nah.' Ezra shook his head. 'Girlfriend though – Tegan.'

'Tegan, nice name.' Yonatan smiled. 'She Jewish?'

'Jewish . . . ah –' Ezra's posture stiffened. 'Well, no but –'

Yonatan laughed. 'Ezra, I'm not your *bubbe*. I don't care if she's Jewish.'

Ezra laughed, relaxed his shoulders. 'Sorry . . . I thought maybe it mattered – you know – that you'd care that I'm a bad Jew.'

Yonatan sat up, kept his expression tight and stern. 'To marry a gentile is to break the covenant with *Hashem*. As it is said in the book of Exodus, "If you will obey Me faithfully and keep My covenant, you shall be My treasured possession among all the peoples."' Yonatan waited for Ezra's features to tighten once more and only then did he laugh. 'Sorry, you're too easy.'

Ezra smiled. 'Glad to see joining the rabbinate didn't take away your sense of humour. What about you – married?'

Yonatan nodded. 'Seven years now. Rivka.' He picked up his shot of vodka, recited *Shehakol* quickly and threw it back. The burn on the swallow was good – like the shock of ice water. He felt awake, alive.

'Sounds lovely. You got any kids?'

Yonatan started to shake his head but stopped himself and then the taste of vodka was back in his throat. He tried to swallow, but his mouth was too dry. He coughed once, and again and again, and was on the verge of a fit when Ezra mercifully passed over his *treif* beer.

It was cool, slightly bitter and refreshing. 'Thank you.' He drank again and passed the beer back to Ezra. 'Rivka . . . she's pregnant with our first.'

'Wow. Congrats, Yoni. That's awesome.'

'And you?'

'Me?' Ezra shook his head. 'Nah . . . but –' He took his elbows off the table, blinked a couple of times and opened his eyes wide as though he wanted to emphasise what he was about to say. 'She's great – Tegan. More than I could ask for. More than a bad Jew like me deserves.' He laughed nervously, raised his beer and finished it.

Ah, there he is. Underneath all that bluster he is the same – sentimental and full of self-doubt. Yonatan smiled. '*Mazel tov*, my friend. I'm happy for you.' And then silence settled on them again, but it was different – Yonatan felt as though they'd regressed to their childhood selves. Ezra, doe-eyed and dependent, always seeking validation, while Yonatan played the part of big brother, happy to take his hand and show him the way, and so he did. 'Tell you what, it's Purim this weekend, but next Shabbat come over to my house, bring Tegan and you can meet Rivka.'

Ezra beamed. 'Seriously?'

'Of course. Don't consider it a favour, it's a mitzvah to invite a lapsed Jew to Shabbat dinner.' Yonatan grinned.

Ezra laughed and stood. 'Actually, you're funnier than I remember.' He offered to grab another round, but Yonatan declined, and Ezra went to buy another beer for himself.

There was history now, a rapport with the bartender, and perhaps he was a bit drunk already. Either way, Ezra was flirting more this time. He flashed his smile relentlessly, and there was a moment where Yonatan swore he touched her hand. There was a gesture back towards Yonatan as well – do you see that Jew over there, he's my old friend, we're reconnecting, aren't I interesting? What about Tegan, Ezra? What about her being more than you deserve? A light panic tickled Yonatan's throat. What did he really know about this man? Hadn't he taken enough risks by sitting where he was at that moment?

Ezra returned, beer in hand, large smile on his thin lips. 'So, what's our old school like? Any of our teachers still around?'

'None now. But the year I started was Rabbi Horowitz's last.'

'Horowitz? No kidding. He must've been a hundred.' Ezra laughed. 'What about the council? I mean – I can't imagine they survived the Hirsch thing.'

Hirsch. It had taken Ezra long enough to broach the subject, considering they wouldn't be there, sitting in that very booth, if not for him. Yonatan had arrived late to the rally, popping out of the underground entrance to Parliament Station in time to hear Avraham's ardent cries for justice. His voice was strong, his speech well-practised, but the skin about his face was grey and loose and he wavered as he spoke like a sapling in the wind.

A passage in *Bereishit* about his namesake came to mind: 'Abraham was old, well-stricken in age.' But this Avraham wasn't stricken by age. His brother suffered, his family suffered and how did the community respond? How did its elders and the school council respond – denial, refuge for your tormentor, ostracisation from the only way of life you've ever known. No, it wasn't age, it was the fight that left him withered, abandonment by a faith that preaches goodwill, virtuosity, kindness to one's neighbour, compassion for those who have suffered.

Yonatan's faith. Yonatan's community. He didn't want to talk about Hirsch or sit in that booth any longer. He'd been gone for too long already. It was time to leave, and so he stood.

Ezra looked up at him, and then at the half pint he had remaining.

'I'm sorry,' Yonatan said. 'I lost track of time. I have to go.'

'No worries, completely understand.' Ezra stood as well and pulled his phone from his pocket. 'Let me give you my number and we can organise that dinner.'

'Sorry.' Yonatan shook his head. 'I don't have a mobile.'

'Ah, right. No worries, you know what, I'll add you on Facebook, we can message that way.' He held out his hand.

Yonatan shook it firmly and stepped out of the booth.

'Hey, Yoni,' Ezra called when he was a few steps away.

He turned around.

'It was great to see you again,' Ezra said, smiling.

Yonatan didn't say anything, only nodded and left.

Chapter 5

Ezra

'I'm looking for a 2016 Cape Mentelle cab sav. Do you have any in stock? Okay, thanks, anyway.' Ezra hung up the phone, tried the next number on his list. It was the seventh specialty wine cellar he'd rung so far. 'Hi, I was just wondering if you had any Cape Mentelle in stock, specifically a 2016 cab sav. You do? And what time do you close? Brilliant, thank you.'

It was coming together. He'd already sourced some black label double cream camembert, and texted Tegan that he might have to work late so she should eat without him. He was relying on her extended history of being unable to resist any kind of dessert, cheese in particular. It was the first step, he told himself, in making amends – alcohol and dairy defibrillator paddles for their relationship.

After six months together – fucking at all hours, going to gigs on weeknights and waking up together, legs entwined, stinking of sex and sweat and wine, late to work every morning – Ezra and Tegan's relationship settled and they submitted to the ease of domestic routine. Around four nights a week, he would go to her place or she his, and they would cook together, recount their days and watch an episode of *Doctor Who* on the couch while eating dinner. Later, they'd have lacklustre, full-time-work-tired sex, sometimes read afterwards and then sleep.

On weekends, one of Tegan's friends usually had a birthday, housewarming or dinner party and then, if he was lucky, Ezra might get to sleep in on Sunday before Tegan hurried him out of the house to catch the tail end of the Prahran Market, when the stall holders began discounting their stock.

Amongst rows of Romanesco broccoli, Jerusalem artichokes, celeriac and other produce he'd never heard of, Ezra would stand guard to their bags, dodging baby strollers and thick, unapologetic grey-haired women, while Tegan spoke to short European men with impossibly thick eyebrows and bargained down the price of sweet potato. And it was in those moments that Ezra often found himself wondering what had happened to them and to the ineffable girl who had taught him what a rim job was.

At the nine-month mark of their relationship, Ezra was restless and increasingly distant. He told Tegan that all of the back and forth made him feel dislocated, that he was losing his sense of himself and didn't feel at home among her Joan Didion prints, piles of clothing and indomitable stack of unread *New Yorkers*. He made clichéd excuses about being too tired from work to see her – choosing instead to share his evenings with the black mould on his bedroom ceiling, Xbox and repeats of *Seinfeld*. It was around then that Ezra had his first blip – Phoebe, petite, amber skin, large fake-lash awnings over blue eyes, light with apathy and mischief. She worked for the Department of Health.

They'd met at a training session in the city. One of those generic public policy events most government employees were forced to attend once a year. In a conference room with several round tables set up cabaret style, Ezra didn't notice Phoebe, sitting across from him, until their overly enthusiastic facilitator repeated the phrase 'paradigm shift' for the third time and she mimed placing a gun to her head. Ezra tried to stifle a laugh, but a snort escaped, and after clapping a hand to his mouth, he found Phoebe beaming at him.

For the rest of the session, they passed Phoebe's notebook back and forth to each other, playing a game of Hangman. Her first phrase read 'I _M SO BOR_D' when he guessed it. He followed that with 'K_LL ME N_W'. Phoebe then wrote 'ALREAD_ DEAD, TH_S _S HELL', and Ezra had to hold in another laugh. He was stumped for a minute then, before he chose 'PARADI_M SHIF_' and it was Phoebe's turn to laugh, attracting a glare from the facilitator. Her final turn read 'DRIN_ AFTER THI_?'

He told himself it was nothing, a drink between new friends, that the only reason he didn't mention Tegan was because she hadn't asked, that after one more pint he'd stand up, tell Phoebe he had to go, that his girlfriend was likely waiting for him, and hold out his hand – platonic. But he didn't. It was two more pints before he stood up and followed Phoebe out of the bar to the tram stop on Swanston Street where they hugged goodbye, a lingering-too-close hug, so that he was aware of her chest pressed against him, of the smell of coconut shampoo, the nape of her neck inches from his lips, but that was still okay, you might hug a relative like that, a good friend even – the line was fuzzy but it hadn't been crossed. They pulled apart, and he was almost gone, blameless, free. And then he leant back in.

Why? Afterwards he would tell himself he was too drunk, that he didn't know what he was doing. But who the fuck was he kidding? He was there. Her mouth was small, swallowed by his. Her lips tasted of cider and her tongue was lean and quick. He thought all of those things, he was aware of them, while his conscience flashed behind his eyes, *Don't do it, don't do it, don't do it,* but he did anyway, and continued, because he wanted to know that he could.

For weeks afterwards, Ezra's stomach felt like he'd been chewing on lightbulbs. He couldn't sleep and was terrified that Tegan could read the guilt on his face. He oscillated between deciding to confess and concluding that it was nothing, would only hurt Tegan and wasn't worth jeopardising their relationship over. But then the landlord of Ezra's share house announced they were selling up and Tegan suggested they find an apartment together. Yes, it was perfect, as though fate had handed him a giant antacid.

Tegan mentioned love first. Soon after they moved in together. One of countless Sunday mornings spent in bed until a purple-hued sky woke and shook off its clouds to bare early afternoon blue. Still half-asleep, there was no telling which were Tegan's limbs and which his, and Ezra knew if he closed his eyes again, he might forget his need to pee and lapse back into a kind of content he was already feeling nostalgic for. But then Tegan turned to him, pressed her dry lips against his and said, 'I love you.'

Unsure if he were dreaming, he said it back. Because, awake or asleep, there was no other answer he could give. For all the discussions they'd had about the importance of communication, how they were both intelligent and receptive to each other's opinions, he knew that if he hesitated, even for a moment, their relationship was as good as over. Not because Tegan was the kind of person to overreact, but because the imbalance wouldn't be sustainable. If he'd given her that second, she would have said, 'I don't want you to feel any pressure. I'm just telling you how I feel. I don't have any expectations.'

But whether or not that was true, he knew himself. If he didn't say it, he would feel as though Tegan were assessing his every smile, kiss and touch, asking herself, 'Does he love me yet?' And the thought of his feelings being expected, sooner or later, to develop into a discernible state of 'love' would get to him, until one day he'd be unable to feel anything other than the ever-present buzzsaw of his own anxiety. And so he said, 'I love you too,' and gave Tegan a long, delicate kiss while pressing his hand to her cheek. A kiss that he imagined you would give someone you loved.

In all honesty, Ezra wasn't sure what 'love' felt like. Was it an animalistic, uninhibited need to fuck the instant you saw someone? Bubbling, frenzied unease over an unresponded text message? The velvet meant-to-be comfort of their body at rest against yours? He'd felt all of those, but each seemed too reductive. If love was anything at all, Ezra imagined it was better expressed as a metaphor – analogous to an experience, something varied and complex that culminated in an intangible sense of peace and warmth and joy. And he did feel that for Tegan; once, or so he thought, on a trip the two of them took to Margaret River to celebrate a year of being together.

It was Tegan's idea. Winery tours, cheese boards and a stone cottage overlooking the calm river surface. 'Like adults,' Tegan had said. 'A real couple.' But still, they'd sculled chardonnay and slurped cab sav, giggling as affronted sommeliers withdrew their glasses and purposely underpoured their requests for something a little less oaky, with a hint of cinnamon and a bolder finish. Half-drunk, Ezra would navigate back-country roads in their rented hatchback, on to the next winery, while Tegan teased at his crotch with her fingers.

One evening out there, the weather turned on them on the way back from a delicatessen. He and Tegan had stocked up on locally produced venison chorizo and double cream camembert when a distant rumbling announced the arrival of a sheet of ashen clouds. Ezra switched on the hatchback's high beams. The wind picked up, and he drove slow as the occasional gust whipped the car into a sway. Around them, a tunnel of pale-barked trees, stretching into darkness, rattled and lashed at each other. Ahead, a snapped branch, thick as a man's thigh, lay across their lane. Ezra made to drive around it, but Tegan told him to stop the car. She got out, hefted it up and threw it into the woods while the wind did its best to blind her with her own hair.

'Someone might get hurt,' she said once back in the car. He felt proud of her, but also a little jealous and ashamed that it hadn't been his instinct to do the same.

After that, they took turns removing the branches from the road, and though it almost doubled their journey back to the cottage, and he was worn with exhaustion when they arrived, it felt like they'd accomplished something together, and that made him feel good, satisfied.

The cottage had a small wood-burner fireplace that he'd been getting better at lighting. He layered it with newspaper and kindling before adding a couple of larger logs. Once they'd cracked and the hiss-pop of the fire tingled his skin, he pulled some couch cushions to the ground and called Tegan over. She brought him a glass of wine and curled up to him, resting on his chest while outside the storm thrummed against the windows and distant lightning bursts illuminated the river beneath them. He kissed the back of Tegan's head and closed his eyes.

That was it, that moment. And with the wine and cheese, Ezra supposed he was hoping to forget about his doubts and indiscretions, bring them back to that place and reinstate the simple pattern of their life together. There were endless episodes of *Doctor Who* after all, and he didn't mind it so much. It was worth it to be with Tegan. Did anyone actually know what kind of life they wanted, anyway?

Tegan had been working late recently, preparing a response to a Senate Committee Inquiry on Crisis Intervention Services, but she'd taken on a side project as well – the Hirsch case. After Ezra told her about it, she'd started researching – newspaper articles, victim interviews, relevant case law. The Kliger family had filed a civil suit against Yahel Academy some years ago for enabling Hirsch's abuse and helping him flee the country, and Tegan was still in the process of combing through all of the available documents. It was all she could talk about, and because of Ezra's proximity to the case, she was constantly badgering him for information.

'Avi Cukierman, did you know him?'

'How many students in a class?'

'What's a *beth din*?'

She had a predilection to take on a cause – it was her nature. But Ezra suspected that it was his intimate distance that drove her frenzy in this instance, as though he was the one searching for justice – asking to be saved.

The wine cellar was out in Belgrave, and the round trip took Ezra almost two hours after work. He was rarely home later than Tegan, and he imagined she would rush him at the front door, where he planned to hold the wine and cheese behind his back and present them to her, rom-com Valentine's style. But Tegan didn't greet him when he entered.

'Tegan?' he called.

'Hey,' she said from the living room.

She was on the couch, hunched over her glowing laptop screen, wearing her Radiohead t-shirt, grey tracksuit pants and cream Ugg boots. To either side of her, spread out on the couch cushions, were printed articles and two of his university textbooks – *International Law* and *Criminal Law and Procedure*.

Ezra took a step towards her and held out his gifts, labels facing Tegan. 'I thought maybe we could –'

Tegan looked up from the screen, glanced at the wine and cheese, then flicked her eyes back to whatever she had been reading. 'I'm all right, thanks – been snacking a lot.' She pointed to an almost empty bowl of potato chips next to her. 'You go ahead, though.'

Ezra sighed and took the wine and cheese into the kitchen. He could go back out there, remind her of what made that particular wine and cheese special, but what was the point? It had been a stupid idea.

'Did you know,' Tegan said, 'the fucker has been claiming he's catatonic now, and that's why he's unfit to stand trial?'

'Sorry,' Ezra called from the kitchen, 'the fucker?'

'Hirsch.'

Ezra found a corkscrew, opened the wine and poured himself a generous glass. It was fruitier than he remembered, but on the swallow he could almost feel the heat from their crackling fire. He remembered Tegan placing a slice of cheese on her nipple, laughing and telling him that was his plate. He scooped up the cheese with his tongue, and Tegan shivered. 'Good boy,' she said, smiling.

'Catatonic?' Ezra asked.

'Yep – unbelievable, right? That was five years ago, and then the Israelis slapped a home detention order on him. Home detention, for a catatonic! But the Kliger family say they have evidence to the contrary. Witnesses in the town he's been living in told them he's been going to the synagogue, at the store, all kinds of shit, so the Kligers hired a private investigator, got video.'

'So what happens now?' Ezra asked.

'There's a chance, if the protest and the new evidence worked, that the Israeli Justice Minister will have him arrested for breaching his detention order and for obstruction of justice. She could arrange an independent psychiatrist's report. And if the psychiatrist declares him fit, he'll finally stand for his extradition trial.'

Ezra refilled his glass, took another drink and remembered waking up to Tegan's baby-rattle snore, the fire reduced to embers beside them, and a small pool of her pink drool on his chest.

'And do you think the Israelis will do that?' Ezra asked.

'I do. From what I've read, the ultra-Orthodox have a lot of sway in Israeli politics, and that's likely what's been holding up the extradition so far. But arguing against a blatant obstruction of justice charge would look bad for them and put a strain on the Israeli Government's relationship with ours.'

The blanket had slipped down, and he pulled it up over Tegan's shoulders. She stirred, her eyelashes tickling him as she woke, raised her head and smiled. A thread of saliva clung to her lip. Tracing it back to him, she swept aside the lake on his chest with the back of her hand, smiled again, and said, 'Whoopsies.'

'The bullshit thing,' Tegan said, looking up from her laptop, 'is that it's been twenty fucking years, the Kligers have been campaigning for all of this time and it hasn't strained their relationship yet. Fucking politicians.'

She craned her neck upwards and kissed him, tasting of cherry, raspberry, a hint of aniseed. She dropped her cheek back to his chest and spoke muffled words into him. 'You know what I think, Ezra. I think you're good and kind and thoughtful. And I think we fit.' She kissed the valley of his chest with the side of her mouth. 'Right here,' she said, 'this is where I'm meant to be.'

Ezra tipped his head back, finished his glass and closed his eyes, but the fire in the cottage was out, replaced by one in his gut. A low-key burn, rising through his chest and into his throat till his mouth was sour with the smoke of it, and he had to run to the bathroom, damming his lips until he reached the toilet and was free to let everything out.

Chapter 6

Yonatan

Yonatan was late to the morning service on Shabbat Zachor. The night before, he'd slept restlessly and woke often, with his deepest, most rejuvenating sleep only arriving once Rivka was already awake, nudging at his prostrate body and chirping in his ear. 'Yoni. Get up, Yoni. A lazy person has nothing to eat, Yonatan.'

Ordinarily, he would walk the few blocks to *shule* on his own and arrive early on Shabbat morning with plenty of time to greet the other members of the congregation and take his seat before the service began. Afterwards, he would meet up with Rivka at *Kiddush* in the hall behind the prayer room. But that morning they walked together, Yonatan in his white shirt, black suit and fedora, and Rivka wearing a white jacket over a long grey dress, and a black cloche with a large white bow on top of her *sheitel*. Sweat ran down Yonatan's face as he quick-stepped along the sidewalk, and Rivka struggled to keep up. Though he couldn't say why, he felt conspicuous walking to *shule* with his wife by his side.

Shabbat dinner, the previous night, had been only the two of them, and he'd told Rivka about inviting Ezra and his partner over for the following week. He explained how he and Ezra went to Yahel Academy together but Ezra's parents had pulled him out, and that he was now somewhat secular. Thankfully, Rivka hadn't asked what had motivated Ezra's parents to take him from the school.

'Is he *halachic*?' she asked.

Yonatan recalled Ezra's shameless flirting at the bar. 'He may be Modern Orthodox, possibly Reform.'

'And his wife?'

'They are not married, and I think she is a *goy*.'

'A *goy*. You're telling me I need to prepare Shabbat dinner for a *goy*?'

'Rivka, please, it's a mitzvah to lead a stray sheep back to the flock.'

'A sheep maybe, but a *shiksa*? Do you want me to go out and buy some ham, prawns perhaps, a cheeseburger?'

'Rivka!' It was unlike her to be so judgemental.

'Where did you reconnect with this *goyishe yid*, anyway?'

Yonatan had lied. What choice did he have? He said they met at Glick's, that Ezra was buying donuts for Tegan, boasting that they were the best in Melbourne.

Once inside the *shule*, Yonatan and Rivka separated without speaking to one another – Rivka heading upstairs to the women's section, while Yonatan approached the door to the main prayer room. He could hear the melodious voice of the *chazzan* within – the service had already begun.

Holding a stiff, apologetic smile on his lips, Yonatan edged past knees and polished dress shoes to his seat, where he took his *tallit* from its bag, donned it and recited the blessing for doing so.

Throughout the service, his mind continued to wander, and he had difficulty following the proceedings. During the silent reading of the *Amidah*, his thoughts strayed to the previous night's argument with Rivka. She knew him too well; lying had been a mistake. He should've consulted her before inviting Ezra over and trusted her with the truth. It would be best if he made amends and apologised. Surely she would understand why he went to the protest, *cherem* or not.

Feeling better, Yonatan was able to ground himself for the Torah reading of *Parshat Zachor* and the *haftorah* afterwards. Then Chief Rabbi Feiner approached the lectern in front of the ark for his sermon. Yonatan was ready to listen. Rabbi Feiner had been appointed chief rabbi a year or so ago. A student of Rav Bloom, he was in his mid-fifties and bald but for sparse hair on the sides of his head. A short, neat beard of grey patched with brown hung from red cheeks beneath puffy, weary looking eyes. He appeared exhausted all the time, a look that was easy to mistake for learned; one that, Yonatan imagined, helped him gain his appointment, along with the favour of the then growing followers of Rav Bloom.

'Today we read *Parshat Zachor*,' Feiner began. 'What does *Parshat Zachor* say? It says, remember Amalek. "Remember the Amalekites and what they did to you on your journey out of Egypt." What did they do? The Amalekites targeted the elderly and feeble at the rear, the most vulnerable, and to them they did unspeakable things. And so the Torah tells us to "erase the name of Amalek from under Heaven" – do not forget.

'On Purim, we tell the story of Haman, the vizier to King Achashverosh, who plotted to destroy the Jewish people. Haman, we are told, was a descendant of Amalek. The Romans, destroyers of the Second Temple, were descendants of Amalek; the Cossacks of the seventeenth century, Amalek; Hitler and the Nazis, Amalek. "Remember," the Torah says, never forget Amalek. But today, in this modern world, where is Amalek? You ask, is there still Amalek?'

Feiner paused and looked from one side of the *shule* to the other. 'Is there still anti-semitism in the world? Of course there is, and until the *Moshiach* comes there always will be, but that is nothing new. Yes, Amalek is here, but he does not walk around with a swastika on his arm, his hand raised in the air. Our Amalek is hidden. He is quiet and subtle and insidious and that makes him more dangerous than any threat we have faced before.

'Again, you ask, where is he? You want to see? You want to know?' Feiner pointed to the adjacent window. 'Go outside. There he is, on the street, in our workplaces, in our very homes. Our Amalek is apathy. He is Jewish boys growing up without bar mitzvah, Jews eating pig and crayfish. Intermarriage. Our Amalek is a worldwide decrease in *shule* attendance, and in this age of immodesty, perpetuated by the Internet and mobile phones he grows more powerful every day.'

The congregation stirred audibly. Reb Feiner paused until they settled. '"Remember," the Torah says. But I say to you remember not just Amalek, remember who you are. The descendants of Avraham, led by Moshe out of Egypt, *am segula*, the people chosen by *Hashem* to receive the Torah. A holy people. A light unto all other nations. For thousands of years we have triumphed through adversity and suffering. While the greatest nations in all of history have disappeared, we have prevailed.

'But what is our survival without memory? What good is existence without identity? Tradition, ritual, faith. These are the cornerstones of life. *Halacha* guides us, and *halacha* binds us together. Look to your neighbour. He is a *Yehudi*. He is your brother and your father and your son. "Remember Amalek." But also remember Avraham and Yitzchak and Yaacov and Yehoshua and Levi and Moshe and Aharon. Remember who you are. Shabbat shalom.' Rabbi Feiner left the lectern.

Yonatan stood for *Musaf*, frowning. It was the most impassioned sermon he'd heard Rabbi Feiner give since being granted his position, and it was no coincidence. *Zachor* was a historically divisive *parashah*; it practically commanded the Jews to commit genocide. It was the perfect opportunity for him to confirm his alignment with the more conservative members of the *shule* board, or for them to indirectly assert the *shule*'s future direction to the congregation.

Shortly after the service came to an end, the congregation sprang to life. All bustle and chatter as men and women filed out of the prayer room towards the hall next door for *Kiddush*.

Yonatan spotted Rivka by the tabbouleh and fattoush, holding a paper plate, likely filled with smoked salmon, falafel and hummus. She was speaking to Shimon Brener. Shimon had studied with Yonatan at his *kollel*. He was a tall man with a thin, dark beard, a high forehead and black marbles for eyes. Largely, he was pleasant enough and well-liked, but he had been a mediocre student at the *kollel*. Shimon was known for lacking conviction, always careful to provide equal weight to contradictory sides of Talmudic interpretation. And that constant avoidance of conflict irritated Yonatan. He'd even blown up at Shimon once over an interpretation of a verse in the Pesach *Haggadah*.

'They can't both be right. Rashi and Nachmanides are saying different things. You have to pick a side, Shimon. Pick a side.' Later, Yonatan would apologise for his outburst, but he still questioned what such a man wanted from life.

‘Good Shabbos,’ Shimon said, holding up his drink.

Yonatan nodded. ‘Good Shabbos.’

‘Last Purim for you two.’ Shimon smiled.

Last Purim. What did he mean by that? It was difficult to hear over all the voices in the crowded room. ‘Sorry?’

Shimon leant in closer and gestured to Rivka’s belly. ‘Last Purim for just the two of you.’

‘Ah . . . yes.’

Shimon smiled. ‘Such *nachas*.’

‘Yes – we have been blessed.’ Yonatan considered the wine on the table behind him. He would need a drink if he was going to be stuck speaking to Shimon. Rivka placed her plate on the table, added some tabbouleh to it. He couldn’t apologise until they were alone. He tried to catch her eye, but she was focused on her food, picking capers off her salmon.

Yonatan knew he should ask Shimon about his family, but for the life of him he couldn’t remember the name of his wife or how many children they had. The silence between them went on for too long, past awkward. Rivka’s mouth was full; she couldn’t save them. Shimon looked from side to side, as though he were about to excuse himself, when Yonatan spotted Menachem edging towards them.

‘Good Shabbos, Menachem,’ Shimon said, with more spirit than Yonatan imagined he normally would.

‘Good Shabbos,’ Menachem said quickly. ‘A profound luminary, our Reb Feiner.’ He turned and looked at Yonatan. ‘Amalek among us.’ He shook his head. ‘A welcome warning.’

Shimon laughed. ‘I’m not sure Reb Feiner was saying Amalek is among us literally. I thought maybe it was a call to arms for spirituality.’

'It is no joke, Shimon,' Menachem said. 'Amalek is indeed among us, literally so, and it is nothing new. In the early twentieth century, Rav Mendel Wollman, a visionary European scholar, suggested that all *mumars* and *apikorsim* are descendants of Amalek. If they did not exist, they could not infect others with their apathy for *halacha*.'

Shimon nodded. 'I see what you're saying, Menachem, but I would've thought that with education and outreach we could –'

'Rabbi Benyamin Grossman of the Echad Yisrael party in Israel has expressed similar views,' Menachem said. 'There is a growing collective in Jerusalem. With globalisation and the advent of the Internet and social media, there has not been such a threat since the *shoah*.'

The colour drained from Shimon's face as if he'd stood up too fast. The poor *schlep*. Yonatan felt for him, but he was also glad not to be the subject of Menachem's vitriol. As it was, he thought it was likely that Reb Feiner was speaking of philosophy and not individual Jews themselves as Amalek. To suggest Jews were instructed to wipe out themselves, only two generations from the *shoah* would be –

'Manny.' Rivka's sharp tone interrupted Yonatan's thoughts. 'A mitzvah for *Yehudim* to erase fellow *Yehudim* – really?'

Menachem appeared slightly startled, but then he composed himself and turned to his sister. 'Some commentators advise that *apikorsim* shouldn't be considered to be –'

'Some?' Rivka shook her head, placed her plate on the table. 'What about Maimonides? Did he not say that when a *goy* converts, and accepts all the commandments, even a descendant of Amalek, they are to be considered Jews for all matters.'

'Yes, he said conversion extends to Amalekites but –'

'So our actual enemies, specified in the Torah, are granted the opportunity to learn from their mistakes and repent, but you would have us stone a *goyishe Yehudi* who drives on Shabbos?' Rivka laughed. 'Oh, Manny. I'm sorry, but I have to agree with Shimon on this one.'

Rivka was right. Yonatan hadn't thought about that line of argument and apparently neither had Menachem. His chubby face reddened. He muttered something about getting a drink and left them.

Shimon, facing Rivka, radiated gratitude. Yonatan half-expected him to drop to his knees and kiss her feet like an idolater. He opened his mouth to speak, but Rivka turned to Yonatan, placed her hands on the back of her hips, arched her back and grimaced. Her forehead beaded sweat; she reached out for his elbow. 'I'm sorry. I'm a bit tired. Would you mind if we went home now?'

At her touch, Yonatan felt a swelling of warmth. Seemingly, all had been forgiven. 'Of course.' He held his hand out to Shimon, shook his and said, '*Shabbat shalom*.'

'*Shabbat shalom*, Rivka,' Shimon called.

She nodded, put her damp hand in Yonatan's, and they left.

Rivka was silent on their walk home. A muggy air had settled on the early afternoon. The first of the season's fallen leaves crunched beneath their feet. Summer's heat had lingered longer than Yonatan ever remembered. His breath was short, chest tight, as though there was sawdust in his lungs. When they reached the shade of the awning above their front door, and he was able to cough himself to relief, he paused with the key part way in the lock, remembering what he had wanted to say to Rivka.

But when he turned to her, her eyes were vague and distracted. The neckline of her dress was darkened by sweat. 'Are you feeling all right?' Yonatan asked.

'Sorry,' she said, smiling lightly, looking straight through him. 'It's the heat.' She reached out for his forearm, and he was surprised by how much of her weight she leant against him. 'I think I just need to lie down.'

Yonatan nodded and opened the door. He couldn't possibly burden her now. They'd talk later, when she was well rested. 'If you need anything,' he said, 'I'll be in my study. *Chalomot paz*.'

Rivka squeezed his hand and shuffled towards their bedroom.

Every Shabbat, after returning home, Yonatan would study Talmud until it was time for the evening service, while Rivka joined other women in the community visiting the sick and frail. No-one would question her absence, though, taking into account her pregnancy.

In his study, Yonatan plucked a copy of the Babylonian Talmud off his bookshelf and opened it to where he had recently been revising. But as soon as he sat down, his attention wavered and the ink blurred on the page. He closed the Talmud, pinched the bridge of his nose with his fingers and reached for his lowest desk drawer and the envelope within it.

*

He'd found the clinic online, a simple search, and made the appointment by phone from his office at Yahel. The clinic was in McKinnon. A corner block of textured concrete and glass with 'MCKINNON FERTILITY CENTRE' written above the entrance. He was thirty minutes early to his appointment, and he used all of those minutes to change his mind more times than he cared to count.

The doctor was a young man – younger, Yonatan guessed, than himself – wearing a white shirt and red striped tie. His short, thick hair was swept to the side in a neat quiff. His name was Doctor Richards.

'So you're after a fertility test, is that right?' Doctor Richards said, turning from his computer screen.

'Yes,' Yonatan said.

'All right, pretty simple. We'll need a semen sample and then we'll do some tests to measure the health of your sperm. Things like the number of sperm, the shape of them and their motility – how they move, that is. Just need to ask you a few questions, and then we'll get you to provide that sample.'

Yonatan nodded.

'Do you smoke?'

'No.'

'Marijuana?'

'No.'

'How often do you drink?'

'A glass of wine or two on Shabbat.'

'Have you ever used steroids?'

'No.'

'Do you work with toxic chemicals or in an extremely hot environment?'

'I am a teacher, so only if you consider teenagers toxic.' Yonatan smiled, but the doctor's face was unflinching.

There were some other questions about his medical history as well, all of which Yonatan answered negatively.

'Are you married?' Doctor Richards asked.

'Yes.'

'Has your wife had a fertility test as well?'

Yonatan shook his head. 'My wife . . . my wife is fine.'

'Okay – can I ask then,' Doctor Richards crossed his legs and leant back in his chair, 'do you have any reason to doubt your fertility?'

'Some.'

There was silence between them for a moment. Yonatan assumed Doctor Richards was waiting for him to elaborate, but he didn't and the doctor seemed to accept that, because he opened his desk drawer and handed Yonatan a small plastic container, before standing up and asking Yonatan to follow him to the collection room.

It is a sin to masturbate. Yonatan knew this, everyone knew this. In the Gemara, Rabbi Yochanan said a man who 'emits semen in vain deserves death' – adultery by hand, they called it, but Yonatan didn't see any choice in this instance. He imagined Rabbi Yochanan might do the same in his position.

A large black leather recliner sat in the corner of the room. To the side was a sink with soap and paper towels. In front of the recliner, mounted to the wall, was a flat-screen television that the doctor offered to show him how to use. Yonatan declined. *Hashem* did not need to see him commit more than one sin at a time.

In his youth, before he knew it was a sin, Yonatan had admittedly experimented with the act. And of late, he had done so again in the bathroom of Yahel, sitting in a stall, half caught up in the motion and half listening for footsteps and the squeak of the bathroom door. He did so to test his ability to meet this moment, because there could be no doubt – his efforts would not be in vain.

Yonatan waited for the doctor to leave, but he stayed by the recliner as if he were waiting for Yonatan to ask him something.

'I was just wondering,' the doctor said, 'if you'd like . . . we get many religious patients here, and I understand there can be cultural difficulties around the provision of a sample. And . . .

you should know that your wife is welcome to come and assist in the procurement of your sample.'

'My wife? No, thank you. That won't be necessary.'

The doctor nodded and left Yonatan in that small room with the lid of the plastic cup digging into his palm.

*

The glue on the envelope's flap was losing its purchase. He didn't know why he was so careful to reseal it after every opening. If Rivka found it, everything would come to light – pleading ignorance of the results couldn't dispute his performance of the test.

For the umpteenth time, he unfolded the paper within and read the words Doctor Richards had recited on his follow-up visit: 'complete asthenozoospermia'.

'It means your sperm have no progressive motility,' the doctor said. 'Rather than swimming in a straight line, they move in a tight circle. It happens to around one in every 5000 men. There are options, though. Studies have shown that supplements can –'

'That's fine,' Yonatan said, standing and extending his hand. 'It's all I wanted to know.'

He put the letter back in the envelope, resealed it, once again, and placed it back in his desk drawer.

Walking silently, in his stockinged feet, Yonatan crept to his and Rivka's bedroom. The door was open and a sliver of light pierced the border of their curtains, so that Rivka's silhouette was visible at the edge of her single bed. Above the covers and still wearing her dress, she lay on her side curled into herself like the leaf of a fern. As though he might trigger an alarm, Yonatan sat on Rivka's bed and gently let the bed's springs absorb his weight. He then swung his legs onto the mattress and inched forward until his chest was pressed against Rivka's back. Her breathing was heavy and rhythmic, a deep carrying-weight-you're-not-used-to sleep, so he didn't fear waking her as he looped his arm over hers, rested his hand on her belly and closed his eyes.

Something touched him.

He snapped his hand back as though he'd been bitten, pushed himself away from Rivka and sat upright. Her breathing remained slow and even. Thankfully, he hadn't woken her. He got off the bed and walked to the hallway where he could see his hand in the afternoon light. There was nothing there. Was it a dream? He didn't think he'd fallen asleep but perhaps he had.

Chapter 7

Ezra

Yonatan's house was a narrow two-storey unit, orange brick with brown terracotta roof tiles, near the corner of Hotham and Inkerman – streets that bordered the Jewish community's self-imposed ghetto. Ezra parked a block away to avoid offending Yonatan and his wife, in case they saw him driving on Shabbat, though he wasn't sure it mattered yet. According to his phone, they had twenty minutes until sunset.

'There's like this thread,' Ezra said to Tegan who was wearing a dark blue shirt, buttoned high, and a long black skirt over stockings. There was a slit on the side, but it was the longest skirt she owned. 'It goes around the whole neighbourhood, running across telephone poles or something like that. It lets Jews carry things in their pockets on Shabbat, which they can't do otherwise – can't remember why, must be considered work in some way.'

Tegan was holding a bottle of Red Concord *mevushal* wine that she'd picked up from the Coles in Elsternwick. She didn't respond, only stared at the flyscreen door as if she were expecting something to jump out from the other side.

A piece of masking tape had been stuck over the doorbell, and a handwritten sign above it read 'PLEASE KNOCK'.

'No electricity,' Ezra said, gesturing to the doorbell before opening the flyscreen and knocking as instructed. He then reached into his pocket, withdrew the small black *kippah* he'd bought years ago for his grandmother's funeral, and put it on his head.

Not a moment later, Yonatan opened the door, as though he'd been standing on the other side the entire time. 'Good Shabbos,' he said, and shook Ezra's hand. 'And you must be Tegan.' He held out his hand to her, but Tegan looked at it as if she were unfamiliar with the gesture.

'Sorry,' Tegan said, finally accepting Yonatan's hand. 'Ezra told me that you might not be allowed to –'

Ezra laughed. 'Sorry, mate. I thought you might be *shomer negiah*.'

Yonatan smiled at Ezra. 'I'm impressed you remember that much.' He turned back to Tegan. 'I am, but for Ezra's partner I think a handshake is okay. Just don't tell my wife.' He laughed and held the door open for them.

Inside, Yonatan led them to the lounge room where two caramel leather couches faced each other across a coffee table. The walls were cream stucco and sparsely decorated. Centred on one was a painting of what Ezra assumed was one of the great commentators – a thick man, dressed in black, sitting with his hands clasped in front of him. A square white beard covered his chin and a black fedora his head. The skin beneath his eyes was slightly puffy and well-lined, and the ends of his thick lips curved with the beginnings of a smile. A friendly man, jolly even.

Slap a red suit on him and take a seat on his lap. He was born for the role.

A framed certificate hung opposite the painting, a few paragraphs of printed Hebrew script followed by handwritten signatures, all enclosed within an ornate floral border. That one Ezra knew. He'd forgotten the name for it in Hebrew, but it was Yonatan and Rivka's marriage contract. He remembered asking Yonatan about the one that hung in his parents' house. He was reminded of being back there now – Mrs Kaplan's furtive glances as she walked past Yonatan's room at least twice an hour, and Reb Kaplan, rarely seen but always a looming, commanding presence that echoed from within his closed study door.

More than the contract, and the musty stench of old furniture, it was the bull-in-a-china-shop feeling that took him back there – best behave in this house, God's watching.

'Would you like a glass of water?' Yonatan asked.

'Yes, thank you,' Tegan said. 'Oh, and this is for you.' She held out the bottle of wine.

'Ah, *mevushal*,' Yonatan said, taking the bottle. 'Perfect.' He smiled and left through a door on the other side of the room.

Tegan sat stiffly on the edge of a couch, placed a hand on Ezra's knee and scanned the room. Nerves, Ezra figured – an intermingling of discomfort and excitement.

After seeing the film *Disobedience*, a year or so ago, Tegan confided to Ezra that she liked his Jewishness, that it was so much more interesting than her boring Anglo background. She even used the word 'exotic', enunciating it slowly as though it were pleasurable to say.

'It's a contract,' Ezra said, pointing to the certificate, 'from their wedding. I could probably read it. He stood up and walked over to the wall. '*Beh-ehchad beh-shabbat beh-shlishi yom le-chodesh* . . .'

Tegan smiled. 'Very impressive. What does it mean?'

'Ah . . . it's a date, I think. *Ehchad* is one and *shlishi* might be the third, so I think they got married on the first Shabbat, on the third day of the month, something like that.'

'On the sabbath? Didn't you say there's all of these restrictions on the sabbath? Why would you get married then?'

Ezra shrugged. 'I don't know.'

Yonatan returned then, with two glasses of water and a woman trailing him. An elegant, long-sleeved, black dress hung to her ankles over a slight baby bump. Her hair was shoulder length, dead straight and dark brown with a heavy fringe. It took Ezra a moment to remember that it was likely a wig.

'Ezra, Tegan – this is my wife, Rivka.'

Ezra nodded and said, 'Nice to meet you.'

Remaining seated, Tegan smiled widely and told Rivka that she had a lovely home. 'Thank you,' Rivka said. 'I was just about to light the candles for Shabbat. Would you care to join me, Tegan?'

'Oh . . . okay, sure.' Tegan stood up, smiled nervously as she walked by Ezra, and followed Rivka out of the room.

Ezra gave Yonatan a sideways glance. 'Rivka knows that Tegan isn't Jewish – right?'

Yonatan nodded and sighed. 'Sorry, I think she wants to test the *goy*. But it's nothing to do with you two – the pregnancy has been hard on her, and she's been cooking all afternoon.'

'No worries, Tegan loves this stuff – will lap it up, whatever Rivka's intentions are.'

'I'm glad,' Yonatan smiled. 'She seems lovely.' He edged forward on his seat, pursed his lips as if he was going to speak but turned to the still-closed door first. 'I just remembered – do me a favour. I told Rivka that we ran into each other at Glick's.'

'Glick's? On Carlisle Street?'

Yonatan nodded. 'You were buying donuts.'

Ezra laughed. 'Okay, sure. But why can't you –'

'There's a *cherem* on Avraham Kliger and his family. I shouldn't have been at the protest.'

'Sorry, a what?'

'It means a ban, excommunication.'

'On Kliger? Why him? What about Hirsch?'

Yonatan sighed. 'Officially, it's because the Kligers went to the secular authorities instead of letting a *beth din* decide Hirsch's fate. But –'

'But what?'

'But the truth is that Yahel Academy had been hearing allegations against Hirsch for years. They covered for his behaviour again and again. So the Kligers went to the police.'

'Jesus.' Ezra shook his head. 'Sorry, but that's bullshit.'

'I know, I know, but please just don't mention that I –'

The door opened, and Tegan re-entered, smiling. She sat down next to Ezra. 'How was it?' Ezra asked.

'Fascinating,' Tegan said. 'Rivka wore a veil, and she showed me how to light the candles. How you cover your eyes and say the blessing. She taught it to me. It was something like *ba-rook ut-ah uh-doh* –'

Ezra nodded attentively but he was still thinking about the *cherem* on Kliger. So Rivka didn't know Yonatan broke the *cherem*. What did that mean? What would she think if she knew? He'd better tell Tegan not to mention Hirsch. Though, because of her fascination he'd already told her it might be a sensitive subject. She said she'd only mention him if it came up, and then she'd be subtle about her interest. Ezra opened his mouth, about to interrupt Tegan, when the door opened again and Rivka announced that the sun had set and it was time for *Kiddush*.

In the dining room, four places had been set on a rectangular table, sheathed with a white woollen tablecloth. At the head of the table were two long candles burning in silver holders next to an ornate matching *Kiddush* cup, the bottle of wine they'd brought, and a loaf of braided *challah* covered by a blue velvet cloth. They each stood in front of a chair while Yonatan opened the wine and overpoured the *Kiddush* cup. He then placed the cup into the palm of his right hand, holding it by the bottom, and recited the blessing. Eyes on the dancing flames, Yonatan sang: '*Va-yehi erev va-yehi voker. Yom ha-shi-shi. Va-y'chulu ha-shamayim v'ha-aretz* –'

His voice was melodious and rich, intonating each vowel with delicate inflection. Across the table, Tegan seemed transfixed in wonderment and Ezra too felt something stir within him. Briefly he was back at Yahel, struggling to read from his Tanach – his speech discordant and staccato until the rabbi had enough of his butchering and asked one of the *frum* boys to pick up where he left off, likely to the relief of the rabbi, the rest of the class and God.

'Amen,' Yonatan said.

'Amen,' they all chorused.

Yonatan drank from the full cup. He then asked Rivka to pass him her glass and poured from the cup into it.

Tegan shifted in her seat and turned to Ezra.

'Nothing to worry about, Tegan,' Yonatan said, without taking his eyes from the glass. 'It's only a thimble for Rivka to sip and sanctify Shabbat.'

'Oh, no worries. Sorry, I was just –'

Ezra smiled at Tegan and shook his head. 'Nothing escapes this guy, just like when we were kids.'

Yonatan laughed and asked for Tegan and Ezra's glasses. He then poured them the rest of the cup and waited for them to have a drink. 'Okay, now we need to wash our hands, but it's important,' he said, looking at Ezra and Tegan in turn, 'that we don't speak after washing them until we have said the *bracha* for the *challah*, and I thought maybe you'd like to give it a go, Ezra. If you can remember it, that is?'

Say the *bracha*? Was it tradition for a guest to do that? Ezra wasn't sure. Maybe Yonatan thought he might get a taste for it, let himself be reindoctrinated? No harm either way. 'Yeah, I remember. *Ha-motzi*, right?'

'That's the one.'

In the kitchen, a silver jug filled with water sat by two identical sink basins, each with its own faucet and taps.

'Why are there two?' Tegan asked.

'One is meat,' Yonatan said, 'the other is for milk.'

Tegan smiled and nodded as though this made perfect sense to her.

Ezra couldn't remember exactly what to do, but he watched Yonatan and Rivka as they took turns pouring the jug three times over each hand and recited the blessing for *netilat yadayim*, which he did remember. Relishing the role of teacher, he showed Tegan, and pronounced the blessing slowly, so she could repeat it after him.

Back in the dining room, Ezra stood in front of the *challah*, and Yonatan motioned for him to pick it up. He focused on the candles as Yonatan had, hoping he would be able to dredge up the blessing from wherever it was buried inside of him. '*Baruch atah Adonai Elohaynu melech ha-olam, ha-motzi lechem min ha-aretz. Amen.*' He spoke quickly and without melody, but it was still there.

'Amen.'

After they each ate a piece of *challah*, Ezra, Yonatan and Tegan sat down while Rivka went to the kitchen repeatedly, returning with a golden roast chicken, honey-glazed brisket, sweet-potato kugel, Spanish rice and curried-salmon fritters. Ezra busied himself by refilling their wine glasses while his mouth watered at the smell of salty meat, and he waited for Rivka to return to her seat.

During the meal, Ezra, Tegan and Yonatan finished the rest of the wine and another bottle that Yonatan brought in from the kitchen. But Ezra wouldn't have said he was drunk. He couldn't describe himself as anything other than full to the point of bursting. Tegan tried to make small talk while they ate, asking if Yonatan and Rivka had been bothered much by the level-crossing removals or the new Metro Tunnel project, but Yonatan said he hadn't really noticed the works, that they didn't drive that often and never took public transport.

Rivka didn't say a word. She took rabbit-sized bites of her food and only looked up from her plate to steal glances at Tegan. Once she finally placed her knife and fork on her plate, Yonatan suggested they move to the lounge room, adding that he had another bottle of wine in the kitchen.

They sat on opposite couches, one couple per couch. From the kitchen, Yonatan brought tea for Rivka, and Ezra refilled the rest of their wine glasses. The silence between them was too prominent to ignore, and Ezra drank quickly and often to fill it.

'So, Rivka,' Tegan said, smiling. 'How far along are you?'

'Nearly six months,' Rivka replied.

'And do you know if you'll be having a boy or girl?'

Rivka lowered her tea and looked up at Tegan. 'We don't do that. *Hashem* did not intend for us to know.'

'Oh – sorry. I didn't realise. I hope I didn't –'

Yonatan smiled. 'No, no – it's nothing really. A *midrash*: "As you do not know what is the way of the wind, just as things enclosed in the full womb; so will you not know *Hashem*'s work." Not everyone keeps the custom, but why spoil the surprise?'

Rivka nodded. 'But when a baby sits low like this, it's usually a boy.' She looked at her bump and overlaid her hands delicately on top of it.

'Oh – I haven't heard that one. Are you a midwife?'

'A doula,' Rivka said. 'I've already assisted in the delivery of fifteen healthy Jewish children.'

'That's fantastic,' Tegan said, smiling. 'Where did you get your certification?'

'The Women's Wellness Centre.'

'In Elsternwick?' Tegan asked. 'Run by Devorah Levenstein?'

'You know it?'

Tegan nodded. 'I helped them with some grant applications last year. She . . . wears a lot of yellow.'

Shit, Ezra thought, that was a gamble – saying something derogatory about a Jew. He watched Rivka carefully, waiting for her to stand up and excuse herself, for Yonatan to follow her and for him and Tegan to hear the distinct sound of muffled arguing.

But Rivka smiled, and her cheeks were red and lovely. 'We used to call her Morah Blintz, because she looked like a big cheese blintz.'

Tegan smiled. 'And those earrings.'

Rivka laughed, squeezed her eyes shut and shook her head. 'Pineapples.'

'No,' Ezra said, smiling. 'Seriously?'

'Yes,' Rivka nodded repeatedly, still laughing, and then wiped at her eyes. 'Mini, dangling pineapples.'

Tegan was laughing too. After nearly spilling her wine, she put it down on the coffee table and slapped her knee.

It was infectious, the two of them like that. Ezra smiled and Yonatan smiled back at him, his hat tilted, blue eyes shining. What a good man to invite them over. It was so good to see him again. With Tegan and Rivka getting along like this, they could have dinner all the time. Wouldn't that be something?

Somehow the wine was gone, but Yonatan said they had plenty more – gifts they'd been stockpiling – so he brought out another bottle and sat back down next to Rivka, who took hold of his hand and grinned. 'So tell me,' Rivka said to Ezra. 'Tell me about this one when you were young.' She squeezed his hand. 'What did he get up to?'

'Me?' Yonatan opened his mouth in mock horror. 'I was a *mensch*.'

'Oh, I bet,' Rivka said. 'Come on then, Ezra.'

Ezra laughed. 'It's true, everyone loved Yoni, teachers, students, everybody. But that just meant he was able to get away with more. In grade six we had this super-strict *madrich*. That's like your homeroom teacher,' he said to Tegan. 'Rabbi . . . Schneider. He would report you for anything. If your shoes weren't polished, if you didn't have hairclips on your *kippah*. He once caught me speaking to Yoni during prayers and gave me a week's detention. But he knew Yoni's dad and respected him, so this guy,' he gestured to Yonatan with his wine glass, 'never got in trouble. He used to do things like replace the whiteboard texta with a permanent marker, change seats in the middle of a class, and convince different sets of students to cough or sneeze simultaneously when Schneider said certain words.'

'What words?' Tegan asked.

'There was one word he always said. It was really pretentious, but I can't –'

Yonatan laughed. 'Ostensibly,' he said.

'That's it!' Ezra stiffened his posture and stroked an imaginary beard. '"Ostensibly, Yehuda didn't complete the homework because he had a stomach-ache,"' Ezra laughed. 'But the best thing he ever did' – Ezra turned to Rivka – 'and this was a work of genius, was sneak an entire Christmas tree into the classroom overnight. Like a full-blown Christmas tree, tinsel, baubles, star on top, presents and everything.'

Rivka's eyes widened.

Tegan looked at Yonatan, eyebrows high, mouth agape.

Yonatan smiled. 'To be fair, it was a fake tree.'

'But how?' Tegan asked.

'I opened one of the class windows before I left, came back after hours, and had to make a few trips in and out of it until I had everything. My only regret is that I didn't have fairy lights.'

Ezra wasn't sure how Rivka was going to react to that one, but when he looked at her again, she was shaking with laughter.

As the level of wine in their fourth bottle sank beneath the label, Ezra felt good and warm and light, almost ethereal as though he were floating above them all, watching Rivka and Tegan chatting like old friends, and himself and Yonatan, jumping from one moment of nostalgia to the next, their speech frenzied with excitement.

'And that time that Ilan Umansky ate a whole jar of *maror* on a bet and was sick for days?'

'Do you remember when Davi Spiegelman borrowed his sister's dress and tried to sit in on a Beth Chana class?'

'How about when Uri Berkovic dislocated his finger while we were playing basketball?'

Ezra nodded vigorously. 'And he asked you to pull it back in?'

Yonatan shuddered. 'I can still feel the joint sliding into place.'

'Do you still play?'

Yonatan laughed. 'Not for years. You?'

‘Not recently, but I was in a social team a few years ago. We should shoot around sometime?’

‘I don’t know. I think those days are behind me.’

‘Afraid I’ll finally beat you?’

Yonatan smiled. ‘Not at all.’

‘Let’s do it then. Promise to go easy on you if –’

‘Crazy to think, isn’t it?’ Tegan said to Rivka. ‘It took twenty years for these two to be reunited.’

Ezra hadn’t been listening to Rivka and Tegan’s conversation, but a part of his brain must have been, because a warning siren sounded in his mind. He tried to figure out why it was going off but there was too much wine fog for him to navigate and then Tegan was speaking again.

‘And that they ran into each other like that – at the protest.’

‘Protest?’

Shit.

Rivka’s mouth tightened.

‘Oh, you didn’t know?’ Tegan turned to Ezra, confused.

The warmth was sucked out of the room, as though they were in a plane that had lost cabin pressure. Ezra was himself again, cold, sober and too aware of everything.

‘What protest, Yoni?’ Rivka asked.

What was he going to say? Whatever it was, Ezra would back him up, go along with the lie as far as possible. What else were friends for?

Yonatan placed his glass on the coffee table and turned to his wife. ‘There was a rally in front of Parliament House,’ he said calmly. ‘It was to encourage the extradition of Rabbi Joel Hirsch from Israel. Rabbi Hirsch was teaching at Yahel Academy when Ezra and I were there as students. The rally was organised by Avraham Kliger.’

'Kliger?'

'That's right.'

Rivka turned to Ezra, not angry or sad but impassive, which somehow seemed worse – the walls were back up. 'I thought you met at Glick's?'

'Actually,' Ezra said, 'we went to Glick's afterwards, but we ran into each other first at the rally.'

'Okay.' Rivka nodded, stood up and smiled politely at Ezra and Tegan. 'I'm quite tired. I think I might go to bed.' And then she dropped her smile and left the room.

Tegan spun to Yonatan. 'I don't understand. Did I say something I shouldn't have?'

'Shit.' Ezra shook his head. 'It's my fault. I was meant to tell you not to mention Hirsch. It's complicated, but basically Yonatan wasn't allowed to be there.'

'Shit,' Tegan said. 'I'm so sorry.'

Yonatan sighed. 'It's fine, really. You have nothing to apologise for. I put myself in this position.' He stood up. Ezra and Tegan followed suit, both a little wobbly on their feet.

'Thanks for having us,' Ezra said. 'Sorry again, mate.' He held out his hand.

'Yes, please tell Rivka I'm sorry,' Tegan said, 'and that it was lovely to meet you both.'

'It's perfectly fine, really. *Shabbat shalom*.'

They were both too drunk, Ezra and Tegan agreed, to drive home, so they caught a cab. Tegan was quiet for most of the ride home, which was rare when she drank. Outside of their apartment block, she flew out of the taxi, leaving Ezra to pay, while she forced her key into the lock and kicked their front door open.

On entering the apartment, Ezra heard the toilet flush.

'God damn, that felt so good,' Tegan said, exiting their bathroom. 'I was worried I was going to wet myself.' She walked into their bedroom. 'I wish you'd told me not to mention Hirsch. Fuck. How upset do you think Rivka was?'

Ezra followed Tegan and started to undress. 'I wouldn't worry about it. They're probably having sex right now.'

'I don't know. She looked pretty upset.'

'Doesn't matter, it's Shabbat so they've got to do it, anyway.'

'What?'

'Ya-huh – it's a mitzvah. Actually . . . I'm not sure if it counts when you're already pregnant. But basically on Shabbat you've got to do it, whether you're fighting or not.'

'Seriously? Like you're not bullshitting me right now?'

Ezra held up his right hand. 'Swear on the Torah, it's true.'

'But that's . . . that's fucked . . . what if she doesn't want to?'

'Doesn't matter. God wants her to, that's all that matters. Thou shalt go forth and accept a penis into your vagina even if thine husband shits you.'

'Jesus.' Tegan shook her head. 'So fucked up.'

'If you knew half the shit they're obligated to do. I mean *oy*.'

'*Oy*.' Tegan laughed. 'And what about us?'

'Us?'

'It's Shabbat, so do we have to fuck?' Tegan let her skirt fall from her waist. She was naked beneath it.

Ezra fumbled with his shirt buttons. 'Ah – technically I think it's only for married couples and –'

'Shhh.' Tegan placed a finger on his lips, tugged at his belt buckle and pulled him to the bed. 'Remember earlier when you said that thing in Hebrew?'

'What, you mean the blessing?'

‘That’s the one.’ She bit his lower lip, hard. ‘Say it again.’

‘Okay . . . bit weird but . . . *baruch atah Adonai Elohaynu melech ha-olam, ha-motzi lechem min ha-aretz.*’

She unzipped him, made him slick with her mouth and took him in her hands. ‘Now slower.’

‘*Ba-ruch at-ah Ad-o-nai* –’

She climbed on top of him. ‘That’s it, that’s it.’

The booze came back to Ezra then, and he wasn’t completely sure if what was happening was real. He could hear himself speaking in Hebrew while, above him, Tegan’s body rocked back and forth, blocking the downlight, so that it flashed on and off. The room spun and he felt himself fading. Tegan was still on top of him and, he swore, that as he went dark she had been chanting, as though in prayer, ‘Fuck me, Jewboy, fuck me.’

Chapter 8

Yonatan

Yonatan's afternoon *shiur* with his Year Eleven class was on *Parshat Vayechi* and the lie of Joseph's brothers – that their father's dying wish was for Joseph to forgive them for selling him into slavery. Yonatan was three-quarters of the way through the lesson, having described how Rashi reasoned that the brothers' lie was not a sin because it was committed in the hope of establishing peace between Joseph and his brothers, when Oren Kamiansky raised his hand. Oren was an obnoxious, quick-witted and insolent student who often tried to obfuscate Yonatan's classes with a piece of arcane commentary seemingly dug up prior to class for that exact purpose.

'Yes, Oren.'

'What if a man were to break a *cherem* for the sake of peace, would that meet Rashi's reasoning?'

'A *cherem*?' Yonatan shook his head. Oren's speculations were usually more on point than that. 'I can't say I see your logic. Breach of a *cherem*, unless it's for *pikuach nefesh*, to save a life – it's a significant offence. Our discussion is primarily about white lies.'

'What about someone who intermarries,' Yaacov Cohen spoke up without raising his hand, 'with a *shiksa*? Would it be okay to cook for them on Shabbat for the sake of peace?'

'Sorry, Yaacov. Why are you –'

Yaacov and Oren smiled at each other, and Yonatan understood. Both of their fathers were members of the Yahel *shule* board, friendly with Menachem and supporters of the late Rav Bloom. Unimpressed with what Tegan had revealed, Rivka must have spoken to her brother, in confidence, about their Shabbat dinner, and in turn Menachem had worked to discredit Yonatan. It was gossip, *lashon hara* even, but Yonatan knew better than to be surprised. The community was small and *lashon hara* was the most accessible and practised of sins – at Glick's buying *challah*, Klein's deli for some salami, in Doctor Rotstein's waiting room. What were you meant to do if you ran into Esther Frankel or Naomi Greenblat? What else was there to speak about? It wasn't slander if you were only passing on information. Was there really any harm?

'I think you're confused, Yaacov,' Yonatan said. 'In Mishnah Berurah it's written that a *Yehudi* may not cook for a gentile on *Yom Tov*. Shabbat, however, is perfectly fine, whether it be for peace or otherwise. For *lashon hara* on the other hand,' Yonatan sharpened his tone, and narrowed his eyes at both boys, 'the Torah tells us that Miryam was stricken with leprosy, and I cannot think of any instance where spreading harmful speech about someone would be required to keep the peace.'

The boys sat up and faced the front of the class, their mouths taut, washed of mischief. He hadn't meant to get cross. Had he been too hard on them? He'd never had to reprimand anyone like that before, not even Oren. Hopefully he wouldn't have to do it again. But as he bent down to read his copy of the Talmud, several seats squeaked with the shifting weight of students, and a sliver of unease trickled down Yonatan's spine.

At lunchtime, Yonatan ignored the cafeteria and teachers' lounge, instead managing the school's maze of corridors in search of the sixth-grade classroom where he knew Menachem would be hunched over a desk, eating a tuna and mayonnaise sandwich and simultaneously preparing for his afternoon class.

Sure enough, on opening the classroom door, Yonatan was met by the odour of fish and the sight of his brother-in-law brushing crumbs off the notebook he was writing in.

'What can I do for you, Reb Kaplan?' Menachem asked, without looking up from his notes.

Reb Kaplan. So he was right. Menachem only ever called him that when other people were around. He was establishing distance, would only talk to him as a colleague and not as family.

'*Lashon hara*, Reb Bloom,' Yonatan replied. 'I'm here because of *lashon hara*.'

Menachem put down his sandwich and looked at Yonatan.

'You're entitled to your views, Menachem, but when you preach them to my students and they interrupt my class because of them, it becomes something I cannot ignore.'

'My views? I don't preach my views to anyone. I educate on the Torah. And frankly, I don't have time to teach your students in addition to my own.'

'Really, Menachem? How then do you explain Yaacov Cohen and Oren Kamiansky knowing about my Shabbat guests? I know you spoke to Rivka.'

Menachem frowned, looked at Yonatan carefully for a moment and then took off his glasses and sighed. 'I can see that you're upset.' He pushed himself up from the desk and shook his head. 'I have heard about your guests, but I haven't spoken to Rivka.'

'You haven't?'

'No. But I think you need to talk to her.'

'Are you saying that she –'

'It's not my place. Speak to her, please.' He placed a hand on Yonatan's shoulder. 'You've been good to me, Yonatan, and I'd like to return the favour. I don't know what this *goyishe yid* means to you, but word travels fast. You need to be careful.'

Rivka. Would she do that? They'd hardly spoken since Shabbat. He'd been to *shule* and then the home of a former student, preparing him for his *smicha* exam. Rivka said she was visiting the newborns she'd helped deliver the past month. He hadn't the chance to explain himself, but even if she was still upset, he would never have thought Rivka would voice her frustration to others before speaking to him. But then again, he could no longer claim to know her as well as he'd once thought, could he?

*

As had always been planned, following his *smicha*, Yonatan met with a *shadchan* in order to find a suitable match. He was twenty-five and it was time for him to marry. Both of his parents had aged considerably as well, and he felt obligated to try for a grand-child before they passed.

For a month, he went on dates with different women, either in public or with a *shomer* present. But Yonatan knew that those outings had only been organised to give him the semblance of choice – at the end of the month, his father and Rav Bloom had arranged for Yonatan to go out with the Rav's daughter, and there would be a marriage, whether Yonatan approved or not.

As to whether he did, Yonatan himself wasn't sure. He and Rivka met only twice before the *shidduch* was agreed upon, and both meetings had been too carefully measured for him to gauge how he actually felt about Rivka. She was petite and slim with large green eyes and thin, bird-like arms that he instinctively wanted to rub warm. But their conversation was too spare and confected – discussions about the weekly Torah portion and questions about his *halachic* observance that, doubtless, Rivka had been instructed to ask by her father in order to determine if Yonatan was a man of good *middos*.

Their wedding was extravagant and exhausting, and throughout it all – the signing of the *ketubah*, the breaking of glass under the *chuppah*, and even during the frantic performance of the *Hora* – Yonatan clinging for dear life as his father, Rav Bloom and Menachem thrust his chair into the air – he was aware of an electric hum of apprehension for what lay ahead, once the festivities were over.

His *chatan* teacher had given Yonatan rudimentary instructions, told him that a lot of men faint on the night of their wedding. It's the years of *shomer negiah*, he said, to go from never having touched a woman in clothes to have a naked body against their own – it was easy to be overwhelmed.

Thankfully, Yonatan did not faint when he and Rivka first entered their bedroom as man and wife. He did feel queasy and lightheaded, but if the room was spinning he could not tell because it was pitch-black. Unsure of how to begin, Yonatan undid his belt and slid off his slacks. Presumably taking the clink of his buckle as instruction, Yonatan heard the shuffle of Rivka also undressing. They still hadn't touched yet, but that knowledge alone was enough to give him a painful erection.

Naked, Yonatan patted about the air until he felt the edge of the two pushed-together single beds and lay down. Not knowing what to do with his arms, he kept them stiffly by his sides and waited for the bed springs to cry out with Rivka's weight. He thought about breaking the silence then, telling Rivka he was ready, or that he wasn't – that he didn't feel himself capable of being an instrument of *Hashem*'s will: man, made in his image, to be fruitful and multiply – that his mouth was dry, his hands clammy, and that the wine from the reception was fighting the chicken they'd eaten, and threatening to reappear at any moment. But instead, he remained silent, assuring himself that it wasn't for him to take control, that Rivka's *kallah* teacher would have advised her of what to do.

Eventually, Rivka's shuffling stopped, the bed sank and Yonatan's heart thudded with the strength of horses' hooves against his ribcage. A shiver traced the hairs on his arms. For a moment, he thought it was Rivka's fingertips until he felt a weight on top of his idle hand. He turned his around, allowing for their fingers to interlock. Her hand was soft and warm and small. Too warm, and he was soon conscious of how moist his palm was, so he worked his fingers out of hers but, not wanting her to feel rebuffed, he turned towards her and hung his arm limply over her side. Rivka placed her hand on his wrist then and lightly stroked his forearm up to the loose skin of his elbow which she pulled gently. A strange gesture. Was he supposed to know what that meant? A signal for him to get on with things? His *chatan* teacher hadn't prepared him for that. Hadn't told him anything about how Rivka's body would feel, or what it would be like to be touched by her. Nonetheless, he obligingly rolled on top of her.

Immediately, Yonatan was flooded with sensation. The heat of her rushed into him, and he could taste a salty musk in his mouth. His erection pressed into the smooth skin of her thigh and spots swam before his eyes. He pushed himself up onto his elbows and felt Rivka's light breath against his face. He waited for her to direct him on how to proceed, but she didn't. Beneath him her breathing quickened, and he was worried he would be unable to support himself and crush her if he took too much longer.

He shifted himself downwards, trying to position his erection between her legs, as his *chatan* teacher had instructed him to do. 'It will fit,' he'd said, 'like a key in a lock.' There was no clear lock, though, and each time Yonatan readjusted and pushed, Rivka would wriggle her hips as a means of letting him know that he was missing the mark. That continued for some minutes until Yonatan was at the end of his tether and almost doubtful that his new wife even had a 'lock', when all of a sudden Rivka clasped his erection.

Nothing could prepare him for that – there was no allegory in the Torah that equated to her touch in that moment, no wisdom from the *Rishonim* or any of the great commentators to prepare him, as she guided him upwards. But he did know something, with prophetic clarity – he knew that he would not be able to control himself, he was going to waste his seed, and their marriage would not achieve *nissuin*. And so he pulled away sharply, rolled onto the empty side of the bed, groaned into a pillow and exhausted himself into the sheets before pretending to sleep in a wet patch of his own shame.

It was a long night. Yonatan listened to Rivka's breathing and, once it seemed regular and slow, he turned onto his back, stared into the dark and contemplated the morning. He would have to call his father, admit his failing and confirm that what he'd done was not *halachically* valid – that in the eyes of *Hashem* they were not man and wife.

In an instant there was light in the room – the morning sun peeking through the edges of their blackout blinds. He must have fallen asleep. A wisp of a dream still circled his head. Nothing he could recall. He turned onto his side and, for a moment, was shocked by the presence of a naked woman lying on her front, facing him. The sheet had slipped, exposing the bulge of her breasts pressed against the mattress, freckled shoulders and the contours of a milky white back. Rivka opened her eyes then, as though she could feel him looking at her. '*Boker tov*, husband,' she said, turning to him.

Husband. At the sound of the word, he thought his shame would return. But there was a lightness in Rivka's green eyes, an honest tenderness, perhaps not for him as her husband, but simply as a person. He was drawn to that, so much so that he propped himself up, leant over and kissed her, for the first time. Their lips stayed pressed together, for he couldn't say how long, before Yonatan withdrew and laughed at the ease of it, of how nice it felt and how stupid he'd been not to have done it earlier.

Rivka reached up, placed a hand on his bearded cheek and looked into his eyes. 'It's nice to see you,' she said. 'My *kallah* teacher told me to imagine the great rebbe's face while we fulfilled the mitzvah, so that we would have righteous children. But you're much better looking.'

Yonatan laughed, felt himself blush a little, and then kissed her again. She urged him on top of her with her hands, then guided him gently with her fingertips, and he was able to control himself this time, enough to at least complete the mitzvah, and afterwards he sought out her hand and held it in his.

*

On the landing of their home, Yonatan sighed and closed the front door behind him. What had happened to them? When they fulfilled the mitzvah on Shabbat now, Rivka would lie on her side, not even facing him in the dark, and he would shuffle up to her and grip onto her hips until the deed was done. She never touched him anymore, and hardly made a sound. Though he was inside of her, she felt distant and unreachable. What did she think about in the dark, listening to his heavy breath and the smack of his skin against hers?

As ever, he was greeted by the smell of her cooking. A fragrant blend of onion and oregano, plenty of garlic. As Rabbi Eliezer says, 'For her husband a wife must grind flour and bake bread, wash clothes, cook food and nurse their children.'

In the kitchen, a large pot was on the stove, chicken soup simmering. In another saucepan potatoes were boiling for kugel or latkes, but Rivka herself was nowhere to be found. On the way to their bedroom, Yonatan heard the toilet flush and stopped dead in the middle of the corridor. He stood a metre from the door, listening to the tap running, the lather and rinse of Rivka's hands, the tap turning off. He didn't continue on to the bedroom or call out, but stood, frozen. Not knowing why.

'*Oy!*' Rivka held her hand to her chest. 'Yoni! You scared me half to death. What are you doing?'

He thought again of their first morning together, of those now incredulous eyes when they had been filled with hope and kindness and the beginnings of love, and he was barely able to choke out the words. 'You told people that I went to the Kliger rally. You told them I invited Ezra and Tegan over for Shabbat.'

For a second, Rivka's lips trembled and Yonatan thought she was about to express regret, but then she stood straight and walked past him, turning sideways to avoid their shoulders brushing.

He followed her into the kitchen where she placed a wooden spoon into the large pot and stirred furiously.

'You broke a *cherem.* And then you bring an *apikoros* and a *shiksa* into our home for Shabbat.' Using oven mitts, she picked up the saucepan and strained the potatoes into the sink, steam rising into her face. 'But worse than any of that, Yoni, you lied to me. I'm your wife. Everything you do is reflected on me. If your friend drags you off the *derech* with him, where does that leave me? If that *shiksa* with her revealing skirt and red lipstick seduces you, where does that leave me?' She placed her hands on her belly and turned to Yonatan. 'Yes, I told. What did you expect me to do? You've been acting strange for some time, but I never thought you would do something like this. A *cherem*, Yoni! In broad daylight, in the city, it's *chillul Hashem*.' She shook her head. 'I was shocked, and I thought that if you saw that your actions have consequences, you would understand. You can't just think about yourself anymore.'

Chillul Hashem, really? What about her? Speaking *lashon hara* against her husband? And the way she and Tegan bonded over making fun of that woman – the cheese blintz. Was that not *chillul Hashem*? He was about to mention it when Rivka reached out, took hold of his hand and pulled it to her. He thought she was going to place it on her belly, but she brought his hand to her chest and looked up at him, while her heartbeat thrummed like a jackhammer beneath his fingertips. She was right.

Yonatan nodded, brought Rivka close to him. 'Okay, *chaim sheli*. Okay. I promise, no more.'

That evening, they sat close together while they ate, their knees touching beneath the table, each of them stealing glances at the other, turning shyly away when caught. Afterwards, in their lounge room, Rivka lay with her back against Yonatan. Gently, he was kneading the knots between her shoulder blades when an unbidden urge struck him. He told Rivka he had to go to the bathroom but, once out of sight, crept to his study and turned on the computer. He shook his head – only hours after their conversation and he'd lied to her again. What was he doing? He stood over his desk, checked that the doorway was empty and loaded Facebook, where a message was waiting for him.

> Hey, Yonatan.
> I just wanted to apologise for the other night. I'm really sorry for bringing up Hirsch. I wish Ezra had told me sooner about the sensitivity there. I hope Rivka wasn't too upset. Thank you again for having us over. You have a lovely home. Give Rivka my best.
> Tegan.
> PS. Let me buy you a coffee some time to make up for any trouble I've caused.

Chapter 9

Ezra

There was no helping it – on seeing Yonatan approach, a bud of laughter planted itself inside of Ezra's chest, and by the time Yonatan reached the bench he was sitting on, beside the Carlton Gardens' outdoor basketball court, Ezra was practically doubled over with tears in his eyes.

'I see,' said Yonatan, smiling. 'Make fun of the *frummer*.'

'I'm sorry . . . I'm sorry, it's . . .' – another bout hit Ezra and he had to wait for it to settle – 'quite a look for you.'

Yonatan's pale arms were bursting from the sides of a Maccabi Tel Aviv singlet like meat squeezed from a sausage. His paunch strained against the yellow fabric as though it were trying to escape. A blue and white *kippah* was pinned to his head and the fringes of a *tzitzit* hung over small blue shorts. 'We'll see if you're still laughing,' Yonatan said, 'once this *frummer* beats you.' He snatched Ezra's basketball up from the bench.

Ezra smiled. 'Where did you get that, anyway?'

'It's my little cousin's,' Yonatan said. 'It's all I could find. Joe Ingles.' He turned around and pointed to the name across his shoulders.

They took some shots to warm up: lay-ups, free-throws, mid-range, working their way up to three-pointers. Yonatan's first attempts missed the ring completely, clapping against the backboard and rattling the rim. Ezra passed the ball back to him, tacking on words of encouragement: 'Next one, flick your wrist, bend your knees.'

On each shot, Yonatan bit his teeth over his lower lip in grim determination, making adjustments as necessary until his shoulders were squared, elbow well tucked and his extension butter smooth. Ezra was quiet then, mesmerised by the rhythm of Yonatan's feet scraping gravel, the smack of the ball hitting his palms and the punchy exhale of his breath as it was released and sailed through the ring.

After hitting four in a row from the three-point line, Yonatan passed the ball back to Ezra and walked to the drinking fountain at the side of the court. He drank long and deep and then placed his face in the stream. When he stood up, rivulets of water dripped through the channels of his beard and darkened the gravel by his feet. If not for the *kippah* still pinned to the back of his head, it would have been easy to mistake him for someone wild and half-crazed, someone Ezra might cross the street to avoid.

'Sorry about the other night by the way,' Ezra said.

Yonatan wiped his mouth with the back of his hand. 'Sorry?'

'Tegan mentioning the protest and all.'

'Ah,' Yonatan said. 'Don't worry about it.'

'Was Rivka upset?'

Yonatan shrugged. 'She didn't mention it.' He took the ball out of Ezra's hands and dribbled towards the ring.

That was odd. Yonatan's nonchalance didn't match the concern he'd expressed before Shabbat dinner. Ezra followed him back onto the court as two young men appeared at the opposite end and dropped their bags beneath the hoop. Both were tall and slim, with short dark hair, and wiry coathanger arms. They were wearing NBA jerseys, long baggy shorts and gleaming black basketball shoes. One of them took a basketball from his bag and passed it to the other, who bounced it between his legs and behind his back in a series of seamless, fluid movements, as though the ball was an extension of himself.

When he was younger, Ezra would have given anything to be able to move like that, to have that kind of talent. He'd never been a top athlete. His movements had always been slow and jerky, refined as much as he could by practice but inevitably flawed. Yonatan was another matter. When they were kids, nothing was a challenge – with his long legs he could breeze past you on the dribble or stop on a dime and cross you up. He had perfect form on his jump shot, and when he got going the basket might as well have been an ocean.

'So,' Ezra said, turning back to Yonatan, 'if you don't mind me asking. How come you came to the protest? With the *cherem* and all?'

Yonatan's shot clanged against the side of the rim and bounced into the surrounding park. A drawn-out '*Oyyy*' escaped his lips, and he chased after the ball, giving no indication of having heard Ezra.

'Hey, how about . . .'

Ezra spun around. The boys were standing behind him, even taller and younger than he'd thought at first glance, both with the same light blue eyes and pale complexion – brothers probably.

'A game?' the taller one asked. His brother was a few inches shorter than him, and though he might have been fifteen at best, he was at least six foot one.

Ezra shook his head and let out a short laugh. 'Sorry, guys. I reckon we're a bit old for –'

'A game?' Yonatan appeared behind him, his breathing laboured and their ball tucked between his arm and waist. 'Let's do it.'

The boys looked Yonatan up and down, undoubtedly surprised by the sight of his curly *peyot*, his *kippah* and the fringes of his *tzitzit*, that they must not have noticed from the other end of the court. They smiled and turned to consult one another in low voices.

A tinge of embarrassment snuck upon Ezra, but he shook it off and approached Yonatan. 'Yoni, they'll kill us.'

'So, they kill us – what else is new for us *yids*?' He walked towards the brothers, still holding the basketball. 'We good, *nu*?' Yonatan said. 'Shoot to start?' Without waiting for a response, he bent his knees and let the ball fly from a good metre behind the three-point line. Like synchronised dolls, the brothers' heads followed the arc of the ball from high in the air down towards the ring and though neither of them spoke both shifted visibly as it snapped through the net.

Ezra and Yonatan started off well. The larger brother was guarding Yonatan at the top of the key, with the smaller – though still two inches taller than Ezra – covering him on the block. Like Ezra when he was their age, defence didn't appear to be a priority for the boys. After checking the ball, the older brother stood flat-footed with his arms down by his sides, half a metre from Yonatan, who made him pay by quickly rising up and swishing the ball through the net with as pure a jump shot as you'd ever seen. The boy was just as lacklustre on the next possession and Yonatan actually smiled before nailing another shot in his face. 'Four–nil,' Yonatan said. 'We're playing to eleven, right?'

The boy didn't seem to like that. He took a defensive stance for the first time and minimised the distance between them to inches. Yonatan responded with a pump fake, which the boy bought, jumping into the air as Yonatan dribbled past him, drew Ezra's man and dropped the ball off to him for an easy lay-up.

That was the end of their luck, though. On the next play, Ezra fumbled a pass and turned the ball over.

Once the brothers had possession, they were simply too tall and long, fast and young. Before Ezra knew it, they were losing five to nine, his t-shirt was a shade darker than when they'd started and his calf muscles were asking for an explanation for the exorbitant stimulation they were being exposed to. Luckily the end was near, or at least it appeared so, as the older brother rose up from behind the three-point line, only for Yonatan to contest the shot and scrape the ball with his fingertips so that it fell loose halfway to the ring.

Yonatan turned and ran for the ball, but the older boy, likely recognising his disadvantage, stuck out one of his bamboo legs and sent Yonatan careening to the asphalt with a sharp thwack.

Ezra forgot the game, their discrepancies in height and age. 'Hey!' He found himself centimetres from the older boy, blood pumping in his ears. 'What the fuck was that?'

For his part, the kid held up his hands and smiled, seemingly unconcerned by Ezra. 'He fell – maybe he just tripped on his beard.' His smile widened.

Yonatan picked himself up off the ground. His knees were red, the skin torn. A gash on his elbow leaked dark blood.

Ezra's whole body tensed. A well had been tapped – one he hadn't realised had been filling, drip by drip, day by day. He didn't feel as though he was in charge of what would happen next.

'Ezra!' Yonatan rushed to his side, the basketball in his hands. 'I'm fine. It's fine. Let it go.'

'No – it isn't,' Ezra said through his teeth. He pictured himself leaping onto the kid and pinning him to the ground, making for his eyes with his fingers, a fist to his smiling face.

'Ezra – please. It's only a game.'

The taller brother held onto his grin, but behind him the younger one was chalk white.

Jesus, what the hell was he doing? Ezra unclenched his fists. 'Fuck!' he shouted, and then he turned to Yonatan, pulled the ball from his hands and kicked it, as hard as he could, into the empty children's playground.

From his perch on a plastic seesaw, with the basketball in hand, Ezra watched Yonatan talking to the boys, likely apologising for his *meshuganah* friend, making full use of those rabbinical conflict resolution skills. He'd compliment them on their skills and thank them for the game. Always calm, always sensible, the ever-wise Rabbi Kaplan.

Fuck.

Ezra gritted his teeth as Yonatan shook each of the brothers' hands and walked over to the playground.

*

In the sixth grade, a new student joined Yahel mid-term. His name was Dimitri, or Dimma as the boys called him. He was a quiet, pale, blond and squat boy with a rectangular head and large ears.

Dimma's family had emigrated from Ukraine and his English was spotty at best, but he was a strong handball player, and his four-square dropshot was unbeatable, so that, even without the ability to communicate properly, he earned the admiration and respect of most of their school year. And then one day, Tzvi Wein took a piss at the urinal next to Dimma.

'It looked like a slug,' Tzvi told the boys at lunchtime. 'There was no head.'

Dimma, as it turned out, had never had a *bris*.

He was different, and the more secular boys took hold of that information as they would have with anyone. They called him 'Slug' and 'Slugger'. Drew pictures of his penis with antennae and passed them around class. David Kamil dacked him at the lockers and pointed at his crotch as he pulled up his pants, chanting, 'Slug, Slug, Slug.'

But what the *frum* boys did to him was much worse. There was an understanding amongst them – if he wasn't circumcised, was he even Jewish? It was a covenant between *Hashem* and Abraham: without it he was unclean, as bad as a *goy*, an abomination.

In class, seats around Dimma emptied. The *frummers* crossed corridors to avoid him. When he entered the bathroom, they left. If Dimma used a door handle, a *frum* boy would open it with his elbow. Amit Cohen threw out his favourite pen, once lent to Dimma. All of the *frum* boys ostracised him; all, that is, but Yonatan.

Yonatan took the seat next to Dimma in class. He asked to borrow his stationery though Ezra knew he didn't need it. He took to eating his lunch with Dimma under the shade of a large elm tree in the corner of the quadrangle.

Ezra was furious. Sure, Yonatan could get away with that kind of thing – everyone loved him, but it would be social suicide for Ezra. What the hell was he meant to do? He took it out on Dimma, bagging him as often as he could to the other boys on the playground. 'Let's douse him with salt and see if he shrivels,' he'd say, or else he'd salute him when he walked past and say, 'Comrade Slug.' The boys laughed at his antics, clapped him on the back and shook him by the shoulder. It was the most popular he'd ever been.

And then, one day, Dimma didn't show up for school. He wasn't there the next day or the one after that. It came out then – he'd been expelled.

'He put a pig's head in the principal's office,' the boys said.

'He was a KGB spy.'

'He snuck into the *shule* and used the Torah for toilet paper.'

Yonatan knew the truth, and Ezra didn't ask how. It turned out that some of the *frum* boys had told their parents about Dimma, and they, in turn, approached the school council who gave Dimma's parents an ultimatum – circumcision or unfortunately they wouldn't be able to provide a place for him anymore.

That was the last time Yonatan ever mentioned Dimma, and afterwards everything returned to normal and it was as if the squat Ukrainian boy had never existed at all.

*

Dimma. That was the embodiment of each of them, wasn't it? Yonatan, thoughtful, compassionate and good. Ezra, the narcissist who did whatever he felt like regardless of how it impacted others – Dimma, Tegan, anyone.

'I'm sorry,' Ezra said as Yonatan approached. 'I overreacted.'

Yonatan sank onto the other end of the seesaw, nodded but didn't say anything.

'I felt like –' Ezra shook his head. 'For a second there, I could've killed that kid.' He rubbed his eyes with the heels of his hands. 'It wasn't the game or him being a shit, I've just been feeling a bit –' Ezra sighed and dropped his hands into his lap. 'I guess it was just the straw that broke the camel's back, you know?'

Yonatan remained silent, managing to maintain an air of learned benevolence, despite the large sweat patch on his singlet and the way his *peyot* were stuck to his cheeks. How much of that steady countenance was learned? Would Ezra himself be like that, if he'd stayed at Yahel? Would he still believe in God? Would he be a better person?

'Sometimes I envy you, Yoni.'

Yonatan looked at Ezra and smiled. 'Me? It's my beard, isn't it? You love the colour.'

Ezra smiled back but shook his head. 'Six hundred and thirteen commandments. A community. A wife. An answer to every question. I'm thirty-two, and I've got no idea what the hell I'm doing.'

Yonatan's smile faded and he looked thoughtfully at Ezra. 'In the Talmud,' he said, taking on an authoritative tone, 'it is said that the right path for a man is whatever is harmonious for himself and for mankind.'

Ezra snorted. 'And what does the Talmud say about me wanting to hurt that kid?'

Yonatan shrugged. '*Yetzer hara.*'

'What?'

'Man's inclination towards evil. *Yetzer hara*. Everyone has it, Ezra. Even a good man is entitled to a bad day.'

Ezra shook his head. 'It's not just the kid. There are other things too.'

'Other things?'

'I haven't been –' But Yonatan looked so reverent and idyllic that Ezra couldn't bring himself to say any more.

'Well,' Yonatan sat up, his face deadpan, 'there's always the chance you were briefly taken over by a *dybbuk*.' He broke into a smile, but when Ezra didn't respond in kind he stood up, sinking Ezra's end of the seesaw to the ground.

Yonatan stepped towards him. 'As a boy, I think you were shy and a little lost, but as your friend I also knew that you were thoughtful and good and kind. And, Ezra, I still see that same person sitting here today.'

Ezra looked up at Yonatan and suddenly they were children again – Yonatan's fingers twirling around his curly red *peyot* as he looked down at Ezra with a mixture of compassion and pity and exasperation. 'To be fair, mate,' Ezra said, pushing himself up from the seesaw, 'we were just a couple of stupid fucking kids back then. You don't know anything about me.' And then he shoved the basketball into Yonatan's chest and walked away.

Chapter 10

Yonatan

Yonatan called Rivka from Yahel and told her that Eli Katz had requested a last-minute private tutoring session for his *smicha*, that he would eat with Eli and be home late. Eli had, in fact, completed his *smicha* the previous week. Rivka could easily have known that, but Yonatan hadn't bothered to come up with something else. Unconsciously, he may have wanted to get caught, hoped that Rivka would press him to tell her where he was actually going, make him come home and confess as to why he felt the need to continuously jeopardise their future. But she only wished him luck and said she looked forward to seeing him later.

Tegan had offered to meet Yonatan somewhere that was easy for him to get to and sent him the address of a bar in Elsternwick. Sitting at a small table with a glass of red wine, she was the only person there aside from a male bartender with slicked-back hair, a white shirt, black tie and suspenders.

It was a crazy thing, his being there after the promise he'd made to Rivka. But on seeing Tegan, he experienced the same nervous elation he'd felt on reading her message – and wasn't faith in that compulsion, in itself, a kind of adherence to *Hashem*'s will?

'Thanks for coming.' Tegan stood up and offered her hand.

'No problem.' Yonatan shook it and sat opposite her. She had already poured him a glass of water.

'Is it okay for you to be here? I mean, meeting up with a *shiksa* and all?' Tegan smiled.

Yonatan smiled back. 'I see Ezra has shared some of our cultural . . . nicknames . . . with you.'

'Some of them.'

'It's fine. There are other people here,' he gestured to the bartender, 'so it's okay.'

'And if there weren't?'

'Then we'd be in *yichud*.' He took a sip of his water. 'It's illegal.'

'But we're just sitting here. Why would it be –'

'It's to prevent . . . temptation.'

'Temptation?' Tegan let out a small laugh. 'Well, I hope you can control yourself.'

She was wearing a grey office dress without stockings. Yonatan glimpsed her bare knee sticking out the other side of the table. He quickly looked away and felt himself blush.

'And is this place okay?' Tegan asked. 'I looked up the menu and they have some vegetarian options, so –'

'It's fine, thank you.' Though technically it wasn't. Even by entering the bar, he'd violated *marit ayin*, but that was *fine* by Yonatan now. Since their argument, Rivka had done her best to retract the harm her *lashon hara* had done, but still his colleagues gave him a wide berth in the staff room, his students were less attentive and engaged, and at *shule* men he used to debate Talmud with glanced at him sideways as he took his seat. And weren't they all justified in doing so? He'd broken a *cherem* and lied to his wife again and again – even just now he'd touched this gentile woman's bare hand, and not for the first time. Sin was becoming second nature.

'I'm glad. So, I wanted to apologise again for –'

'No need.' Yonatan waved his hand in the air. 'You already have and Ezra passed it on as well. Rivka's fine, really.'

'Oh good.' Tegan paused, picked up her glass, drank and then looked at Yonatan. 'The truth is I might have had an ulterior motive in asking you here.'

'*Nu?*'

'It's about Rabbi Hirsch. I don't know if Ezra told you, but my work often involves dealing with victims of domestic violence and sexual abuse. And ever since he told me that Hirsch was a teacher at your school –' She paused, as though carefully choosing her next words. 'I guess I feel like I have a vested interest. Have you been following the case?'

'No, not really – other than the rally.'

'You'll be pleased to hear then – it worked. The extradition hearing was last week. They're sending Hirsch home to face criminal charges.'

'Oh.'

'Yeah, brilliant, isn't it? Hopefully the bastard gets what he deserves, but the precedents here aren't great – six years here and there, only half that before being granted parole.'

'You seem to know so much. How can I help?'

'Ah, but I don't know anything about Judaism.'

'Why don't you just ask Ezra?'

'I don't think he wants to talk about the case with me.' Tegan picked up her glass and brought it to her lips, but then she set it back down without having a drink. 'Whenever I bring up Hirsch, Ezra kind of fades out of the conversation.'

Yonatan nodded. 'Okay. What would you like to know?'

'Tell me about the . . . how do you say it, the *hairem*?'

'*Cherem*.'

'Right, the *cherem* against the Kligers.'

He explained *lashon hara* to her, then the rabbinical court, a *beth din*, and the sin of *mesirah* that Avraham Kliger was accused of committing. 'Have you heard of the term *moser* before?'

'No,' Tegan said.

'That's the name given to someone who commits *mesirah*.'

'So, like a snitch then?'

Yonatan smiled. 'I've never thought of it that way, but yes.'

'And so what does the community do to someone when there's a *cherem* put out on them?'

'They're completely ostracised. Your landlord might evict you, no-one will hire you, the butcher won't sell you meat, friends you've known your entire life might walk straight past you in the street, and your family mourns as if you had died. Invisibility is the punishment. And you might say, "So what? Move somewhere else, start over." But you have to remember that from the moment we open our eyes in the morning to when we close them at night, our lives are guided by *halacha*. Our strength comes from our collective nature. No *Yehudi* is ever alone. We have very little to do with the outside world. Even for a grown man or woman, can you imagine the devastating loneliness, the terror of being thrust into secular life, left to fend for yourself?'

Tegan shook her head. 'Shit.' Her eyes widened and she raised her hand to her mouth. 'Sorry.'

Yonatan smiled. 'You can swear. I'm a rabbi not a monk.'

Tegan finished her wine, sat there for a bit, eyes downcast as though she were dwelling on what he'd told her, but he had a sense, as he often did when his students came to him after class, querying a particular *halachic* quandary, that something else was troubling her. 'Does Ezra seem all right to you?'

Ah, there it is. 'All right? It's difficult for me to say – it's been twenty years.'

'I know, but it's just that lately he's been a bit –' She shook her head. 'It's hard to know what he's thinking these days. He says nothing happened with Hirsch and I believe him but –'

Nothing happened.

Yonatan felt something settle inside of him. A part of himself that he'd been reluctant to acknowledge – one that had been quaking since he first saw Ezra outside of Parliament House.

'He had to move schools,' Tegan continued, 'leaving behind his friends, his community, you, and I just . . . I think it had a bigger impact on him than he's willing to admit.'

Yonatan thought again of the Yehuda HaNasi quote he'd told Ezra and an immediate conflict came to mind – what if your path was chosen for you? One wouldn't be able to ensure harmony for themselves, let alone mankind.

'Has he said anything to you?' Tegan asked.

Yonatan recalled the sight of Ezra at the basketball court, elbows on his knees, head in his hands, sweat pooling onto the ground as he asked Yonatan about morality in the Talmud. But Yonatan could tell Ezra didn't really want answers. He was showing that he was penitent, and he was asking for absolution. He wanted Yonatan to assure him that his sins would be forgiven, that he wasn't a bad person. Yonatan had seen that look on him before – when all he wanted was to be told that everything was going to be okay.

*

It was the height of bar mitzvah season. Noam Abrahams at St Kilda *shule*, Yosef Markowitz at Caulfield, Eitan Fried at the Yahel Academy *shule*. Every weekend of Yonatan's was booked for half the year. Services on Shabbat, and receptions on Sundays, held in function halls all over the city. There Yonatan and the other boys from his grade got drunk on cheap wine, sang 'Hava Nagila' until their voices were hoarse, and tried as hard as they could to flip the bar mitzvah boy from a tablecloth into the ceiling.

Yonatan was invited to more of the celebrations than Ezra, on account of his being *frum*, he told Ezra. But they both knew that wasn't the entirety of the truth. Ezra was, however, invited to Yehuda Gindle's bar mitzvah. *Everyone* was invited to Yehuda Gindle's bar mitzvah. Having survived the Holocaust, Yehuda's grandfather arrived in Melbourne with little. He worked as a tailor in Fitzroy and eventually saved enough to open his own clothing store. Fast-forward sixty years and Yehuda's grandfather was a majority shareholder of one of the largest clothing chains in the country. Yehuda's house took up half a block in Toorak and his birthdays were always the highlight of the school calendar. Yehuda's Torah reading was at Toorak *shule* – an ostentatious building of imposing size, complete with pillared entrance and a striking copper dome. Once inside, the sight of the lustrous red and gold interior only added to Ezra and Yonatan's anticipation for the reception at Crown Casino the following evening.

They were not disappointed. Upon entering the reception hall, guests were greeted by 'Y-E-H-U-D-A' spelled out in giant gold helium balloons. The room was at least as large as the Toorak *shule*'s impressive interior, but with plush purple carpet and a ceiling covered with crystal chandeliers. Two sets of seemingly endless round tables were separated by a glowing dance floor, upon which lights flickered in a pattern to form Y-E-H-U-D-A. Each table was draped in a purple silk tablecloth and held a centrepiece of ice carved into Yehuda's likeness. At the head of the dance floor, the family table sat long and raised above all else, like royalty. On the opposite side, there stood both a deejay and an eight-person band, and by the far wall the bottles of a fully stocked open bar rose, like Yaacov's ladder, to the heavens.

Yonatan and Ezra were seated at different tables. Yonatan had been grouped with the other *frum* boys, while Ezra sat on the other side of the dance floor with the more secular boys and other mixed tables. There was no *mechitza* to separate men and women, and the table arrangement was likely a compromise. Yonatan recognised many of the black-hatted, long-bearded ultra-Orthodox men who arrived and greeted Yehuda and his father with loud exclamatory *mazel tov*s. His own father had allowed Yonatan to attend but politely refused his invitation because of the lack of *mechitza*. These men, however, didn't appear bothered.

During the first *Hora*, Yonatan and Ezra met up and stood together at the corner of the dance floor, watching Yehuda's over-exuberant uncle pull their classmates into the circle and drape his extraordinarily sweaty armpits over their shoulders.

Entrée followed the *Hora*, along with speeches where Yehuda was presented with a personalised Essendon footy jumper, signed by the entire team. Over the course of the evening, Yonatan often looked for Ezra across the way. For the most part, he had his head down and his hands in his lap, likely playing Snake on the Nokia his parents gave him when he was away from home. The rest of Ezra's table were up and down, chasing each other with cloth serviette whips, stealing bread rolls and popping squares of margarine into unprotected glasses of water.

When the bow-tied wait staff brought out the chicken schnitzel mains, Yonatan made his way to the open bar to grab a Coke and take advantage of the absent line. Metres from the bar, he was joined by David Kamil, who greeted him with a wide smile on his ruddy cheeks. 'G'day, Kaplan, after a drink?'

'Just a Coke,' Yonatan said.

'Get a slice of lemon.'

'But I don't –'

'Fucking hell, Kaplan. Just get a slice of lemon.'

Yonatan shrugged and asked the bartender for a Coke with a slice of lemon.

After pouring the Coke from the bar gun, the bartender turned around to grab a lemon from a bowl behind him, and that's when Kamil reached over the bar and pulled out a bottle of Smirnoff from beneath it. He tucked the bottle under his jacket and walked back to his table – Ezra's table.

There was more dancing then. A second *Hora* in which Yehuda and his parents were placed on chairs and lifted up and down by his sweaty uncle and others, and then dessert was served – dairy-free cake and dark chocolate mousse. On the other side of the floor, Ezra had forgotten his phone and was speaking to the boys on his table, gesticulating animatedly. Across the table, Kamil pointed to Ezra's glass, and he handed it over. A few seconds later, Kamil returned it, half-full.

After dessert, one of the ultra-Orthodox men took to the lectern to lead *Birkat Hamazon*. In the centre of each table were laminated copies of the *bracha achrona*, and as Pinchas Singer passed him one, Yonatan caught sight of Kamil exiting the bathroom and smiling to himself in an unsettling way. He sat back down at his table. Ezra was nowhere to be seen. *Birkat*

Hamazon began. Yonatan stood up, ignoring the what-are-you-doing eyes of Pinchas, and walked to the men's bathrooms.

Inside, one stall door was closed. From within there was rustling and the repeated jingle of a belt buckle. 'Do it! Why won't you do it?'

'Ezra – Ez, that you?' Yonatan asked.

The rustling stopped. 'Yo . . . Yoni?'

'Yeah – you okay?'

'I can't . . . Yoni . . . I can't do it.' His speech was slurred.

'Do what?'

'Spoof.'

'Spoof?'

'Yeah – Kamil bet me that I couldn't, and I said that I –'

'Ez – could you open up?'

'I could . . . and he said . . . show me.'

'Ez – I think you should open the door –'

'I shook it and pulled it – but nothing, then he –'

'Ez. You're drunk. Open the door. C'mon.'

'He took his out – and it was big – and really pale, and he had all these dark pubes – so many – I don't have any pubes.'

The floor vibrated. 'Oh shit,' Ezra said. There was more rustling and buckle clinking. 'My mum's calling. What do I do?' His voice went high, panicked.

'It's okay. Open the door. I'll take care of it.'

'Okay – one sec.' Yonatan heard him pull up his pants, zip up and fumble with the lock. The door opened. Ezra's eyes were glassy, wandering. His shirt tails were untucked. He held out his Nokia in the palm of his hand as though it were a spider in a jar.

Yonatan took the phone. It had stopped vibrating, and there was a voicemail waiting.

'Yoni –'

'Yes, Ez.'

'I need to . . . wait tell me . . . I want to – do you have pubes?'

'Ez, I don't think that –'

'Wait.' Ezra held up his hand, turned around and threw up violently onto the toilet seat and stall floor.

Yonatan stayed with Ezra for the next hour until his mum arrived. He brought him glasses of water between his bursts of dry retching and handed him paper towels. When people came into the bathroom, Yonatan told them it was something Ezra ate, but the boys from their year knew better and either smirked or offered boastful advice on how to deal with the next day's hangover. For the most part, Ezra was an unintelligible mess, holding his head under running cold water, muttering to himself, seemingly on the verge of tears. But at one point he sparked up, shot into a brief moment of lucidity in which he let go of the sink basin, sought out Yonatan and fixed on him with a desperate, pleading gaze.

'I couldn't do it, Yoni. Tell me. Tell me, Yoni – is there something wrong with me?'

*

Sitting in the bar across from Tegan, Yonatan shook his head. 'No,' he said. 'Ezra hasn't said anything to me.'

They stayed at the bar for another half hour, discussing the position of religious parties in Israeli politics, until Yonatan said he should be getting back to Rivka. Together, Yonatan and Tegan walked to the parking spaces opposite the Classic Cinema, where they'd both parked their cars.

'Thanks again for coming,' Tegan said.

'It was a pleasure.' Yonatan smiled and shook her hand goodbye.

Tegan opened her car door and ducked to enter, before quickly standing up. 'Could you do me a favour? Maybe don't tell Ezra I asked to meet. I don't think he'd understand.'

More secrets, *oy*. 'Not a word.'

Yonatan walked to his own car, unlocked it and sat down heavily. 'Ezra, Ezra, Ezra,' he said aloud, shaking his head. Tegan clearly loved him, but for how long could a person withstand the stubborn, silent suffering of their partner? He started the engine and looked in his rearview mirror to reverse, but something stopped him – two boys were having a conversation outside the cinema. They were wearing *kippot*, white shirts and dark slacks. Familiar looking, possibly from Yahel, but he couldn't be sure. Had they seen him leave with Tegan? Shake her hand? They must have gone there to see a secular film, a prohibited activity. Even if they were from Yahel, surely they wouldn't say anything for fear of him doing the same. Nonetheless, Yonatan reversed quickly, threw his car into gear and sped off without looking back.

Chapter 11

Ezra

Standing outside of his and Tegan's apartment, Ezra rocked back and forth on his heels, swayed by rolling waves of self-loathing. He rested his forehead against their front door, resisting the temptation to pull his head back and smash it repeatedly until the wood splintered and he was gifted with unconsciousness. The effort of raising his keys to the lock was almost overwhelming and by the time he turned the door handle, his breathing was heavy and laboured.

It'd been a rough day. For the past month, he'd been working with the Victorian Office of Parliamentary Counsel on the drafting of a bill to assist with the implementation of reforms promised by the state government in the last election. It had been a tight race but ultimately the more conservative Liberal Party had won on a platform of corporate tax cuts and the streamlining of what many considered to be a bloated public service. For Ezra, the result meant working on legislative changes that cut social services in order to produce savings that would help make up for the money lost in the promised tax cuts.

Yes, he'd agreed with Tegan, it was an abhorrent, short-sighted policy, but it was also his job to serve the democratically elected government of the day. To counteract the guilt of what he did, and admittedly to impress Tegan as well, Ezra would sometimes photocopy the Cabinet-in-Confidence documents he was working on, slide them surreptitiously into his bag and then show them to Tegan when he got home.

Ministerial briefings, new policy proposals, legislative drafting instructions – anything that might help her in her work at Australia Without Violence, where she could draft a response to a Senate committee inquiry or produce a better position statement.

Getting caught would mean losing his job, possibly even a criminal charge. But on those nights, when the two of them were huddled over the documents on the couch, sharing a bottle of wine and speaking in hushed whispers, as though someone might be listening, Ezra felt a little bit better about his job and himself, and more importantly, he felt closer to Tegan. They were in it together – like when they were lifting those branches off the road in Margaret River, they were a team.

Two weeks ago, Ezra had brought Tegan a copy of the draft bill sent to him by the Office of Parliamentary Counsel, based on his drafting instructions. Specifically, the bill was to amend existing legislation that detailed the income tiers for people receiving housing assistance. The bill lowered the tiers, meaning that countless people who relied on that funding and earned a salary near the threshold would find themselves suddenly ineligible for assistance.

After half an hour poring over the bill on the couch, Tegan stood up excitedly, ran to their room and returned with her laptop.

A minute later, she clapped in celebration. 'I knew it!'

'What?' Ezra asked.

'Take a look at section four and compare it to the current act,' Tegan said, handing him the laptop.

Section four was the repeals section, provisions that would no longer be relevant under the new version of the act, but Ezra couldn't see what she was talking about. 'And?'

'Anything missing?'

He scanned the document again, checked the provisions it referenced in the act, but still couldn't find anything. 'Sorry – I've got no idea.'

'Look, look!' She pointed to the current act and the section titled 'DEFINITIONS'. 'It's not listed – they've forgotten to repeal the current definition of ELIGIBLE APPLICANT, but the new one is being inserted anyway.'

'Oh – right. They must've made a mistake, but what does that have to –'

'There'll be two definitions.' She jumped up and paced in front of Ezra. 'We'll wait for the bill to pass, and then we'll contest the new provisions as being invalid.'

'Okay, but –'

'I know – they'll change it, but it's going to take time. And we can use that time to lobby the opposition and independents to oppose the lower thresholds. Even if all we get are a couple more months before this shit actually hits, at least that's a couple more months of women and children having the money to afford somewhere safe to sleep at night.' Ezra couldn't remember the last time he'd seen Tegan that excited. 'This is brilliant.' And then she leant over and kissed Ezra hard on the mouth.

Since then, he'd been in constant email and phone contact with Laura Sellars, Assistant Parliamentary Counsel, about the bill. She hadn't picked up on the error, and earlier that day, they'd had a meeting to finalise the bill before it was given to the minister for introduction into Parliament.

The meeting was held in a boardroom at the Office of Parliamentary Counsel, near the Old Treasury building in East Melbourne. Steven accompanied Ezra, as his director and project lead for the implementation of the bill.

At the security desk in the building's lobby, Ezra gave Laura's name and then took a seat beside Steven on a bench by the entrance. A minute later, a slim woman in a fitted, dark business suit came to collect them. She wore her blonde hair in a ponytail, and dark rimmed rectangular glasses that covered extraordinarily large blue eyes. 'You must be Ezra,' she said, holding out her hand.

Ezra shook it and smiled.

'Nice to put a face to the name,' Laura said, smiling back.

Steven introduced himself, and they both followed Laura through the door she'd appeared from to the lifts.

The boardroom had paisley carpet, upon which sat a long table of dark, varnished wood surrounded by black leather chairs. Sitting in one of the chairs, with a laptop and multiple copies of the bill spread out before him, was an older, heavyset man wearing a navy suit and a thick grey tie. He stood as they entered and Laura introduced him as Ian Macpherson, a senior drafter who'd been assisting her with the bill. There were no windows in the room, and as Ezra approached the table, he noticed the shine of the halogen downlights on Ian's large forehead. Laura walked around the table and sat next to Ian. Steven and Ezra sat across the table from them, and Ezra smiled to himself, feeling as though they were entering into an interrogation.

'Thank you for coming,' Ian said.

'Least we could do,' Steven replied. 'Thanks for drafting the bill.'

'Actually – it was all Laura.' Ian turned and smiled at her. 'First one on her own. I dotted some i's, crossed some t's, but this was her baby.'

Laura returned Ian's smile and two small dimples etched into her cheeks. 'I like to think of it as more of a team effort.' She picked up two copies of the bill, stood and handed them to Ezra and Steven across the table. 'Ezra's been a big help.'

Feeling his face warm, Ezra opened his copy of the bill and ducked his head into it. 'Job's not over yet,' he said. 'What've we got left?'

'Not much,' Laura replied, opening her own copy and glancing over at Ian's laptop screen. 'Some minor revisions for you to look over, changes to the numbering that'll affect the Explanatory Memorandum and a question Ian had about the minister's power to expedite an application.'

Ian elaborated on the issue he had in mind. Steven identified it as being a matter of the minister's preference and fortunately he was able to get a hold of the minister's adviser and confirm what they wanted. They went over the other revisions for the next forty-five minutes and then Ian shut his copy of the bill and lowered his laptop screen. 'That's it.' He stood up and held out his hand across the table. 'Job well done,' he said, shaking Ezra's hand and then Steven's.

Laura stood, did the same and sat down, then she took off her glasses and smiled. She looked down at the completed bill in front of her, and the lights shone off the moisture in her eyes as she took a deep breath and exhaled. It seemed to Ezra that he was privy to a private moment of pure, uninhibited satisfaction and he should look away, but he didn't.

'Fantastic work, everyone,' Steven said. 'We'll have to get lunch, once this thing passes and –'

Ezra had a vision. Laura being asked into Ian's office, her upturned lips, eyes shut as she learned of the bill passing Parliament with errors she failed to see. And then Ezra had another – her gratitude for his discovery of the error, the pop of shirt buttons, the clink of his belt, her taking out her ponytail and him sweeping the hair out of those blue eyes.

'Wait – sorry, Steven. Could we just –' Ezra picked up his copy of the bill and opened it to the repeals section. 'Sorry, Laura, would you mind quickly checking something for me in the current act? I just have a hunch.'

Half a bottle of wine to quell his anxiety, a long shower and maybe a toasted sandwich if he felt up to it. That was Ezra's plan for the evening, but when he opened their apartment door, he was greeted by the sultry voice of Etta James and the sound of Tegan singing along in the kitchen. He stood in the doorway, paralysed. He considered stepping back outside, walking in the exact opposite direction until his legs cramped and his feet blistered, but then the music stopped.

'Ez, is that you?'

Shit.

'Yeah, I –'

'I'm in the kitchen,' Tegan called. 'Come here.'

That was it – there was no going back. He'd have to tell her that the drafters found the error in the bill, and though he'd leave out his part in it, he doubted he could hide the shame that had his insides curdling into tar.

In the kitchen, Tegan had her back to him, pouring Prosecco into two champagne flutes. Her hair was out, hanging over her shoulders, and she was wearing the silk, animal-print dress he liked. He called it her Africa dress, for the miniature elephants, giraffes, zebras and lions that chased each other about her legs and waist. Between the two of them, on their kitchen island cart, were small bowls of chopped lettuce, tomatoes, cheese and a plate of tortillas. Tegan turned, smiled on seeing him and held out a glass. 'How was it?'

God damn she was beautiful. His throat closed – he might cry if he spoke, so he rounded the island, took the glass from her hand and kissed her instead. A long, delicate kiss, as his free hand slid against silk. He shut his wet eyes tight, and kept his mouth occupied for what he hoped was long enough to stifle the confession brimming on his lips.

'It was good,' he said. 'Glad it's all over.' He waited for Tegan to pull away, hold him at arm's length and search his eyes for the glimmer of a lie, but she only smiled and held up her glass.

'Cheers,' she said.

They clinked glasses. Ezra took a sip of his drink, savoured the tingling of bubbles on his tongue and was surprised to feel his shoulders relax, pulse slacken. There was no trace of the gut-churning guilt that had him nearly doubled over at the door. Instead, what he found was an extravagant, untended hunger as Tegan unlidded a pan on the stove and the mouth-watering smell of cooked mince wafted to him.

It was a nice evening. Tegan didn't ask anything further about the meeting or bring up the Hirsch case. During dinner, they polished off the rest of the Prosecco and Tegan told him about her colleague's custody dispute, asking for his thoughts, though she knew ten times what he did about family law. They left the dishes for a change, and full and tipsy, settled on the couch to stream an episode of *Doctor Who*.

Lying with Tegan's weight gently resting against him, everything was good and easy. Ezra's eyelids were heavy, as he was lulled to sleep by David Tennant's voice and all of that dalek nonsense. Half-conscious, with colours sparking behind his eyelids, Ezra was on the verge of blissful ease, when Tegan's hand brushed against his crotch and the day flooded back – Laura.

His heart thundered. He was too hot. He couldn't breathe. How could he have done something like that? How many lives had he impacted? How much suffering would he cause, and for what? A chance with a woman he hardly knew. A fantasy.

Ezra raised himself slightly and looked down at Tegan, hoping her glancing fingertips had been an accident and nothing more. He wouldn't be able to – there was no way he could have sex now. But what would he say if she grasped for his zipper? Worse still, if she kissed him gently, made him look in her eyes, and said in all earnest, 'I love you, Ezra.'

Fuck.

He could tell her the truth – let Tegan see him for how pathetic, small and weak he was. The words were there, all he had to do was open his mouth and let them out. But then again, who was he kidding? If he could do that, he wouldn't be the kind of person who fucked up in the first place. No – the only thing left to do was to close his eyes and pretend to sleep.

Chapter 12

Yonatan

It was Yonatan's turn to laugh, as he caught sight of Ezra on the other side of Swanston Street, waiting for the lights to change. His tie hung loosely around his neck, and his suit jacket was draped across his arm. Semi-circles of sweat darkened the pits of his light blue shirt.

'Seriously,' Ezra said on arriving at Yonatan's side. 'I don't know how you bloody stand being dressed like this all the time.'

Yonatan shrugged. 'You get used to it.'

'I see you've gone full Jew today,' Ezra said, gesturing to Yonatan.

He was wearing a long black *bekishe* that he usually reserved for *Yom Tov*, along with a circular fur *shtreimel*. In his hands was a velvet *tefillin* bag embroidered with a silver *Magen David*. 'I was feeling . . . theatrical,' he said, smiling.

Together they turned and walked past the Sidney Myer Asia Centre into the grounds of Melbourne University.

After what Tegan had said to him, and the experience at the basketball court, Yonatan decided to reach out to Ezra and invite him to a *mitzvoyim* visit at the university.

'It's outreach,' he explained to Ezra on the phone. 'We try to find Jewish students and help them perform *mitzvot*, like putting on *tefillin*.'

'Lapsed Jews, you mean,' Ezra said, 'like me.'

'Well . . . anyone who hasn't performed the ritual that day.'

'Uh-huh, and this is to get their mitzvah points up – keep them out of hell when the *Moshiach* comes?'

'Hell is a Christian concept, it's more of a –'

'I know, I know – purgatory, I remember. And will helping these kids increase my mitzvah points?'

'It couldn't hurt.'

'All right – I'll come, but only because Melbourne Uni is around the corner.'

It had been a long shot, but Yonatan had suspected Ezra would be keen to make amends for how he left things at the basketball court. And here he was, wiping sweat off his forehead with the back of his hand. Yonatan reached into his pocket, withdrew a small black *kippah* and offered it to Ezra. 'In case you forgot.'

'Thanks,' Ezra said.

Yonatan had been to the university last *Sukkot* with Menachem. They came armed with a *lulav* and *etrog* and soon found themselves inundated with questions from *goy* students whose interest had been piqued by the strange Jews waving about a lemon and a tree branch. From that experience, Yonatan knew the best place to find students would be on the South Lawn by the Old Arts building.

On their way through the campus, some students glanced up from their phones or conversations and watched them as they passed. But not with the lingering, accusatory gaze Yonatan had grown accustomed to in public. These were young, inquisitive minds, still receptive to ideas and experiences that were foreign to them. It was one of the reasons Yonatan had chosen the university for Ezra's first *mitzvoyim*. Elsewhere, it was more likely they would encounter the hostility of prejudiced individuals with opinions cemented by a lifetime of anger and hate.

Stretched across the well-tended bright green grass of the South Lawn were countless students – lying on their backpacks, eyes skyward, young men and women sitting in mixed groups, throwing a frisbee, kicking a football. Ezra would have been one of them once, living like this, without Torah, without *halacha*, without *Hashem*. 'Bring back memories?' Yonatan asked.

'Some.'

'Good or bad?'

'Honestly, I was pretty drunk most of the time.'

Yonatan laughed.

'So, what do we do now?' Ezra asked.

'Simple – we ask if anyone is Jewish.'

'How do we know who to ask?'

'Oh, you know, dark hair, dark eyes, big *schnoz* – the usual.'

Ezra raised his eyebrows.

Yonatan smiled. 'You're too easy, my friend – we'll ask everyone.'

For fifteen minutes they wandered from one end of the lawn to the other, approaching several clusters of students, all of whom received them warmly, but none of which were Jewish. Yonatan was near the point of giving up, and thinking of ways to salvage the day, when they spotted a small group in a shaded corner of the lawn.

There were three of them, two boys and a girl. The girl had very short brown hair, not unlike Rivka's beneath her *sheitel*. She was wearing a tight-fitting blue top and shorts. Yonatan averted his eyes from the bra straps, visible on her exposed shoulders.

One of the boys was thick and muscular. He wore a singlet, maroon shorts and sunglasses. The other was slim and dark skinned, in black jeans and a t-shirt despite the heat.

'Excuse me,' Yonatan said. 'Are you Jewish?'

'No, sorry,' the girl said.

Yonatan smiled. Of course she wasn't. If she had been, she'd have recognised the bag he was carrying, known that women did not put on *tefillin*.

'And you?' he asked the boys.

The skinny one shook his head, while the other turned to the girl, smiled and then looked up at Yonatan. 'Yeah, I'm Jewish.'

'Bayden,' the girl said with a hint of reproach.

'Excellent, would you like to stand up?' Yonatan said.

'No worries.'

'Bayden, is it?'

'Yep.'

'Okay, Bayden. Have you put on *tefillin* this morning?'

Bayden shook his head.

'Have you put them on before?'

'Ah . . . yeah – few years ago.'

Beside Yonatan, Ezra watched their exchange with narrow eyes and stepped towards him. 'Hey, Yoni. Can I speak to you for a second?'

'Excuse me,' Yonatan said to Bayden.

'I don't think this kid is Jewish,' Ezra said quietly.

'Of course he is,' Yonatan said, loud enough for Bayden to hear. He turned to the large boy. 'You're Jewish, yes?'

'Yeah, mate. Jewish.'

'See, he's Jewish.' He smiled at Ezra, a 'Trust me' smile.

'Okay,' Yonatan said, taking another small black *kippah* from his pocket, 'could you please place this on your head?'

Bayden did as he asked, and Yonatan removed the arm *tefillin* from the velvet bag. 'Now hold out your left arm for me.' He slipped the leather strap attached to the box over Bayden's left hand and placed it on his bicep. 'Inside the box is parchment inscribed with a passage from the Torah. We place the box on the bicep, facing the heart. Now repeat after me, *ba-ruch a-tah Ado-nai* –'

Bayden struggled through the blessing, looked relieved when it was finished, and held out his arm towards Yonatan.

'Not yet,' Yonatan said. 'We still need to do the rest of your arm and the head *tefillin*.' Bayden's smile fell and he lowered his arm, but on turning to his friends and seeing their enraptured stares he re-engaged, and asked Yonatan what came next.

'We wind the strap seven times around the forearm and the excess around the palm.'

Bayden laughed as Yonatan wrapped his arm. 'It's like I'm tying one off.'

'Jesus, Bayden,' the girl said.

Yonatan retrieved the head *tefillin* from the bag, placed it on Bayden's forehead and helped him through the blessing. 'Nearly done – I'm going to wrap your fingers now. We form the shape of the Hebrew letters *shin*, *dalet* and *yud* for the name of the master of the universe.' From his pocket Yonatan withdrew a card that had a transliterated version of the *Shema* on it. 'Now read from this card to recite the *Shema*, just do the best you can.'

The *Shema* was an effort. Bayden pronounced each syllable on the card individually in a halting, staccato fashion, so that it took him twice as long as Yonatan would normally expect.

'– *Elo . . . hay . . . khem*.' Finished, Bayden looked up from the card, turned to the girl and smiled. He looked proud.

'That's it, Bayden. Well done.' Yonatan unwound his arm.

'So what was that about then?' The skinny boy spoke for the first time. 'What'd he just say?'

'It affirms that there is only one *Hashem*, and that you are commanded to love Him with all of your heart.' Yonatan held out the card to the boy. 'There's an English translation on the card, if you'd like to read it.'

'Take care lest your heart be lured away,' the boy read aloud, 'and you turn astray and worship alien gods and bow down to them. For then the Lord's wrath will flare up against you, and He will close the heavens so that there will be no rain and the earth will not yield its produce, and you will swiftly perish from the good land which the Lord gives you.' He looked up at Yonatan and Ezra. 'That's pretty intense.'

Yonatan nodded. 'In Judaism, the Almighty is ruthless to the faithless and wicked. But it also says, there,' Yonatan pointed to the card, 'that if you abide by His commandments and serve Him with all your heart and soul, He will take care of you.'

The boy handed the card back to Yonatan and thanked him. Yonatan wished them all *yom tov* and thanked Bayden for performing the mitzvah.

Walking away from the group, Ezra was quiet and seemed thoughtful. He spoke once they were out of earshot of the students. 'There's absolutely no way that guy was Jewish.'

'I know,' Yonatan replied.

'But then why did you –'

'Everyone is a child of *Hashem*. Why should he be excluded from performing a mitzvah under His gaze?'

'But aren't we the chosen people? Isn't there a prayer that thanks God for not making us gentiles?'

Impressive. He hadn't expected Ezra to remember that. 'There is. But there's also a mitzvah for not selling a beautiful woman taken captive in war.' He smiled. 'The modern context is important.'

'But not everyone thinks that way, right?'

Yonatan nodded. 'It's true. But if they had it their way, we'd be stoning everyone who touched a light switch on Shabbat.'

'Woah.'

'That's right.'

Yonatan surveyed the grounds for a group they hadn't approached.

'Do you reckon I could get a look at that card?' Ezra asked.

'Of course.'

Yonatan pretended to shield his eyes from the sun while actually watching Ezra.

What was his pensive, sad-eyed friend thinking as he read the translation of the *Shema*? He held out the velvet bag to Ezra. 'How about you, young man? Have you put on *tefillin* today?'

Ezra smirked and handed back the card, then his lips tightened into a line and he pulled the *kippah* from his head. 'I think it's a bit late to save me from the Lord's wrath.'

A shadow darkened the lawn – a sudden blanket of clouds had been laid out over the sky. No rain yet, but most students, accustomed to Melbourne's weather to the point of premonition, had already left in search of shelter. Yonatan hurried to the arched openings of the cloisters by the Old Arts building, Ezra close behind him.

Together they watched the rain come down in a great, unrelenting surge and quickly pool in pockets of the lawn. Yonatan muttered a quote from *Parashat Noach* to himself. 'And the floodgates of the sky broke open and rain fell on the Earth for forty days and forty nights.'

'Guess we'll be here for a while,' Ezra said, raising his voice over the rain. 'Did you hear about Hirsch by the way?'

Yonatan recalled what Tegan had said to him. 'No. What happened?'

'He's finally being extradited. He'll be arrested as soon as he lands in the country. There'll be a trial.'

'Glad to hear it,' Yonatan said.

'Do you reckon you'll go?'

'I'm not sure.' Yonatan traced the *Magen David* on the *tefillin* pouch in his hand. 'I don't think it would be a good idea.'

'Because of the *cherem*?'

'Yes.'

'Did something happen – because you went to the protest?'

'It's nothing.' Yonatan paused. 'But it was noticed.'

'Jesus Christ.' Ezra shook his head. 'But Hirsch is the paedophile, not Kliger.'

'I know, but –' How could he best make Ezra understand? 'There's a city in Ukraine, Uman, where Rebbe Nachman, a great *tzaddik*, was buried in the early nineteenth century. And on Rosh Hashanah every year, hundreds of thousands of ultra-Orthodox *Yehudim* go on a pilgrimage to his grave. While they are there another group also flocks into the city to meet the demands of the *charedim*. Can you guess who?'

Ezra shrugged.

'Prostitutes.'

'Seriously?'

Yonatan nodded. 'The most devout and respected members of the community make the yearly journey to Uman and say nothing about their exploits to their wives. As you're beginning to understand, the community can be quite selective when it comes to breaches of *halacha* and deciding who should be reprimanded for what sins.'

'Shit.' Ezra paced and kicked at the stones beneath his feet. 'I'm sorry, Yoni. Sorry we got you into trouble.'

Yonatan waved away his apology. 'Don't worry about it. I'll be fine.'

Ezra stopped pacing, looked up at Yonatan and smiled.

'*Mah zeh?*' Yonatan said.

Ezra took off his jacket and rolled up his shirt sleeves. 'Least I could do is give you some more mitzvah points.'

In Ezra's last year at Yahel, all of the boys in their grade had to put on *tefillin* for morning prayers. It was preparation for the time after their bar mitzvahs, when they would do it every morning for the rest of their lives. As he did back then, Yonatan helped Ezra place the first box on his bicep, say the blessing and wrap his arm. And then, in a confluence of time, he was back with that child, winding the leather tight around his fleshy bicep, and simultaneously touching this man's large, dark-haired forearm.

Ezra the boy, and the man, looked at him – the boy, bashful and innocent, smiling with affection, and the man reticent and withdrawn, attempting to placate him with a mask of interest. Once again, Yonatan was reminded of the inner turmoil Ezra had hinted at on the basketball court. Was it abandonment of the Torah that led his old friend to suffering? His life as an atheist, an *apikoros*? *When you forsake the Lord and serve strange gods, then He will turn and do you evil, and destroy you*. But if that were true, what about himself? Though he'd been no better of late, what sins had he committed when his own life began to unravel? Had he not been an exemplary servant of *Hashem*? He had never taken a trip to Uman or let himself be led by *yetzer hara* – not since Ezra left Yahel and he gave up all mischief. Would *Hashem* destroy a man over a fake Christmas tree?

'I've got it from here, Yoni,' the boy, and man, said as one, before placing the second *tefillin* on their forehead. '*Baruch atah Adonai Elohaynu melech ha-olam. Asher kidshanu . . .*'

Chapter 13

Ezra

In his first year of university, at the age of eighteen, Ezra questioned his sexuality. It wasn't a particular event, or somebody he met – if he were honest with himself, the question had always been there, lying dormant and unexplored because asking it had never felt like an option. Glen Eira High School had been a feeding ground for early developed, overstimulated boys who were shaving before Ezra even had hair in his armpits. The school was their labyrinth and if you hoped to navigate it, you'd best prove yourself. Tell them of all the pussies you'd fingered, what a girl smelled like down there, did she spit or swallow, wait for them to make a joke about your mum or sister, laugh and take it, don't dare throw it back at them.

Then there were his parents. Ezra imagined they would be shocked and offended at the thought of being called homophobic, but it was an unspoken truth that such things simply didn't happen in the Steinberg family. In high school, his mum would often probe him about his 'situation'. Were there any girls he liked? Did anyone like him? Don't rush into anything – when the right girl came along, he'd know.

In 2006, his dad went to see all of the Oscar-nominated films, as he did every year, except for *Brokeback Mountain*, saying to Ezra's mum, when Ang Lee won Best Director, 'It just makes me uncomfortable. Why should I do something that makes me uncomfortable?'

In the change rooms of the Harold Holt Swim Centre, after a trip to the pool, Ezra recalled his dad berating an older man for walking around naked in front of Ezra. His penis was a thick stump surrounded by willowy white hair and, as he grabbed a towel, his sagging, unsupported breasts flapped in front of him like two deflated balloons.

And Ezra was Jewish. Despite his family's use of light switches on Shabbat, and the occasional flake fillet they ate in the summer holidays, one's Judaism was derived from matrilineal descent – as much a part of you as your blood type. And how could a Jew be gay when the Torah so clearly declared the homosexual act to be an 'abomination'?

For Ezra, the trouble started with porn. When he began watching it, in his mid-teens, when their Internet was finally good enough to download video, he would shield his eyes from the parts with a penis in it. Like the childish attitude he once held towards the opposite sex – dicks were gross.

But, with time, he lowered his hand from his eyes, reasoning that he was only picturing his penis in the place of the ones on screen – though he knew full well there was no mistaking nine inches of dark wood for a circumcised Jewish teenager.

One day, when he didn't have any university classes, and his parents were at work, Ezra turned on his laptop, eager to take full advantage of his solitude the same way he always did. Everything started off normal. Stiff as a board, Ezra worked himself towards climax in tandem with the couple on screen, until the man suddenly withdrew, the camera focused on the woman touching herself alone, and Ezra felt himself soften. He tried to work himself up again, but it was no good. Then the man returned to the scene and Ezra was all steel. He let go of himself and slammed his laptop violently shut. That was the beginning.

All day, every day after that – during classes, eating lunch, while watching a movie – Ezra would tally up the evidence he had for and against his being gay. Was he attracted to men? He didn't know. Had he ever got an erection from looking at a man? No. He did sometimes dream about having sex with men and wake up with an erection. But he also woke up with an erection every morning, even when his dreams were nonsensical romps involving people he didn't know, speaking languages he didn't speak, defying all physical and natural laws.

He would test himself by looking up pictures of naked women and try to force an erection without touching himself. He avoided urinals and would bite hard on the inside of his cheek if he so much as glanced at a man's crotch. He couldn't focus. His grades slipped. Every waking moment of every day he assessed and reassessed the information. Do you like looking at naked women? Yes. Naked men? Unsure. Do you want to touch breasts? Yes. Do you want to touch a dick? Unsure. Do you like kissing women? Yes. How about kissing a man? Don't know. He couldn't sleep. He had no appetite. His mum asked if he was okay, and he told her it was just the stress of upcoming exams. But he was cracking up. He couldn't bear to face people and had to lock himself in his room, terrified of closing his eyes, the images he might conjure up and then have to interpret. Yes, no, yes, yes, no, no – *yes*!

And then, after months of agonising over his every thought and feeling to the point of complete debilitation, a spontaneous idea, unthinkable to the tenets of his upbringing and religion, occurred to him. So what? So what if he was gay? Men or women – it didn't matter. It didn't change who he was as a person, and it wasn't the eighties anymore, he could survive. And that was all it took. He slept soundly that night and regained control of his life.

To date, Ezra still hadn't had a sexual experience with a man, but he was no longer opposed to the idea, and sometimes thought about it when he was alone. Acceptance brought him solace, but the experience in his teens also taught Ezra that he was capable of unhealthily fixating on something to the point of dysfunction, that he would have to learn to mediate his anxiety to the best of his ability and remember that if something like that happened to him again, it would pass.

It had been fifteen years since that incident, but of late Ezra was aware of a stray thread of disquiet once again building at the base of his mind. He didn't know what it meant or was related to, only that he needed some time alone to let it fizzle and pop. Socialising was the last thing he wanted to do, but Tegan was attending a conference in Sydney for a week and he had already promised to go to her colleague's housewarming party that Saturday before she left.

The party was themed 'Australian politics'. Not feeling festive, Ezra wore a suit and told Tegan he'd pick one of the old prime ministers at random, tell people that was who he was. He picked out Frank Forde from Wikipedia. For her costume, Tegan found an oversized camouflage jacket online, stuffed it with pillows and said she was the Bloated Defence Budget.

The party was in Northcote. They caught a cab there and brought a six pack of beer to split between them. The house was a single storey, white brick Victorian with one of those small metal gates you could just step over, and indoor furniture sitting in the overgrown front garden. The front door was open, Men at Work whooping down the narrow entranceway from somewhere inside.

Ezra took the beer to the kitchen while Tegan looked for her colleague. Most of the attendees had gone all out. There was a bald-cap and bespectacled John Howard, a short red-wigged Pauline Hanson and a longer red-wigged Julia Gillard, as well as a couple of guys in suits wearing Akubra hats who could have been either Bob Katter or Barnaby Joyce.

Two beers in hand, Ezra went out the back in search of Tegan. The backyard was big, crowded with people chatting in small groups. Fairy lights had been strung up along a verandah at the back of the house and Australian flag bunting hung from a Hills hoist in the middle of the yard. Tegan stood by a table of food, talking to a girl in a t-shirt and jeans. On her shirt was a map of Australia broken up into hundreds of different coloured parcels. Ezra recognised it from someone's Twitter feed, knew it was a representation of the Indigenous nations that existed prior to the arrival of the First Fleet. Above the map, in capitals, written by hand were the words 'TERRA NULLIUS MY ARSE'.

Tegan was biting her lower lip – the way she did when she was concentrating. Ezra walked over. The girl beside Tegan said something about a Senate inquiry but stopped on seeing him. 'Sorry to interrupt,' Ezra said, holding a bottle out to Tegan.

She took it and placed her free arm around his back. 'Lydia, this is Ezra.' She turned to him. 'It's Lydia's place.'

'Pleased to meet you.' Ezra held out his hand. 'Thanks for having us.'

'The infamous boyfriend.' Lydia took his hand and smiled. 'You work for the government right, for the man.' She mock scowled.

Ezra held up his hands. 'Guilty as charged.' He smiled but also got the feeling she wanted to continue their conversation and would rather he wasn't there. He squeezed Tegan's hand and sidled away.

Hung up on a crossbeam of the verandah's awning was a giant piñata head, unmistakably made to look like Tony Abbott. Two large plastic ears had been glued onto each side of the head and a red and yellow swimmer's cap had been placed on top like a *kippah*.

'Papier mâché,' said a voice behind Ezra. It was a guy wearing a suit and rimless rectangular glasses. His hair was swept to the side in a fringe and dyed white with powder – Kevin Rudd. 'Took me a whole bloody afternoon.'

'Looks good, though,' Ezra said. 'Do you live here?'

'Nah, but my girlfriend does.' He turned and pointed to Lydia.

'Oh, cool,' Ezra gestured to Tegan with his beer. 'I'm Tegan's boyfriend.' He stuck out his hand. 'Ezra.'

'Tom,' Kevin Rudd replied. 'What's she uh –'

'Oh, she's the Bloated Defence Budget.'

Tom smirked. 'Clever.' He reached into his jacket breast pocket and took out a fat joint. 'All right if I –'

'Yeah, no worries.'

A lighter appeared in Tom's other hand. He held the joint to the flame and rotated it with his fingertips until the end was glowing, then he brought it to his lips, drew deeply and blew the smoke away from Ezra. Tom held out the joint. 'How 'bout it?'

Ezra didn't like weed. It rarely did anything for him, and when it did the soft calm was often too short and the heightened anxiety too long. Still, he had nothing else to do and a quick drag might loosen him up, make the next couple of hours more bearable.

Drawing on the joint, Ezra let the smoke fill his mouth, and then he breathed in again, the way some classmates from university had taught him in the back of an old Corolla. Shit – it was too much. His lungs burned. He tried to hold in the cough but that only made it worse – it came out, dry, hacking.

'You right?' Tom asked.

Ezra nodded, small coughs still sputtering from his lips. He smacked his chest, spat on the ground. 'Been a while,' Ezra said, clearing his throat and handing the joint back to Tom. He took an extra long pull from his beer. Tom had another toke from the joint and Ezra held up his near-empty bottle before Tom could offer him another hit. 'I'm gonna get a beer. Do you want one?'

Tom shook his head, and Ezra went back inside. He took his time, picking at chips and a cob loaf spinach dip on the kitchen counter before grabbing another bottle from the fridge. He was all right – one hit wasn't enough to affect him.

Back outside, Tegan and Lydia hadn't moved but Tom and another guy, wearing a '#STOPADANI' t-shirt, had joined their conversation. Ezra went over and slid into a space next to Tegan. #STOPADANI, as it turned out, was another housemate, and he was telling the story of why their final housemate, Marcus, wasn't at the party. Marcus had wanted to invite his brother, Jez, and the rest of the house said he could only come if he didn't bring his best mate Lynden. Lynden was on parole from prison. He had been caught selling drugs out of a Flemington commission flat.

'Don't get me wrong,' Lydia said to Tegan and Ezra. 'I believe in rehabilitation and reintegration. It's just that –'

'It's that he's a junkie,' Tom interrupted, 'and he brought ice into the house.'

'He what?' Tegan said.

'A few weeks ago,' #STOPADANI said. 'Jez and Lynden came over – they were watching a movie with Marcus – *Blade Runner*, the new one, having a couple of drinks, comparing it to the

Harrison Ford version, when Lynden takes out a glass pipe, asks if anyone wants some.'

#STOPADANI shook his head. 'Look, I get it. Addiction is a thing. Some people are predisposed towards it. We can't pretend to understand what Lynden's going through, but –'

'But some people are just shit,' Tom said. 'For whatever reason. I mean the second the guy gets out of prison for doing drugs, he's back doing drugs.' He looked at Lydia. 'Jez has a choice about who he spends time with, and if he wants to hang out with that deadshit, that's his prerogative. But we don't have to spend time with bad people.'

Ezra felt the muscles at the back of his head tighten. His cheekbones were numb, his teeth mossy. What about him? How would this group feel if they knew the things he'd done? If they could read his thoughts? All those women and children who were going to suffer because of him. He felt sick. His stomach boiled acid. He was bleeding sweat. There was no air in that damned backyard.

'You okay, mate?' Tom asked. 'Look like you had a stroke.'

Jesus! He knew, everyone knew.

'Ez?' Tegan's eyebrows were pinched with concern.

'I've just gotta . . . go to the bathroom.'

He ploughed through the house and into a thankfully empty bathroom. It was too hot, unbearably hot. The bathroom had a deep basin, large enough to fit his head under the faucet. He shut his eyes and spun the cold tap. The shock of water was fucking heaven, and he would've stayed there till his skull was soggy with it had there not been a knock on the door.

'Ez, is everything okay?' It was Tegan on the other side.

'One sec!' He let the water run, gripped the sides of the basin and faced himself in the mirror. His eyes were wild and red. Jesus Christ, it was happening again, just like when he was eighteen. He shut his eyes, shook his head. No, no, no, no. Fuck, fuck, fuck. Was he losing his mind? Okay . . . focus, deep breaths, deep breaths.

Inhale.

Exhale.

Inhale.

Exhale.

It'll pass, like last time, everything does. He turned off the tap and used a hand towel to dab at his soaked hair before opening the door.

Tegan entered and closed the door behind her. He rested his wet forehead on her chest, and she put her hands on the back of his head and held him there. 'What's wrong?'

'I had some weed. I feel funny. I'm sorry.'

'Weed?'

'Yeah, Tom, he –'

'It's okay.' She removed her hands. 'Do you want to go?'

'Yeah – I mean if that'd be all right?'

Tegan nodded. 'Okay.' She took his hand, led him out of the bathroom and to the front door.

'Don't you want to say goodbye?' Ezra asked.

'I'll text them from the cab.'

God damn she's incredible. Look at her. Not a moment's hesitation. All she cares about is you and your wellbeing. If she knew the truth, though – if she knew what you'd done, who you really were, would she still be there? She'd spit on you, tell you to go fuck yourself, drown in that sink basin, make the world a better place.

Tegan held his hand the entire ride home, and while he had a cool shower, she put fresh sheets on the bed – because she knew he liked that – and then she went to bed with him, though it was still early and she'd probably rather stay up reading or get some work done.

Ezra shut his eyes, knowing there'd be no sleep – his mind was a beehive. But it was good to rest, and better to let Tegan think he was sleeping while he tried to make sense of the chaos in his head.

Who was he? Was he inherently bad? Why did he do bad things? He'd been through this before. Order helped – he made a list.

The Good: He gave change to a homeless guy on Bourke Street sometimes, he made the mitzvah rounds with Yoni, he was going to buy Baz that teacup of the Royals.

The Bad: Cheating on Tegan, lying to Tegan, telling Laura about the mistake in the bill because he wanted to fuck her.

But what weight should he give each action? How did you attribute a numerical value to good and bad? God would know, or Santa Claus, if either existed. Tegan was tied up in all of it. She was a good person. He didn't need a list to know that. She loved him, but he couldn't love her back. She deserved better. What kind of life was he preventing her from living by tangling her up in his mess of an existence? How many points would he lose for that?

Once he was sure she was asleep, Ezra sat up and let his eyes adjust to the dark. He watched the rise and fall of Tegan's chest. What else was he capable of? He'd dated a girl once who asked him to choke her during sex, smack her around a bit too, but he couldn't do it, said it made him uncomfortable. Was he afraid he would like it? Would he? Could he do that to Tegan if she asked? Or even if she didn't? Squeeze on her windpipe till he felt a pop. Pick up a pillow, smother her in her sleep. Jesus Christ. What the fuck was wrong with him? He shuffled away, to the edge of the bed. His heart beating so loud he swore Tegan would wake. Why would he think something like that? A good person wouldn't have those thoughts. He was fucked. He had to get away from her. Thank god she was leaving in a couple of days.

Chapter 14

Yonatan

Yonatan's thirty-third birthday fell on a Thursday. That morning, a few members of the *shule* congregation greeted him when he arrived for *shacharit*, but not warmly, and no-one appeared willing to engage him in conversation beyond that. No matter. He wasn't at *shule* to socialise. Let them have their prejudice. Only *Hashem* could cast judgement on his worth, as He would on them for their discrimination.

After *Tachanun*, when the Torah was taken out of the ark, Yonatan stood and moved to the end of his pew. Chief Rabbi Feiner picked up the Torah, resting it against his body so that the velvet, gold-embroidered covering faced outward. Reb Feiner then paraded the Torah throughout the *shule*. The bells of the crowns sitting atop the Torah rang out with his movements and the congregation chanted.

Yonatan added his voice to those around him while wrapping the fringes of his *tallit* around his fingers. He then pressed the *tzitziyot* to the Torah as it passed and kissed them. Once the

Torah was placed on the *bimah*, Yonatan remained at the aisle, listening to the *gabbai* call up the first *aliyah*. As it was a weekday, there would only be three *aliyot* – the first two being a Cohen and a Levi, leaving Yonatan for the third. He watched as Reuven Cohen approached the *bimah* and the first Torah portion was read. Natan Levy followed. Yonatan started up the aisle, barely listening to the voice of the *gabbai* as he called for Shimon Brener. Halfway to the *bimah*, Yonatan stopped dead. Shimon? What? Embarrassed, he turned around, shuffled past the men in his row, with apologies, and returned to his seat.

A mistake – that's all it was. The *gabbai*, Lior, was a relative of the chief rabbi's and new to the *shule*, having recently moved to Melbourne from Sydney. He had probably forgotten Yonatan's request. Yonatan would remind him after the service, arrange for the *aliyah* on the coming Shabbat morning. He did so, and though Lior didn't acknowledge that he'd forgotten about Yonatan, he did repeat the request for the coming Shabbat and his name 'Yonatan Kaplan', as though he were trying to remember it.

The next day, as with every Friday, there were no afternoon classes at Yahel, so students and teachers alike might have time to prepare for Shabbat. Yonatan was eager to get home himself and help Rivka – Menachem was coming over for Shabbat dinner. But following his final class, while Yonatan was packing up his things, a request was made over the PA for him to visit Principal Margolis' office.

That had never happened before. While Yonatan liked Principal Margolis, he couldn't help but acknowledge an unnerving thought, prompted by the announcement – first his students and then the *shule* congregation – they were going to make it official, rebuke him in a professional context. But how?

Rather than a traditional office layout, with a desk in the centre of the room, a high-backed leather chair behind it and two smaller visitor chairs in front, Principal Margolis opted to have his desk pressed against the side wall, facing a window and the grounds outside. The principal preferred to conduct his student meetings on a smaller round table at the side of the room. He wanted students to feel as though he were more a peer than their principal. Such a gesture was indicative of Principal Margolis' thoughtful and intelligent nature, and the reason why he held a position of respect and reverence in Yonatan's mind.

Upon entering the office, Yonatan found Principal Margolis sitting at his desk with a folder open in front of him. 'Ah, Yonatan. Take a seat,' Principal Margolis said.

Yonatan sat at the round table and wiped his palms on his slacks.

Principal Margolis closed the folder and carried it over to the small table where he sat opposite Yonatan. There was no labelling on it, but Yonatan suspected it was his personnel file. Nothing good could come of this.

'How have you been, Yonatan?' the principal said.

'Good, thank you.'

The principal nodded. 'And Rivka – she's with child, *nu*?'

'Yes.'

'Your first?'

'Yes, our first.'

'*Baruch Hashem, b'sha'a tovah*.' Principal Margolis smiled.

'Thank you.'

'Okay – onto business.' The principal placed his hands on top of the folder and sighed. 'I suspect you know what this is about, Yonatan.'

Lashon hara, a *cherem*, sacrificing morality for the sake of tradition. 'I have an idea.'

Principal Margolis nodded gravely. 'The decision has been made, Yonatan, to remove you from the school's list of teachers participating in *mitzvoyim* visits. It was suggested that it would be best if you weren't representing Yahel when visiting the wider community.'

Mitzvoyim – it was an insult, but he'd expected worse. Yonatan nodded. 'I understand.' He pushed himself up from his seat.

'I'm afraid there's more.'

'Sorry?'

'After this term, you won't be teaching *Derech HaYashar* anymore. A position has opened up in the primary school and –'

'What? The primary school. But I –'

'I'm sorry, Yonatan. I really am. But some concerning behaviour was brought to the attention of the school council and your commitment to *halacha* has been . . . questioned.'

'My commitment?' What *mishegoss*! His crimes were nothing compared to those of Hirsch, and yet the council had protected him. 'I've done nothing that –'

'Yonatan, listen I –'

'With all due respect, Reb Margolis, this is discrimination. It's –'

The principal opened the folder and read from it. 'It has been confirmed that Rabbi Kaplan knowingly violated a *cherem* by attending an event at Parliament House run by Avraham Kliger. Rabbi Kaplan was also seen exiting a *treif* restaurant with a woman who is not his wife. There was physical contact.' He shut the folder. 'I'm afraid my hands are tied, Yonatan. The school council has been placing increasing pressure on me lately.'

Yonatan took a deep breath, forced himself to calm down. Reb Margolis was only the messenger. It didn't matter, none of it mattered – the machine was too great for him to fight against.

'May I ask, who will be taking over for me?'

'It hasn't been finalised, but Reb Bloom has been highlighted as the most likely to –'

'Menachem, but –'

The principal held up his hand. 'I know what you're going to say. But there is a lot of support for him.'

What was he going to say? That his brother-in-law lacked experience. That he'd been too aggressively steeped in a narrow-minded way of thinking by his father? Why bother?

Principal Margolis stood up, walked to his office door and turned to him. 'Yonatan, I urge you – these things that have been spoken. You have a child coming. The grandson of Rav Bloom. You must think of your family.'

Yonatan met the old principal's earnest eyes, paused for a moment and nodded. 'I will.'

The trip home was a blur. Yonatan replayed the conversation with Principal Margolis on loop.

'Concerning behaviour.'

'Commitment to *halacha*.'

'Think of your family.'

'*Your* family.'

On arriving home, he couldn't bear to face Rivka and retreated to his study before she could call for him. He needed time to compose himself for dinner with Menachem, to present himself for the meal as though it were merely another Shabbat. But was there any point? It was all bound to come out sooner or later. What would he say once Rivka discovered the truth and confronted him? You were right – I didn't listen and it happened, just as you said it would.

On his bookshelf was an unopened bottle of Chivas Regal – a gift from a former student. He would need courage to get through dinner. Halfway through his second glass, Rivka called for him, announcing that Menachem was at the door. He held his glass up to his study window – the horizon was the same dark orange as his drink, and when he looked through it the whisky swallowed the light as though he might be able to drink it away.

Yonatan let Menachem recite *Kiddush*, and, unsure of what he might say, remained quiet throughout their meal, focusing instead on drinking wine. Largely, Rivka and Menachem spoke of her pregnancy and plans for the birth – everything had been arranged with Liat Berkowitz and the birthing centre. Rivka was over eight months now, and she had back aches and trouble sleeping – what a relief as well as a blessing it would be to welcome their child into the world.

Their child. *Feh!* Eight months and still she sticks to the story. Did Menachem know? Yonatan could tell him now. See the look on both their faces. That's right – stupid, ignorant Yonatan knew all along, and yet he was the *apikoros* in the family. Ha!

Maybe Menachem did know; it could have been their plan all along – to send Yonatan off the *derech*. A new child for one, a new job for the other. What a family! He poured himself another glass of wine, ignored the look Menachem gave him and drank as their conversation continued.

'– and if Yonatan needs some respite after the birth,' Menachem said, 'I'd be glad to cover some classes for him.'

Yonatan laughed. 'Cover my classes?'

'Yes, I'd be glad to –'

'Why don't you jussst take them all?'

'Take them? *Slicha?* Yonatan, I don't –'

'Wait. You already have!'

'What?'

'I'm not a *putz*, Menachhhem. I know it was your plan. Well, *mazel tov*, the job is yours. Reb Margolis confirmed it today. You have succeeded.'

'What?' Rivka said. 'Yoni, what are you saying?'

'Don't worry, Rivka, Menachem can provide for the child. I won't –' The room spun. The knishes weren't sitting well. He needed more wine to wash them back down. But when he reached for his glass, it tipped along with the room, spilling a lake of Concord Red on Rivka's stark white Shabbat tablecloth.

'Yoni!' Rivka chided.

Let the waters under the heavens be gathered together into one place, Yonatan thought. Look – he had created too. Waters of wine.

'I think you've had enough wine,' Menachem said. 'Let me take you to your room.'

Pssht, he didn't need help getting to his room. Yonatan stood up, wavered on his feet and steadied himself on the table. And then he was lying in bed, shoes off, clothes on, voices murmuring in the distance, but he couldn't quite make out what they were saying. Perhaps he would be able to focus better with his eyes closed.

It was dark when Yonatan woke with a catch in his throat. He'd been dreaming of another Shabbat dinner. One where he'd tilted the *Kiddush* cup to his lips only to find it had been filled with salt. A trill of pain echoed from behind his brow as though a fine needle had been lodged there. He remembered Menachem coming over and asking him to say *Kiddush*. Beyond that there was nothing but a foreboding sense that he had shamed himself more than having fallen asleep in his clothes without saying the *Shema*.

According to his bedside clock, he had two hours until *shule* opened for the morning Shabbat service, but there was no returning to sleep. Across the room, in her bed, Rivka's guttural snores raked at Yonatan's ears. What was the point in waiting for her to wake and confront him with more of his sins? As deftly as possible in his state, he prepared for *shule* and left the house. And though the light was bare in the early morning, and his steps were matched by a cutting cold, he felt better for it.

Yonatan teetered on the brink of sleep throughout the morning service, digging his fingernails into his palm in order to stay alert for his coming *aliyah*. After the procession of the Torah, Yonatan perched himself on the edge of his seat, not leaving it this time as the *gabbai* called a Cohen up for the first *aliyah* and a Levi for the second. By the time the fourth of seven had approached the *bimah* and their assigned Torah portions were read, Yonatan knew he would not hear his name called and slumped back in his seat.

What would he tell Rivka, watching from the women's section above? That he'd been forgotten again? She'd know better. He needn't tell her about his job; here was her evidence. If he insisted on breaking a *cherem*, on associating with lapsed Jews and their *shiksa* partners, this is what he could expect, what their family could expect. Who knew how she was similarly being spurned by the women upstairs?

For the remainder of the service, he was unable to focus on his prayers and thought only of what he would say to Lior afterwards. He would be pleasant, affable, make as though he assumed it was another mistake, say he'd be happy to receive an *aliyah* the following week, and if it would help the *gabbai* to remember, he could speak to Principal Margolis of Yahel Academy, ask him to remind Lior, as he understood the principal was a member of the *shule* board. He hoped to not have to resort to such tactics, that the *gabbai* would instead recognise the wrong being committed and agree that a mistake had been made.

But after the service, Lior saw him coming and spoke before Yonatan had a chance. 'I've been asked to inform you that the *shule*'s policy is only to grant an *aliyah* to those in a position of *chiyuv*. As no-one in your family has recently passed, you do not qualify for an *aliyah*. Please excuse me.'

And then he was gone, lost among a throng of black coats and dark beards, leaving Yonatan with his accommodating, *simple misunderstanding* smile stuck to his face.

His hands shook, and his tongue was thick with an acrid swell of bile. Bullshit! He wouldn't stand for this humiliation from this *fakakta gabbai*. He'd been a member of this congregation for twenty years, and he always received an *aliyah* on his birthday. It was obviously Reb Feiner's doing, that *mamzer*. If he expected Yonatan to lie down and take this kind of insult, he had underestimated him.

At the post-service *Kiddush*, Chief Rabbi Feiner stood with a cup of wine in his hand, flanked by Lior, Aron Belovski, treasurer of the *shule* board, and its secretary, Nir Weiss. Principal Margolis had not been in attendance that day. It would have been nice to have some support, but nonetheless Yonatan approached the group. 'Reb Feiner, could I have a word?'

The group went silent, all turning to Yonatan.

'Shabbat shalom, Kaplan.' Reb Feiner did not refer to him as *rabbi* or *reb* – a purposeful sign of disrespect.

'If I could just –'

'My office hours are listed on the *shule* noticeboard.' He turned back to the men around him.

'I'm afraid it cannot wait, Reb Feiner.' Yonatan pronounced his name loudly and clearly. He would not be provoked into engaging in childish tactics. 'I know you have not been chief rabbi for very long, but I have been a loyal *mispalel* of this congregation for over twenty years, and on every birthday since the age of bar mitzvah I have received an *aliyah*. But all of a sudden, this year I am being denied one. Why, Reb Feiner?'

Rabbi Feiner looked to Lior and then back to Yonatan and smiled. '*Slicha*, I was under the impression you had been made aware of our policy not to grant *non-chiyuv aliyot*.'

'I was told,' Yonatan said. 'But I also saw that Shimon Brener was granted a *non-chiyuv aliyah* on Thursday.'

Rabbi Feiner's smile dropped and he sighed. 'The *shule* and its *gabbaim*,' he looked at Lior again, 'reserves the right to exercise discretion when granting *non-chiyuv aliyot*. For example, if a *mispalel* is not believed to be of good *middos*.'

Of good *middos*? Did he say that? Accuse him of having bad character, amongst these men? '*Middos*. I should be one to talk of *middos*.' Yonatan laughed. It was too much – what was the point of holding back now? 'What about your treasurer?' Aron's mouth fell open. 'Everybody knows if you give a large enough donation, he'll refund ninety per cent, but tell you to claim the full amount on your tax return.' Aron made to speak but Yonatan kept on, louder still. 'How about Uman? How many men here have made the pilgrimage?' He stretched out his arms, aware of more eyes on him than those of the group. 'What would their wives think, if they knew they were sleeping with prostitutes? Good *middos*, *nu*? Or how about the *Yehudim*, who actively helped Rabbi Hirsch, a known abuser of children, flee the country rather than face his crimes, or the members of this *shule* board, yourself included, who continue to punish the victims of that abuser for speaking out. Are those good *middos*, Reb Feiner?'

He turned from the men, not waiting for a response, and walked to the exit. Black coats parted before him like an apostate Moses. He smiled at the thought and held with him the image of Reb Feiner's bloated red face and incredulous stare, looking as though he would strangle Yonatan if granted the opportunity.

Somewhere behind him, Yonatan knew, Rivka would have made a subtle but expeditious exit. Hand under her belly, shuffling as fast as her weight would allow. He had a lot of explaining to do, but so did she.

Chapter 15

Ezra

For as long as he could remember, most mornings, on waking, there was the briefest moment before the neurons in Ezra's brain made the requisite connections across the relevant synapses to inform him of who he was, so that, like an amnesiac, he floated in an identity-less limbo. And lately, it was that half-conscious moment of blissful ignorance that he came to look forward to most in his day.

The rest of the time, when he was actively Ezra Steinberg, his composition was a cocktail of anxiety and self-loathing which took considerable effort to mould into something that resembled a functioning member of society. At least with Tegan away for the week, he was at liberty to forgo all pretence of capability at home and indulge in his contemptibility until his outward form better matched the discord of his mind. Dark, puffy circles underlined his bloodshot eyes and patches of black beard sprouted from his cheeks and neck. When he ate, which wasn't often, it was something microwavable with 'INSTANT' in its name. He bought slabs of beer to keep his hands occupied, and his mind dull, from the moment he got home from work until he passed out at night. Empty bottles marked his way from the couch to the bathroom and back like breadcrumbs.

Work was hell. Since the completion of the housing assistance bill, he had hardly anything to do, and it was difficult to keep his mind off Tegan's return and the obsessive thoughts swarming about his head. He didn't feel fit to converse with his colleagues – concerned that if he opened his mouth his ramshackle brain would let spill his secret conflict. He wore headphones at his desk and ate lunch outside, despite the frosty Melbourne winter and his body's shivery protests.

By midweek, Baz was pointing out his crumpled shirts and saying, 'Remind me to buy you an iron for your birthday.' His smile was gapped with missing teeth.

On Thursday afternoon, Steven asked Ezra for a quick catch-up before he headed off. Earlier in the day, he'd walked past Ezra's desk while he was meant to be writing a response to a piece of correspondence to the minister. But his chest felt as though it was full of cotton, so Ezra hit Caps Lock on his keyboard and slammed on his keys till he was facing:

FUCK FUCK FUCK FUCK FUCK FUCK FUCK FUCK
FUCK FUCK FUCK FUCK FUCK FUCK FUCK FUCK
FUCK FUCK FUCK FUCK FUCK FUCK FUCK FUCK
FUCK FUCK FUCK FUCK FUCK FUCK FUCK FUCK
FUCK FUCK FUCK FUCK FUCK FUCK FUCK FUCK
FUCK FUCK FUCK FUCK FUCK FUCK FUCK FUCK

Ezra made sure to put his jacket on and have the strap of his bag over his shoulder as he entered Steven's office. No time to chat.

'Please, take a seat,' Steven said.

Ezra sat but kept his jacket on and placed his bag on his lap.

'I . . . some of the staff have –' Steven shook his head. 'Look, is everything okay? You seem a bit off lately.' He gestured up and down at Ezra's appearance. 'What's going on?'

What's going on? I don't want to be here. I don't want to be anywhere. I'm a piece of shit. I spend every waking moment of every day wondering if my existence is a stain on those around me. I'm cracking up. What isn't going on?

'Sorry, Steven. It's my . . . grandfather, my *zeyde*. He died. And this,' he repeated Steven's gesture on himself, 'is part of the Jewish requirement for mourning. "And thou shall rend thy garments and not shave thy cheeks."' The mourning traditions were real, but his *zeyde* was alive and well. Ezra didn't know where the lie came from, but he was happy with the way it made Steven's face drop.

'Shit.' Steven shook his head. 'I'm sorry. I didn't realise – so sorry about your grandfather, Ezra. You should've told me. I . . . you're more than welcome to take some time off. There's a provision for compassionate leave in the EBA.'

Leave? More time in the apartment, surrounded by pictures of him and Tegan, by Tegan's clothes and the sweet, sometimes salty scent of her. No. 'I'm okay, thanks – it's good to stay busy.'

Steven nodded. 'Okay, but if you need, there's counselling available through the Employee Assistance Program.'

'Thanks, Steven. I'll think about it.'

On Friday, two days before Tegan's return, unable to bear the sight of his screen, Ezra opened the cabinet next to his desk, withdrew a stack of papers, encyclopaedia thick, and headed for the photocopy room.

Lift the cover, put a sheet in the corner, press the button, flash. Lift the cover, put a sheet in the corner, press the button, flash. Lift the cover, put a sheet in the corner, press the button, flash, flash, flash.

'You know you can put the whole lot in the feeder?' Danny was standing in the doorway. His beautiful, flawless face was the embodiment of youth – a life without worry, stress or suffering.

'What?'

'The feeder. You don't have to do them one by one.'

'Oh, I can't.' Ezra plucked out the paper and pointed to the corner. 'Staples.'

Danny looked at the pile next to him and frowned. 'Well, you're going to be here for a while then.'

'It's okay. I don't really mind.' The mound of documents was actually composed of copies of a ten-page report on the distribution of housing benefits that Ezra didn't need anymore. But there was something cathartic about photocopying hundreds of pages and then shredding them all.

Danny remained in the doorway, shuffling his feet. 'Steven told me about your grandad – sorry to hear. Hope you can still make it tonight.'

Ezra nodded. 'Yeah, no worries. Thanks.' He turned back to the photocopier. Tonight? Wait, shit. He spun back to the doorway, but Danny was gone.

Danny the grad was moving on – his four-month rotation in their division was up. All of the department's grads were meeting at Garden State to celebrate the end of their rotations, and as a convenient means of goodbye to them, Danny had invited the whole team as well.

The grads had hired out the middle of Garden State – a platform above the speakeasy cocktail bar below, with a few wooden tables, hanging orb lanterns and two incongruously placed palm trees. Aside from their team, the attendants were fifteen or so smiling twenty-five-year-olds, buoyed to joy simply by the company of friends and the end of the week. Ezra sighed. What a life.

Steven made his excuses after one drink – wife and kids, expected home by dinner. Danny was engaged in conversation with two young women, and Steven asked Ezra and Baz to give Danny his best. That left them alone while Danny played host with the other graduates at another table.

'I don't see why all of them have to be here too.' Never comfortable with a change to his routine, Baz was whingeing.

'Come on, Baz. He just wants to celebrate with his friends.'

'I went ahead and told Mum I'd be home late for this.' Baz gestured to Danny and the other grads, laughing, flirting, gossiping.

It had been like that when Ezra was a grad too – who's hooking up with who, who's got what for their next rotation, which supervisors are good and who's just going to send you for coffee and photocopying.

'I don't know why he asked us to come if he's just gonna ignore us the whole time,' Baz said.

Jesus Christ, Ezra couldn't take it anymore. He finished his pint and returned to the bar.

Wanting to limit his time with Baz, Ezra continued to drink quickly, and soon he was drunk, but that was okay – it seemed like the right thing for him to be. At pint four, or maybe it was five, he decided to join Danny and his friends at the other table. But once he got there, beer in hand, he realised he had nothing to say. The day's light had faded and the noise of excited voices was a weight, so he stood there – at the corner of Danny's table, sipping his beer and trying to ignore Baz's lingering eyes – when someone smacked him hard on the back.

'Ezra!' It was Danny, and he was also drunk. 'Glad you came, mate. And sorry . . . uh, about your grandad again.' He turned to a girl, who Ezra hadn't seen standing behind him, and explained, 'Ezra's grandad died recently, that's why he looks like shit.' Danny laughed.

'I mean that's not –' Ezra began.

'Oh – are you Jewish?' the girl asked.

'Yeah, I . . . yes.'

She had short platinum blonde hair, pale skin, bright blue eyes and high cheekbones. Nothing like anyone in his family.

'Are you?' Ezra asked.

'No, but my ex-boyfriend was. I'm sorry about your grandad.'

'Thanks.'

'No wonder you looked so sad.'

That was all right. He didn't mind if he looked sad, but standing there, talking to that girl, he suddenly realised he didn't feel that sad anymore. Actually, he felt quite good, and he reckoned she might be the key to maintaining that feeling, and maybe even improving on it.

'Imogen's next rotation is in Legal and Governance,' Danny said. 'You worked there for a bit, didn't you, Ezra?'

Ezra nodded. Speaking still felt like an effort. 'Yeah.'

Imogen smiled. She had perfect, toothbrush-advertisement white teeth. 'Where did you go to law school?'

'Melbourne Uni.'

'Oh, me too. What year did you graduate?'

'Two thousand and ten.'

'Ah, I was twenty-sixteen. Did you do the Juris Doctor?'

'Nah. Undergraduate, double degree.'

'Oh wow. Straight outta high school. Clever then.' She smiled again.

'Me . . . nah, I just –'

Danny wrapped his arm around Ezra. 'Don't listen to him, Immi – proper legal genius, this guy. We had a budget measure to implement, required legislative change, and this guy practically wrote the bill.'

Back at their original table, Baz was staring at his phone – elbows on the table, shoulders slumped. He looked up from his screen, and Ezra quickly turned away. Imogen spoke again, but Ezra couldn't quite hear her. He knew he should go back to Baz, tell him these kids were boring as hell, suggest they go to the Imperial. He nodded to whatever Imogen was saying and turned, but Baz was gone – left without saying goodbye, because his 'friend' ditched him for a pretty girl.

Fuck. He wasn't feeling very good anymore – he needed another drink.

At some stage, Ezra didn't know when, one of the graduates suggested they move on from Garden State and head back to their place. Embroiled as he was, by drink and a desire to be close to Imogen, what choice did Ezra have but to join them?

There was a table in the centre of the kitchen. Bottles of wine and half-full glasses littered across it. Ezra couldn't remember how he got there, let alone whose house it was or who had given him the glass of red wine he was holding. From where he stood, leaning against the kitchen sink he could hear voices in the backyard – no-one he recognised. He should leave, figure out where he was and call a cab. But before he could take out his phone the door opened and two guys entered, both in tan chinos and tight shirts, manicured stubble on their cheeks and their hair combed back – thick and slick. They could've been twins except one was practically a foot taller than the other. He didn't know either of them.

'Ezraaa!' the shorter one called. Apparently, they knew him.

'Wanna line, mate?'

'Sorry?'

'It's good stuff. C'mon.' He opened his hand. A baggie of coke sat on his flat palm. The taller one cleared some space on the kitchen table, extracted his wallet and racked up some lines with his credit card.

The table was wooden – a dark brown veneer, chipped and dented and stained. On top of it the coke was a glowing zebra crossing and it seemed obvious to Ezra that he had to get to the other side, so he waited for the taller guy to finish his line and accepted a rolled-up fifty-dollar note from him.

Straight away, Ezra knew he'd made the right decision. He felt good, optimistic even – he was where he needed to be, wherever that was, and these guys, they were such good guys, sharing their coke, he wanted to tell them that, so he did and they reciprocated the compliment and he felt like it was true – he was a good guy – he never meant to hurt anyone, things got out of hand, but life was a miraculous and complex interaction of incomprehensible factors that led him to situations he couldn't control.

He told the guys that as well, and they vehemently agreed and offered another line, a great idea, god they were such good guys, and then the coke was done and it was clear that something else had to happen because they were young and brilliant and filled with potential. They discussed that for a while, each of them agreeing that they were all destined to accomplish the extraordinary, when an idea came to the shorter one. 'Shots!' he shouted. 'Imogen's got some tequila in the backyard.'

Imogen. He'd forgotten about her. He should definitely see her, so he told the shorter guy that shots were the best idea he'd ever heard.

The only light in the room was a soft glow from a bedside lamp. Imogen was laughing and taking off her clothes, till she was in a black bra and panties. Ezra wasn't sure whether or not he was in the room or if he were disembodied and seeing into it somehow but, looking down, he too was only in his underwear.

'Are you coming?' Imogen asked.

Was he? Is that what he'd meant to do? Was he still in the same house as before? If not, how did he end up there? Had he kissed Imogen? He must have, otherwise they wouldn't both be nearly naked. He stepped towards the bed, stopping at the foot of it, still not feeling like he was quite all there. 'I feel weird,' he said.

Imogen lifted the bed covers and jumped into bed. 'It's warm in here.'

She mustn't have heard him. Was he saying what he thought he was saying? 'I don't . . . I should tell you . . . if you can hear me . . . the thing is –'

'Come on in.'

'My grandfather isn't dead.'

'What?'

Ah, she could hear him. 'I told Steven that – but he's alive. He lives in Caulfield.'

'What the fuck!' Imogen sat up, covering her chest with a blanket like girls do when they're mad in bed on TV, which only made Ezra question again if it was actually happening. 'That's sick – lying, so I'd pity you, so I'd fuck you.'

'No – I wasn't . . . it was Steven and I –'

'Get the fuck out! Get the fuck out now!'

Ezra shook his head. If she'd just let him explain – if she was real that is – he could help her understand, but she kept shouting at him, so he rummaged around the floor for his clothes, pulled them on and hurried out of the room.

He tumbled out of the house and into the street. The air was cool and the pavement was slick. It must have rained. In the distance, the city skyline propped up a purple early morning. Where the hell was he? His phone, of course. Luckily, it was still in his trouser pocket, the battery nearly dead. He had a missed call and a text message from Tegan. Shit. Had he called her while drunk? Did he confess, tell her everything? His hands were shaking. Fuck, fuck. It could all be over. He checked his call history first and exhaled long and slow with relief – he hadn't contacted her.

Her message read: *Hey just called to see how you're going, figured you might be out. I've had a long day of schmoozing. Looking forward to seeing you. I'll text you my flight details tomorrow xx.*

The message was a sobering gut punch that nearly levelled him. He'd done it again, and it was clear that he was going to keep doing it. He'd made excuses as though he wasn't in control, that things happened to him and he was a helpless participant, but it wasn't true. No-one made him drink as much as he did. He could've gone home when Baz left, and he didn't have to follow everyone to that house, or accept the cocaine, and then there was whatever had happened or was about to happen with Imogen. God damn it. He sank to the ground, raised the sleeve of his jacket to his mouth and screamed as hard as he could.

He needn't have done any of it, but he had – he was sick and weak. What was it Yoni had said? *Yetzer hara*, an inclination towards evil, that was him. He re-read Tegan's message and put his phone away. There was no avoiding it – he knew what he had to do. He stood up and walked towards the burgeoning dawn.

Chapter 16

Yonatan

Yonatan went straight to his study, intent on steadying his shaking hands with Chivas Regal. He took the bottle and a glass with him to the lounge room, where he placed his suit jacket over the back of a couch, took off his fedora and dropped it onto the coffee table. He sat with his hands folded in front of him, listening for the squeak of the front door hinges, Rivka's exasperated, heavy breathing and the inevitable shout of his name.

One minute. Five minutes. Half a glass of whisky. Half a glass more. Nothing. Even with the pregnancy, the walk from *shule* shouldn't have taken her that long. She could have been making excuses for him to Reb Feiner, saying, 'Please excuse his behaviour, take pity on him, he hasn't been well of late.'

But the more he drank, the more unlikely that seemed. She was still there after all, with them and not him. 'He's well off the *derech*,' she would say. 'No respect for Torah. You cannot imagine what he subjects me to in our home – *shiksas* and *apikorsim*. I work hard to make a kosher home and this is how

I'm rewarded.' He refilled his glass and drank deeply. Off the *derech.* He laughed, sprang up from the couch and took slow, deliberate steps to the light switch by the kitchen door.

Why disappoint them? Off the *derech* they wanted, so off the *derech* he'd give them. He flipped the switch. The downlights flickered on. *Whoever does any work on the Sabbath day must surely be put to death.* He flipped the switch again, picked up his glass of whisky and drained it. What next? He put his glass down and walked to the bathroom. After relieving himself, he washed his hands and was halfway through reciting *asher yatzar* when he caught himself and clamped his teeth together.

In the mirror above the sink, a red-eyed *putz meshuganah yid* stared back at him. For the first time in his life, his red tubular *peyot* felt like strange adornments – hallmarks of an image that didn't match who he was anymore. He ran his fingers through his thick auburn beard, took a hold of the end in a fist and tugged as though there were a chance it would come off. A few strands stuck to his hand. He shook them off in the sink and went to the kitchen. He opened drawers and cupboards, rifled through trays of utensils, even looked behind the silver candlesticks, *Kiddush* cup and tablecloths in Rivka's Shabbat cupboard. He slammed the door shut. Where were they? And then he saw them – nestled into the front of a wooden knife block, Rivka's chicken shears.

The first of his *peyot* struck the bathroom basin like a stone: a lifetime of hair and yet he'd never thought about its weight, anchoring him to a way of life, a community – The Chosen People. It lay limp, the ends unfurling slowly in the sink like roots to water, a leaf to the sun. Only once the hairs were still did he let the second fall and get to work on his beard.

When he was done, the sink looked like the top of a man's head, as though a stranger were crouched beneath it, somehow sticking his head through the drain. The idea bothered him and, without thinking, Yonatan turned the tap, soaking the hair into a red sludge that sank for a moment before the drain clogged and the water rose. He turned off the tap and watched as a flotsam of scraggly hair drifted to the edge of the sink.

He'd done a decent job, but you could only cut so fine with chicken shears. His face was fatter without the beard, chin and cheeks more rounded than how he saw himself. He looked younger too. A little *pisher* having a crisis of faith, challenging thousands of years of entrenched custom and tradition. He forced a smile and was pleased by the prominence of his pink mouth on his pale face and the appearance of dimples that had been long hidden. Here was the face of a once precocious youth and prankster, filled with life and endless opportunity – who he might have been had he left Yahel with Ezra all those years ago.

It was time to go and be that man but even without the beard and *peyot* he still might be recognised as a *yid* and that was more concerning than being recognised by someone he knew. In his and Rivka's bedroom, he unbuttoned his shirt and flung his *tzitzit* over his head and onto the bed.

After the rally in March, Yonatan hid his purple Purim shirt in an old *tallit* bag for fear of Rivka finding it wrinkled and wondering why he'd worn it. He unzipped the bag and removed the shirt. There were so many wrinkles, they almost resembled a pattern, and it smelled too, a bitter tang of body odor when he brought it to his nostrils. It would have to do. He put on the shirt, not bothering to tuck it into his slacks, and was about to leave the room when he remembered his *kippah*. He unpinned it from his crown and was going to throw it on the bed with his *tzitzit*, when he suddenly felt queasy and opted instead to shove it into his trouser pocket.

Despite the whisky, Yonatan was sure he was fine to drive. It was still light out after all, and what kind of off-the-*derech apikoros* would he be, if he didn't drive on Shabbat? He turned down Orrong Road, no destination in mind, away from Yahel was all that mattered, away from Rivka and Reb Feiner, *mitzvot* and *aveirot*, *Hashem* and all Yonatan had ever given Him. He turned down another street at random, turned again and again and found himself too close to the back end of a tram. Foot to the brake, his tyres skidded on the tracks, stopping only when his bonnet was inches from crumpling. *Oy*. He closed his eyes and light flashed beneath his lids. Maybe he shouldn't be driving after all. Where was he anyway?

Once the tram started again, he looked for signs but saw none. Fifty metres more, and the familiar skyward golden 'M' of a McDonald's filled his windscreen view. He realised he was on Glen Huntly Road in Elsternwick, around the corner from where he'd met up with Tegan. Pulling into the McDonald's parking lot, Yonatan laughed to himself. It was as though he had been guided there. No restaurant was more *treif* than McDonald's, and he hadn't eaten all day.

Inside, a handful of people sat at rows of grey tables and chairs bolted to a tiled floor. An obese man wearing a baseball cap, tracksuit pants and a stained hooded jumper stood in front of a large vertical screen, slowly trailing his fingers down the images, his mouth agape, lips glistening with saliva. Beside him, an Indian couple stood at another screen, bickering in a language Yonatan didn't recognise, each jabbing violently at the screen before them. Past the screens, at the front of the restaurant, was a counter and the kitchen in which youths in short-sleeved red shirts and black hats shouted commands at each other and slunk about with round shouldered apathy.

Yonatan approached the counter, above which were more screens, showing images of various burgers and fries with strange names and exclamations.

'BIG MAC – THE ORIGINAL AND THE BEST.'

'MCANGUS – SORT OUT YOUR BEEF.'

'THE SPICY MCCHICKEN – IS IT TOO HOT FOR YOU TO HANDLE?'

'WelcometoMcDonald'scanIhelpyou?' A skinny boy with considerable acne and tufts of bleach-blond hair sticking out the sides of his cap stood behind the counter. His nametag read 'JAYDEN'.

'Ah – sorry?'

'Can I help you?'

'Ah, yes. Thank you.' Yonatan looked up at the pictures again. 'I'm looking for ah . . . something with pig in it?'

'Pig? You mean bacon?'

'Bacon is pig, yes?'

'Ya-huh.'

'What has bacon then?'

'The double beef 'n' *bacon* burger has *bacon* in it.'

'Double beef and bacon – what does that . . . what else is in that exactly?'

Jayden sighed, inhaled and rattled off the ingredients in one breath. 'Twobeefpattiesrasherofbaconsliceofcheeseonionketchup mustard.'

Cheese and bacon. Meat with milk and *davar acher*. A two *aveirot* for the price of one burger. 'Perfect. One of those, thank you.'

The boy punched his fingers into the screen before him, asked Yonatan for five dollars and then handed him a receipt. 'You're Order 149.' It was just like the butcher's.

A few minutes later, Yonatan's number was called, and he was handed a warm brown paper bag. He sat at one of the grey tables by the window, looking out onto Glen Huntly Road, welcoming the chance that someone he knew would pass by. The burger was in a box with its picture on it. But there must have been some mistake – his burger looked nothing like that picture. It was flat, two pieces of compressed beef between squashed bread. A yellow liquid that might have been cheese. Where was the bacon? He peeled off the top bun. Stuck to it was a flat piece of pink meat, brown at the edges. He raised it to his nose. A sweet, meaty smell, not as intense as beef but more so than chicken. Was that bacon? He replaced the bun, took the burger in both hands and ate.

Salty, smoky, fatty. It was like a lighter pastrami. He took another bite, tasted the caramelised onion buried beneath the beef. The cheese was warm and thick. All together the burger was juicy and sweet, tender and rich. Like having salty *knishes* with a *blintz* filling and . . . he'd nearly finished the burger without realising, what a waste. Contritely, he placed the remaining piece back in the box and took care to chew what was in his mouth slowly. He understood now how the *Yehudim* crossing the desert must have felt – if ever there was a food akin to *manna*, this was it. He picked up the last bite, let it sit in his mouth, savouring the flavour.

Finished, there was a moment when he felt furiously unsated and considered charging the counter, demanding another. But he also knew he'd eaten fast, and so he waited a minute for the food to settle and, sure enough, the craving passed only to be replaced by a desperate thirst. A considerable queue had built up at the counter, while Yonatan's tongue sat like a dry sponge in his chalk mouth. Rather than wait, he stood and left the restaurant, unsure of where he was headed, until he remembered that he was around the corner from the bar where he'd met Tegan.

Yonatan was the only patron this time, and he chose to sit on a stool, in front of the same slick-haired bartender who had been there when he met Tegan. He began with a beer to quench his thirst. It was a relief to not have to think about the ingredients before ordering. After that, he opted for a whisky with ice and then another and another. Sitting there, his stomach churned on the burger and bacon and bloated uncomfortably with bubbling gas – punishment for his sins? The curse of *davar acher*? Did *apikorsim* feel this way all the time? Did Ezra? His poor apostate friend. Clearly, Ezra had his own troubles. Now would be a good time to reach out to him, without fear of reprimand from the community. Perhaps they could eat burgers with bacon together, celebrate in their joint exclusion from the world to come.

*

Soon after Ezra left for Glen Eira High School, the then principal of Yahel Academy, Reb Kahn, had called Yonatan into his office. Though he'd never been caught for his pranks to date, Yonatan assumed someone had finally dobbed him in, and it was with that on his mind that he entered the principal's office.

Reb Kahn was ancient. No-one knew exactly how old, but he'd been on the verge of retirement for as long as Yonatan could remember. His large black coat tented his skeletal shoulders. Long white *peyot* hung as low as his chest, and a wizened grey beard rolled off his chin well beyond them. He'd been reading from the Talmud when Yonatan entered. He spoke slowly as though it took tremendous effort for him to produce each word. 'Sit, Yonatan.'

Yonatan did, hanging his head and casting his eyes downward in what he hoped was an adequate portrayal of remorse.

'You are a . . . good student – *nu*?'

'I . . . I have straight A's, Reb Kahn.'

Reb Kahn nodded. 'Tell me, Yonatan. What do you want for the future?'

'I want to complete my studies, maintain my grades.'

'And you want *smicha*, *nu*?'

'*Smicha?*' Yonatan nodded. 'Yes, Reb Kahn.'

'Good. Your father too was a good student.'

'Yes, Reb Kahn.'

'Ezra Steinberg.'

Ezra? Where did that come from? Was he expected to respond?

'He left the Academy – last term. You were *chaverim*, *nu*?'

'Yes. We're friends.'

The principal's brow furrowed. 'You are still in touch with Ezra?'

'Yes. I mean, he was away with his family for a while, but then he came back and –'

Reb Kahn shook his head. 'You wish to get *smicha*, Yonatan? Attend *kollel*?'

'I do. But what does that have to do with –'

'You must be a *mensch*, Yonatan.'

Yonatan waited for the principal to elaborate.

'Maybe you don't see Ezra so much as you did. *Nu*?'

'Don't see Ezra?'

'Maybe not so much.'

'But Ezra's –'

'Enough, Yonatan.' Reb Kahn held up his hand. 'You must study Torah. Be a *mensch*, get *smicha*.' Reb Kahn smiled and hunched back over his Talmud. The meeting was over, and Yonatan was left too confused to realise that no-one had dobbed him in after all.

*

What a *schmuck* he had been. Yonatan finished his drink, stood and headed for the bar's exit. Reb Kahn was one of the men instrumental in organising Rabbi Hirsch's escape to Israel. Though he finally retired not long after, it was revealed that he'd been hearing allegations against Hirsch for years and had worked tirelessly to sweep them under the rug.

Outside, somehow, it was night. How much time had passed? It could've been as early as six or as late as midnight. He was drunk – enough to not think twice about urinating in the darkness of the nearby train station car park, but not so to face the stifling winter wind with brash disregard. Hands in his jacket pockets, chin to chest, Yonatan's shoes clapped with increasing rhythm against the sidewalk.

He couldn't say for how long he walked. The cold was sobering, but he wasn't quite ready to turn around, drive home and face Rivka's inevitable, hypocritical chastisement. It must have been late – all the businesses were closed, and the street was bare of people but for a large man in a puffy jacket standing outside a black building with its windows painted over. Above the doorway, a sign displayed the pink silhouette of a woman holding a red heart. Yonatan understood – a *beit boshet*, for fallen men and women. Perfect. What were the sins he'd accumulated compared to those of the men who went to Uman? Those of his own wife even. The very least he could do was try to match them.

Inside, a large woman in a black blazer with dark red hair and long fake nails stood at a desk surrounded by posters of near naked women. She smiled at him and said it was twenty dollars to enter.

After he paid, Yonatan continued on to a large room, dimly lit by hanging lanterns. Small round tables and gold seats surrounded a glass stage that ran the length of the room. Two silver poles cut into the stage near its rounded ends. A handful of middle-aged men sat alone about the room. Loud, pervasive music played from hidden speakers – a thumping, pounding beat that rumbled across Yonatan's skin. A girl appeared on the stage, naked but for scant sparkly underwear. She strutted around a pole in rhythm with the music, then dropped suddenly to her knees and rolled backwards onto her forearms, before swinging one leg around the pole, gripping it between her thighs and leveraging herself upwards, so that she was hanging upside down.

Fixated, Yonatan didn't notice the woman standing in front of him until she spoke. 'Hey, honey,' she said, 'would you like a dance?'

'Sorry?' She was tall with long, straight black hair. A striped halter top barely covered her large breasts, and a piece of white cloth was tied around her waist, not long enough to be called a skirt.

'A dance. Would you like one?' she said, smiling.

Dance? That must be what they call it in this place. Was he ready? No. But he'd come this far, and if *Hashem* was watching Yonatan wanted Him to see.

'Yes. Thank you.'

'Great.' She reached for his hand and on her touch, he almost pulled away. Her skin was dry, fingers long, palm large. How odd, that not all women's hands felt like Rivka's.

She led him across the room down a corridor lined with small partitions, like stalls in a bathroom. At the front of each were red velvet curtains held apart by rope. They walked into one. Inside was a red leather couch, and she told Yonatan to sit. She untied the rope on the curtain outside their booth and pulled it closed.

'Have you had a dance here before?' she asked.

Yonatan shook his head.

'Okay, I'll just go over a few things. First off, no photos or videos, no kissing, licking or touching below the waist, but above is fine. Got it?'

She'd spoken so quickly he wasn't sure he'd heard her correctly. Yonatan nodded.

She smiled. 'Oh, and that'll be fifty dollars.'

‘Yes, of course.’ Yonatan fumbled for his wallet, squinting in the dim light to read the notes before handing over fifty dollars.

‘Thanks.’

She tucked the bill into an invisible pocket somewhere in her skirt. ‘Now just sit back and relax.’

A foot from him, she turned around and danced, swaying her hips from side to side. Her underwear hardly covered anything and the bare skin of her *toches* glistened before his eyes. She turned back then and placed a hand on each of his shoulders before wrapping them around the back of his neck and pulling herself towards him. She stepped over his spread legs, bringing her breasts inches from his face, before letting herself drop onto his lap. With one hand behind her back, she undid the string of her top, but pressed her hands into her chest before it could fall off. She held it there, bit on her lower lip and straddled his lap back and forth, back and forth. The motion reminded Yonatan of a man's shuckling as he *davened.* Perhaps it was her own kind of worship, to Lilith, the first wife of Adam, mother of demons.

Yonatan could feel an erection budding in his trousers, but his penis was pressed to the side of his leg, at an awkward angle. With each thrust of the woman's hips, his body sparked with a unique blend of pleasure and pain. Her pace increased, and it was too much – the warmth of her body, the pressure of her crotch against his. His seed was building, ready to be spilled in vain – and then something pricked him. A short, sharp pain at the tip of his penis – so unexpected at a moment of near ecstasy that Yonatan jolted in his seat and would have leapt into the air had the woman not been on top of him.

What was that? A sign from *Hashem*?

He placed his hand into his trouser pocket and felt the pointed tip of a pin from his *kippah*. He almost laughed – in a way it had been *Hashem*.

'You all right, honey?' she asked, slowing her grind on him.

He nodded. 'Yes, it's nothing.'

'You a black hat, honey?'

A black hat? But his *peyot*, his beard. How did she know?

'It's okay if you are, honey. I don't judge.' She smiled and picked up her pace.

'I –' Yonatan shook his head.

'Being in this area, they come in all the time.'

Of course they did. Why go all the way to Uman when you could commit adultery on your own doorstep?

She let go of her top then and flicked it to the side of the booth. He thought her breasts would hang lower without the support, but they sat exactly where they did before, large, almost too round, centred with dimpled nipples and small brown areolae, barely bigger than a twenty-cent piece. Nothing like Rivka's. Leaning back against the couch, he kept his hands down on the seat, not sure what to do with them.

She smiled, as though sensing his unease. 'No need to be shy, honey.' She leaned forward, picked up his hands and guided them upwards, leaving them to rest on her breasts. 'That's better.' She smiled again and continued to dance.

Her breasts were firm, hard. So unlike Rivka's. Could a woman nurse a child with breasts like that? He squeezed them slightly to make sure he wasn't imagining. Yes, they were like unripe fruit, like Rivka's swollen, bare belly, the nipple being her stretched *pupik*. The child within kicking with impatience, insisting upon its existence, screaming *'IMA! ABBA! I AM HERE.'*

Yonatan dropped his hands, jerked them away and stood up abruptly. The woman fell from his lap. An apology was forming on his lips, but by the time it came out he was already in the street, arm raised, shielding his face from *Hashem*'s ubiquitous gaze.

Chapter 17

Ezra

It was months until Yom Kippur. Months until the Torah said Ezra could atone for his sins, have a clean slate, be forgiven for every bad thing he'd ever done. He couldn't wait, but did it matter? Would God have heard him anyway? The sinner, the lapsed Jew. What was the ultra-Orthodox word for it? *Apikoros*. Was there any fucking point?

Across the road, the iron gates of South Caulfield *shule*, imprinted with *Magen Davids*, stood open. Atop a small stoop of concrete steps, the *shule*'s large teal doors beckoned the pious and observant – the worthy.

After the events of Friday night, Ezra's anxiety had manifested into a tinny whine that emanated from somewhere behind his eyes and had him blinking repeatedly for prolonged lengths of time. He sighed, looked both ways and crossed the road. Tegan would be back in eight hours. He was out of time and out of options. Prayer couldn't possibly make things any worse.

The last time he'd entered that *shule* was his own bar mitzvah nearly twenty years ago. It had been an awkward time. A term had passed at Glen Eira High School, and he was on the cusp of making new friends, but when those boys asked him if he was doing anything for his thirteenth birthday, he told them he wasn't. His parents made the decision to go ahead with his bar mitzvah to appease his grandparents and because he'd already completed most of the necessary study at Yahel before he left.

Leaving Yahel meant leaving the school's associated *shule* as well, so instead of stepping up to the *bimah* he'd practised at, Ezra would read the *maftir* and his *haftorah* at the smaller, musty Modern Orthodox *shule* in South Caulfield. Of his former classmates, he invited a handful, who were only coming, he suspected, because Yonatan had asked them to.

At Yahel, they'd been taught how to put on *tefillin*, and that the bar mitzvah was the mark of being a man, after which they would have the obligations of a man, wear the sins of a man. Until then, you weren't accountable – for typing 'BIG TITS' into AltaVista, for taking five dollars out of your mum's purse or sneaking sips of the brandy in your dad's liquor cabinet. At that age, everything you'd ever done was attributed to your father, who should have kept a better eye on you and learned how to delete his own Internet history.

On the day of Ezra's bar mitzvah it rained heavily; so much so that his parents abandoned their plans to walk to *shule* and bundled him into their car – one final sin to add to his dad's tally, though the drive home would be on him. Half the pews were empty that day, and that seemed about right to Ezra: proportionate to his significance and representative of life as he knew it – about half-full.

For the morning service, he sat with his father and *zeyde* on a pew close to the *bimah*, fiddling with the ends of the *tallit* on his shoulders, scanning the *shule* every five minutes for Yonatan, in case he'd missed him. And then his name was called, and after making one more hopeful glance towards the entrance, Ezra recited his *maftir* and *haftorah* with a small voice, and unzealous accuracy.

It was only when he finished his *haftorah*, and successfully avoided the few hard lollies that were lobbed at him, that he spotted Yonatan and some of the boys he'd invited, at the prayer-room entrance, shaking the rain from their coats and black hats.

Following a simple *Kiddush* in the *shule*'s adjoining room, Ezra's parents had arranged for a small reception in their home with kosher catering for select friends and family, opting to avoid a costly 'whizz bang' – as his father put it – reception like Yehuda Gindle. There was no band, no speeches, no wild linking of arms *Hora*, or his friends lifting him up on a chair, or tablecloth – only foil trays filled with chicken skewers and kugel, bowls of hummus and baba ghanoush, plates of rugelach and babka.

Knowing Yonatan and the other boys would be walking, Ezra kept one eye on the front door while shaking hands and bearing cheek kisses from his extended family. Even though it was still Shabbos, his uncle argued with his mum about switching on the TV to watch the Carlton and Essendon preliminary final.

Soon after, the rain abated and Yonatan and the other boys filed into the house – each of them approaching Ezra with short, seemingly reluctant steps, as though they were making a parentally enforced apology. One by one they shook his hand, mumbled '*mazel tov*', and practically ran back to the others. And then it was Yonatan's turn, and the two of them stood facing one another for the first time in months – Ezra unable to hold back a smile, Yonatan shifting awkwardly in silence.

'Hey,' Ezra said.

'Hey. Um . . . *mazel tov*.' Yonatan held out his hand.

'Ah, thanks.' Ezra had never shaken Yonatan's hand before. It didn't feel right. 'So . . . how's it going?'

'Good,' Yonatan said. 'How's Glen Eira?'

'It's all right. I don't have to do Hebrew or *Chumash* anymore. So that's good.'

Yonatan nodded and looked back to the other boys who stood together in a corner of the living room.

'Hey, so my parents finally got me a Nintendo 64 for my bar mitzvah. Maybe later we could go upstairs and –'

Yonatan shook his head. 'It's Shabbos.'

'Oh, yeah. Of course – I know. I meant . . . tomorrow?'

'I can't tomorrow. I've got to study and –'

'Ezra,' his mum called from across the room. 'Your *bubbe* wants to congratulate you, come here.'

'Okay, Mum. One sec! I gotta go,' he said to Yonatan. 'Just let me know whenever works.'

'Sure,' Yonatan replied.

'Great.' Ezra smiled at his friend and turned away, bolstering himself for his *bubbe*'s kisses.

Yonatan must have left shortly after, without saying goodbye. It was the last time they would speak for, as it turned out, close to twenty years.

This time, Ezra entered South Caulfield *shule* as an actual man. Thirty-two years old, wearing his good suit and tie and the small black *kippah* Yonatan had given him. He opened the great teal doors and entered the *shule*'s lobby, where two similarly bearded men were in conversation. Ezra didn't know either of them, but on seeing him they stopped talking, smiled and wished him '*boker tov*' before resuming their conversation.

Ezra was surprised. Despite his years away from the fold, he'd been readily recognised as one of their own. Passing the men, Ezra crept inside the main prayer room and sat in an empty back pew. About the *shule*, thirty or so men were spread out sporadically, praying in their seats, while a man with a beautiful, lilting voice led them on the *bimah* before the ark.

The prayer ended, and the congregation stood as one. Ezra joined them, resting his hands on the empty book stand in front of him. A small, elderly man, who must have been watching him, approached Ezra's pew, muttering silently in prayer as he walked. The man placed a *siddur* on Ezra's book stand, flicked it open and pointed to what must have been the relevant section.

'Thank you,' Ezra said.

The man nodded and left Ezra with the *siddur*, all the while his lips still moving, his prayers unbroken.

Ezra could still read the Hebrew text, but he had no idea what it meant. '*S'lach lanu avinu ki chatanu* –' He muttered the words like the men around him, adopted their slightly hunched, reverent posture. It wasn't any good – he felt silly. Maybe if he read the English translation on the adjacent page. Surely prayers had the same value, whatever language they were read in.

'*Forgive us our Father for we have sinned, pardon us our King for we have wilfully transgressed; for You pardon and forgive. Blessed are You, O Lord, Who is gracious and ever willing to forgive.*'

Yes, that was good – exactly what he needed. Ezra read on.

'*See our affliction and contend for our strife and redeem us quickly for the sake of Your Name, for You are the mighty redeemer. Blessed are You, O Lord, Redeemer of Israel.*'

Ezra read the words, shut his eyes tight and pictured the darkness seeping out of his pores in a fine mist. Goodbye, *yetzer hara*. Hello, redemption.

There was nothing relevant in the next few paragraphs, until he read: '*Quickly uproot, smash, and cast down the arrogant sinners and humble them quickly in our days. Blessed are You, O Lord, Who breaks enemies and humbles arrogant sinners.*'

What the hell? Why the sudden contradiction? He couldn't say those things, damning himself. Was that what every man here was saying, what they said every day? What about the promised redemption, His great forgiveness?

Ezra read further: '*May Your mercies be aroused, Lord our God, upon the righteous, upon the pious, upon the elders of Your people, the House of Israel, upon the remnant of their sages, upon the righteous proselytes and upon us. Grant ample reward to all who truly trust in Your Name.*'

Well, fuck that! Ezra slammed the *siddur* shut and walked out of the pew, not caring if the men around him stared. It was all bullshit anyway. What had he been expecting? A light that shone through the synagogue window onto him? The thunderous voice of God, excusing him for what he'd done, telling him that he was good, that he need not continue to live in shame, that he was worthy of Tegan's love?

Idiot. He shook his head and left the prayer room. He didn't believe in the revelation of the Torah on Mount Sinai, or any kind of monotheistic god. Chosen People, my arse. A self-titled proclamation to conveniently justify the obtaining and expansion of power. But he did believe in suffering – the plagues of Egypt, the trials of Job, Miriam's leprosy. The fragmenting of his own mind, the dull ache of not sleeping and the piercing buzz of unrelenting anxiety.

But God didn't do that to him. There was a lack of culpability in punishment by God. It was his own conscience, wrestling with his actions, that had him ready to pull out his own fingernails. He was the cause of his own suffering, and he had to be the one to end it. There were no answers in that *shule*, only nostalgia and the last vestiges of a faith he had long since abandoned. And so he left.

On the Tullamarine Freeway, Ezra's dashboard told him that Tegan's plane was due to land in thirty minutes, and according to his GPS it was twenty more to Melbourne Airport.

You don't have to pick me up. I can get a cab, her text had read. But he wanted to – he needed to get it over and done with.

You're the best. Looking forward to seeing you xx.

If only she knew.

The radio was all fake enthusiasm, sound bites and bass he could feel in his chest. The freeway lanes wobbled at the edge of his vision, and the line-haul truck drivers couldn't be trusted. Fuck knew what they were on – a gram of speed, a handful of No-Doz, their heartbeats a drum solo on elephant ribs, just like his.

He was in the wrong lane. Fifty metres ahead a large green sign told him he'd be heading to Bendigo if he didn't get over to the right. He could do that – go to Bendigo, turn off his phone, change his name, get a job that paid cash. Tegan would never find him. A fresh start. It was possible, but he was already indicating right and changing lanes, without bothering to head check.

He had a bag packed and ready in the boot, along with a motel reservation in Fitzroy. Sorting through his things and methodically putting them in that bag had been the only time in days that he'd felt anything close to solace. It could have been the banality and repetitive nature of the task, but he chose to take it as a sign – it was the right thing to do and there would be no turning back this time.

A logjam of cars filled the arrivals lane. He was already there. Where had the minutes gone? God, if only he could stop time, never have to go through this, or fast-forward to when it was over.

Unable to bear the idea of circling the pick-up area, he opted for the multi-level short-term parking. He turned off the engine, took a deep breath, undid his seatbelt and rested his forehead on the leather steering wheel.

The terminal was packed. Husbands picking up wives, middle-aged parents waiting for their children, young women with a handmade sign – glitter and bubble writing that read 'WELCOME HOME CHELSEA'. Not a person there who felt as he did – teeth dull from grinding, guts a mash of twisted wheel spokes, woodpecker in his chest. He had to piss twice in ten minutes – both times the stream was crystal clear.

And there she was, exiting arrivals. Freshly applied red lipstick, hair combed, no glasses – likely contacts. All for him. Small suitcase in tow, shoulders slumped, eyelids puffy. She looked tired, worn from a long trip. Until she spotted him, and her cheeks lit up like a forest fire, her back straightened, eyes sparked, incandescent with joy.

And then she was on him. Lips, teeth, tongue. She even put a hand in his jeans' back pocket – he felt her nails dig in.

There was no time to think. To react in any way that might suggest that things weren't okay, to lessen the brunt of what he had to do.

'I missed you,' she said, finally pulling away.

'I . . . missed you too.' Shit. What else could he say with all of those people around?

Shit, shit, shit. It was wrong to mislead her, but what choice did he have?

For the walk to the car, before she could grab hold of his clammy hand, Ezra insisted on taking Tegan's suitcase, and he worked to stay a step ahead of her, darting in and out of the crowded arrivals area to the carpark lift.

In the car, Ezra was quick to turn on the radio, but Tegan said she had a headache, asked if he'd mind having it off. As he reversed out of their car space, she reached for his left hand, and he let her take it but managed to pull away soon after, saying he needed to grab the ticket for the boom gate.

Back on the freeway, he glanced at Tegan and she smiled, leaned against her headrest and closed her eyes. 'Can't wait to sleep in my own bed. You wouldn't believe the week I've had.'

The week she'd had? Shit. Was he really going to dump this on top of her now?

'Ez – you okay?'

'What, yeah. I just . . . I didn't sleep well. Bit tired, that's all.'

'You look a little pale. I could drive if you'd like?'

'Nah, I'm all right. So, what happened at the conference?'

'Holy shit – I don't really want to get into all of it now, but basically you know how I had that presentation on the shared service delivery model . . .'

Fuck. What was he doing? With every second that passed, they got closer and closer to home – to their shared bed and the promise of Tegan's warmth, where Ezra knew he would cave, convince himself to leave it for another day and then another, while his thoughts slowly drove him mad. Tegan's voice trailed off, and the whine behind his eyes increased, louder and louder. His hands were shaking. He wrung them on the steering wheel. God, he couldn't do it.

'WATCH OUT!'

Traffic had come to a halt in front of them, and he hadn't noticed.

'Shit!' Ezra slammed on the brakes, their tyres squealed in protest, and both Ezra and Tegan lurched forward only to be slung back by their seatbelts. Miraculously, they stopped short of the truck in front of them by what must have been a hair's breadth.

'Jesus, Ez. What was that?'

Bells rang between his ears. His stomach lurched. Traffic started moving, but rather than follow the cars in front, he indicated, turned the car into the emergency stopping lane. He parked and threw open his door as the meagre contents of his stomach hastened upward, spattering the bottom of the door and freeway gravel.

'Ez – Ez, are you okay?'

Hanging half out the door, Ezra felt the rush of cars passing at a hundred kilometres an hour, metres from his face.

'Was it something you ate?' Tegan stroked his back, as he continued to retch.

After another half-minute, he wiped his mouth with the back of his hand, flicked spittle onto the road, closed the door and sat back in his seat. Tegan ran her hand through his hair.

'Switch with me,' Tegan said. 'I'll drive the rest of the way.'

He grabbed her fingers, pulled them away from his head.

'Ez – what's wrong?'

He couldn't do it. He couldn't, he couldn't, he couldn't. He had to. FUCK. 'I . . . we need to break up.'

'What?'

'I'm sorry. I'm so sorry . . . I just –' His voice wavered, and his entire body shook.

Tegan stiffened, blinked rapidly.

Shit, shit, shit. What had he done? He tried to swallow but only gagged. He couldn't breathe. Mouth open, he gasped for air.

'Ez – Ez.' Tegan sounded far away. 'You need to calm down. Listen to the sound of my voice, Ez. Hold your breath for a few seconds, let it out slowly, do it again.'

He shut his eyes tight, did as she said, again and again and again, and then he tried to breathe normally and felt his lungs fill and empty, fill and empty.

'That's it.'

His breathing steadied, but he kept his eyes closed, terrified of how Tegan would be looking at him when he opened them.

'Is it better now? Are you feeling all right?'

Even now, after what he'd just said, all she cared about was his welfare. He opened his eyes.

Tegan was leaning back against her seat, staring out the windscreen. 'Did something happen while I was away? What's going on?'

God, he wanted to tell her – Phoebe, Nineties Night, Laura Sellars and the bill, Imogen. All of it. But he couldn't. He was small, weak and selfish. He couldn't face Tegan knowing him for who he truly was – despicable and worthless – so instead he shook his head and cried.

'Ez. It's okay.' She placed a hand on his cheek. 'It's okay. Talk to me. Please.'

'I've just . . . I can't eat. I can't sleep. I don't know what to do anymore, it's killing me –'

'Have you been thinking about this for a while?'

He nodded.

'Why? Was it something I did?'

He shook his head. 'No – of course not. You're perfect. I'm sorry. I'm just not in a good place.'

'Have you met someone else?'

'What? No.'

'What's wrong then? Ez, talk to me.'

'I'm sorry . . . I . . . I can't.'

Tegan's lower lip curled upwards, as it always did when she was going to cry. He called it her doggy bone, and often tried to temper her sadness with teasing. But not this time. 'What . . . what am I going to do now?' she said, tears flowing. 'What am I going to think about now? . . . I think about you all of the time.'

She did? Jesus Christ. Why? Of all the people in the world for her to love, to want, to care for – why him?

Tegan sobbed silently for another minute or two, and then she sucked in her breath and wiped her eyes. 'We should probably get going – it's dangerous for us to be sitting here like this. I could still drive if you'd like.'

'No,' Ezra said. 'I think I'll be fine.'

They drove without speaking. Twenty-five minutes of squeaking brakes and the tick-tick of the indicator. Ezra was cold but also worried that turning the heater on might break the spell. When they pulled up to their apartment block, he let go of the steering wheel, flexed his hands and exhaled heavily, as if he'd been holding his breath for the entire drive home.

'So what . . . what do we do now?' Tegan asked.

'I . . . I've booked a room in a motel. I've got a bag so –'

Tegan nodded, as though she already knew what he was going to say. Tears slipped down her cheeks. Maybe she thought if she just got him inside she could change his mind. Have it out – a long night of arguments, aggressive sex and revelation. Get to the bottom of what was really going on, address his concerns, get on with their life together. So much of him wanted that, but it wasn't right, and he'd made it this far. He didn't know what to do next, didn't feel as though he had the energy to say anything else. It wasn't a moment, he wanted to wade in, but Tegan didn't move and neither did he. And then he did the unthinkable – he smiled at her.

Jesus, why did he do that? Now she probably thought he was happy – that he'd lied about there being no-one else and planned to drive to the waiting arms of another woman, that he'd enjoyed the sad choke in her voice, her face scrunching up with pain.

But no – of course she didn't think that. She was Tegan, and she was good and honest and trusting and lovely, and when he smiled at her she smiled back, because she loved him, and that's what you do when the person you love smiles at you.

Chapter 18

Yonatan

The house was warm. Either Rivka was still up, waiting for him, or she had recently gone to sleep. A ribbon of light shone beneath the door to the lounge room – still awake then. On closing the front door, Yonatan expected to hear her stomping towards him, for the lounge-room door to explode open, a rigid finger pointed at his face as she shouted and screamed. But he heard nothing. Perhaps she'd fallen asleep on the couch while waiting? A pulsating headache made itself known at his left temple – the whisky had long worn off, but he'd been granted a glimpse of tomorrow's hangover. Not quite ready to face Rivka's inevitable berating, he went to their bedroom, confirmed her absence, and changed into his bedclothes.

After taking a moment to steel himself, Yonatan walked into the lounge room. Rivka was standing by the wall, seemingly reading their *ketubah*.

'Have a seat, Yoni,' she said, without looking at him.

He sat on the couch nearest to her.

She sighed, turned from the *ketubah* and sat opposite him with her hands in her lap. She did not stir at the sight of his shorn beard and absent *peyot*.

'*Nu?*' he said.

Rivka closed her eyes, exhaled slowly and opened them. Her lips parted as though she were about to speak, but then she closed them again. Still waiting.

Oy. Well, there was no holding back now. What would be the point? 'I know, Rivka,' Yonatan said. 'I know the child isn't mine.'

*

The year before, on Simchat Torah, Yonatan had the honour of being *Chatan Torah*, and received the *aliyah* to complete the reading of the Torah for that year. He did so after the *hakafot*, where the Torah scrolls were removed from the ark and men and boys formed circles and broke out into exuberant song and dance. *Peyot* swinging, *kippot* flying, each man taking the hands of his neighbour, raising them high with joy. Arm over arm they were all *Yehudim*, and together they were one, they were strong.

Elation tingled from Yonatan's fingertips to his toes at the sound of the *gabbai* speaking his name, '*Rav Yonatan Kaplan ben Rav Aharon Kaplan*.' He walked to the *bimah* more embedded in his faith and love for *Hashem* than he thought possible until, that is, he saw Rivka after the service.

He asked her about the women's *hakafot*, knowing that without the Torah to carry on their side, the women's dancing often fizzled out within minutes.

'It was nice, but I didn't dance,' Rivka said.

'Why not?'

'Because, Yoni. I didn't want to risk falling down and hurting the baby.'

'Whose baby?'

She smiled. 'Ours.'

'What? Ours? You're saying that –' He looked at her flat stomach.

She nodded.

'*Baruch Hashem*.' He wrapped his arms around his wife, hugged her tight, pulled away and kissed her. 'How did this happen?'

'We have been blessed, *ahuvi*.'

There were tears in his eyes. He nodded and held Rivka again. 'Yes, we have. *Baruch Hashem, baruch Hashem*.' What joy! What an incredible gift! What a world! What a life! He had been lucky and loved – his cup was already full, and now it was overflowing.

For six years, Yonatan had told himself that if *Hashem* willed it, they would have a child, and if He did not they would not, and that was fine because it was His will. As time went on, he urged patience and faith to Rivka, reminding her that they were not in a position to question why *Hashem* grants to some and takes from others.

But in truth, when Rivka told him of their blessing, he had long given up hope that they would have a child of their own. Six years of performing the mitzvah every Shabbat without pregnancy – it should have happened by now. Yes, in the Torah Sarah did not fall pregnant until the age of ninety, Hannah was barren for nineteen years before *Hashem* heard her prayers for a son, and He did intervene to open the womb of Rachel. But those were the matriarchs of their faith, wives of the great prophets. Who were he and Rivka for *Hashem* to intercede?

At the time, they were surrounded by friends and family, a close and supportive community. He was progressing well at Yahel Academy and Rivka was in demand as a doula. The connection between them was greater than either he or Rivka could have hoped for out of an arranged marriage and it was strengthening every day. Life was good, and he was content. But if Yonatan were honest with himself, he had been harbouring an unexplored notion for some time – that something was keeping him from a more immediate knowledge of *Hashem*'s providence, and now he had an answer. It had been the absence of his own children.

For three months, he and Rivka kept the pregnancy to themselves – a private light and source of joy. When they finally spread the news, it was not celebrated, as doing so might bring bad luck, but there was a discernible energy in the community. Rivka's pregnancy was as near a miracle as they'd ever had, and the people around them responded collectively with warmth and attention.

And then an idea manifested in the recesses of Yonatan's mind – an abhorrent, sinful absurdity from his subconscious that he refused to initially acknowledge. But with each *b'sha'a tovah* he received, and as the bump at Rivka's stomach grew, the thought nagged at him like the ticking of a hidden clock, until, one day, he had no choice but to bring it to the surface – what if the child wasn't his?

To begin with, the thought would strike Yonatan like a sudden sickness, leaving as quickly as it arrived. And he came to accept it as an occasional aberration of the mind, not to be indulged. But soon the idea grew of its own will, like an unpruned vine, winding about the contours of his brain, until the notion, no matter how implausible, threatened to consume his waking life. He barely slept and couldn't focus in his classes. Despite the distraction of the pregnancy, Rivka noticed the change in him, and he was terrified she would find a way to read the shameful thoughts beneath his brow. He started taking long walks alone at night, and that was when he knew there was nothing for it. He had to do something, lest he truly become a *shoteh* and destroy what had been given to him – his beautiful wife, his unborn child.

*

'I've known long enough to come to terms with what you've done,' Yonatan said.

Rivka met his eyes and would not turn away. Her look was stern, not shocked or penitent. What *chutzpah*. Was she denying it? Or did she think his transgressions outweighed hers?

'You judge me for breaking a *cherem* and spending time with an *apikoros* and a *shiksa*. You say I have committed *chillul Hashem*, but what about you and your hypocrisy? You're no better than Reb Feiner and his flock. Strict adherence to *halacha* where it suits you, looking down on the Modern Orthodox and Reform, *goyishe yids*, but what about your morality? Is adultery not worse than breaking a *cherem*? Is it not one of the three sins which cannot be excused under any circumstance? You chastise me for lying to you, but that child is a lie!' He pointed to her belly. 'How long have you been lying for? A year . . . five?' He stood up, walked over to their framed *ketubah*. Had he not given her all he had promised? He should pluck it from the wall, raise it above his head and smash it, as Moses did the *Luchot HaBrit*. But he didn't. 'How am I meant to know what to believe?' He slumped back down onto the couch, suddenly exhausted.

Rivka shook her head. A thin smile formed on her lips and she laughed. 'I can't believe you, Yonatan. I can't believe you're going to sit there and proselytise with that sanctimonious rubbish.'

'*Slicha?*'

'Tell me what you know about being a woman – a Jewish woman. My hair is shorn, and I cover it lest I cause a man to have immodest thoughts. I go to *mikvah* every month and cleanse myself because I have been told that I am impure, and my husband cannot touch me otherwise. What do you know of the pain of performing a *bedikah*, inserting a cloth inside myself and looking for a stain of my uncleanliness? What do you know of the humiliation of presenting my *bedikah* cloth to Reb Feiner so he can confirm that I am clean or declare me *niddah*?'

Rivka pulled her long brown *sheitel* and the cap beneath from her head and threw it onto the couch. Tufts of her short hair pointed out in all directions. '"Be fruitful and multiply." *Hashem* does not need my prayers, but he needs my womb. What was I meant to do? Keep delivering other people's children, blessing their health and happiness?'

She shook her head, tears formed at the edges of her eyes. 'Do you know what the other women were saying behind my back? Cursed by *Hashem*, they said, *akarah*. I know that many chose other doulas over me, because they feared I would somehow infect them, cause stillbirth or sterility in their children. For six years I prayed for *Hashem* to grant us a child. Every Shabbat for six years when I was not *niddah* I opened up my heart and my body, and for six years *Hashem* refused me. Have I not otherwise lived a *halachic* life, been an ideal *akeret habayit* and created a Jewish household, a sanctuary for *Hashem*? "Give me children, or I shall die!" I know how Rachel felt. What do you know? Do you not thank him every day for not having made you a woman?'

She wiped her eyes and glared at Yonatan. 'But you – you run into an old friend and need to have this grand, mid-life crisis of faith. You need to experience the world, separate yourself from us luddites, because your mind is too grand, your experiences are too important. How could I, with my narrow-minded beliefs, possibly understand? You think I haven't thought of leaving, dreamt of wearing a short-sleeved top in public without feeling ashamed, having a conversation alone with a man who is not my husband without looking over my shoulder, of brushing my own shoulder-length hair, going to university, learning about the world outside of this *fakakta shtetl*?'

Rivka paused for a moment and placed her hands upon her rounded belly. 'But my life is here, Yoni. My family, my community, my husband.' She lowered her eyes, took a deep breath and looked at him again. 'You call me a hypocrite but look at yourself.' She gestured to his face. 'You're like a teenager with this *narishkeit*. How selfish you've been acting, using your newfound enlightenment to look down on me and the way of life we have practised since we were children. The man I married always put others before himself, a true *ba'al chesed*, but it's not your appearance I don't recognise now, it's your soul.'

Yonatan reached for one of his phantom *peyot*. She was right about his selfishness. What could he say? She'd reminded him that she would be judged for his actions, but he went ahead and committed *aveira* after *aveira* anyway. She was right about everything.

The colour in her eyes had dulled to moss. He wanted to hold her, but he could not, because for all she had said, she had not admitted the truth about the child. Yonatan sighed. 'The child, Rivka.'

Rivka narrowed her eyes at him. 'I could tell them, you know. Everyone knows there is something wrong, that you're halfway off the *derech*. After that display at *shule*, Reb Feiner will talk to the *beth din*. They would force you to provide a *get*. But who would want me with the stain of your leaving on my name?' Rivka sighed, closed her eyes for a moment and then continued. 'Fatherless, you know this child will not be accepted by their peers, life will be difficult and despite whatever love I can give, he or she may grow to resent me and the world. Yes,' Rivka nodded, 'I have sinned. The child is not yours, but unlike us it does not have a choice – they are coming into this world innocent and do not deserve the stigma of being a *mamzer*. Would you put that on them?'

So, she admits it. But intimidation, guilt – she must have been thinking he was half out the door. But he was – wasn't he? 'Who is the father?' Yonatan asked.

'Does it matter? He is nothing to me – a seed to harvest. I did it for us. For you. The child is yours to raise, Yoni.'

'Is it Shimon?' Yonatan asked.

Rivka maintained her expression, too carefully and for too long.

Yes, it was Shimon. 'I see.'

'He has his own wife and children. He was never going to be part of the child's life. We had an agreement. The child is yours.'

'If anyone found out –'

'He would never tell.'

'I don't understand, Rivka. If you knew I could not have children, why not ask for a divorce? Had you spoken to me, I would have understood, given you a *get* so you could be a mother.'

Rivka's stolid expression broke then. Her lips collapsed, cheeks shook. She wept openly. 'Because I love you, Yoni. I didn't want a divorce and another husband. I wanted to be with you and to have a family. To grow and change and live, Yoni. To have a life with you.'

He heard her, and he didn't. What life? How could he go back now, after everything? 'You could leave. Start over with the child. Away from prying eyes and restrictive doctrine. You wouldn't be the first. I'm sure the Modern Orthodox *shules* are filled with –'

Rivka shook her head. Wiped the tears from her face. 'Stop, Yoni. My life is here. Your life is here.' She leant towards him, close enough for him to touch her if he reached out. 'Stay with me, let's raise this child together. You will find renewed meaning in them.'

Oy. How could she? Shimon. She had been intimate with Shimon. How many times? How long did it take to make a child? How should he respond to that? What was he meant to do? He shook his head. 'It's not my child.'

'Does it matter? If you leave, you will irreparably alter their life. The responsibility is yours and has been since the moment you married me. Please, Yoni!' She reached forward, grabbed his wrists. 'What would you do if we had a child of our own already? Would you still leave? What if we had several? Did you know you couldn't have children when we met?'

He pulled his hands away from hers. 'I did not.'

She stood up, raised her hands to her short hair and pulled. 'I get it, Yoni. It's easier. It's easier to run away, tell yourself your wife is a *sotah*. It's not your child and not your responsibility. Though I did it for you, Yoni. I did it for us and the life we have built together for the past seven years.' Her shoulders dropped and she shook her head.

What was he meant to say? What was he meant to do? How did it come to this? Rivka approached the lounge-room door.

'Where are you going?' he asked.

'To get my things. I'm going to stay at Menachem's. Let me know when you've come to a decision.'

Chapter 19

Ezra

An unseasonably warm June Sunday meant the Carlton Gardens thrived with people. Couples toasting wine on picnic rugs, students sitting in circles in the sun, tinnies in hand. Dogs and children running everywhere, spouting a pervasive cry of joy, joy, joy. In hindsight, it was a terrible place for Ezra to meet Yonatan.

Admittedly, since breaking up with Tegan there'd been a significant drop in Ezra's anxiety, but he still didn't need a deluge of happy families reminding him of what he'd potentially thrown away. He was a shit person. *Tegan deserves better*. He repeated the words to himself as a mantra whenever he thought of her, and it worked to quell the welling concern that he'd made a giant mistake. He recognised, now, that he'd been delusional in attempting to seek divine guidance at *shule*, but he also figured he'd been on the right track – hadn't he recently renewed friendship with a rabbi, a professional listener, trained to provide advice to the lost and discontent? There was more too. Despite his staunch atheism, Ezra was aware of a thread of belief that remained from the spool of theology he had been indoctrinated in, and when he thought about it some more, he knew why.

For the most part, when Ezra and Yonatan played together as children, it was at Ezra's house, where they could run and chase and jump and scream without fear of reprisal, without disrupting anyone's study of Talmud, impeding their reverence for God. But every now and then, when Ezra's parents were busy, Yonatan's would return the favour and agree to host Ezra.

On one of those occasions, when they wouldn't have been more than ten, there was a frantic, repeated knocking at Yonatan's front door. His mother was out, and Yonatan was in the bathroom, leaving Ezra to answer it or dare interrupt Reb Kaplan in his study. Needless to say, Ezra chose the former.

Standing on the stoop of Yonatan's house was a *frum* man Ezra didn't recognise. His thin, short beard told Ezra he was too young to be the father of one of the boys from school, but also too old to be a student at Yahel.

The man hesitated at first – likely surprised to see a boy without *peyot* and the ends of a *tzitzit* sticking out from beneath his shirt in the home of Reb Kaplan. '*Shalom*. Is Reb Kaplan home? It's a matter of urgency.'

'Ah, he is but I –'

'Please – I have to speak to him.' The man took off his hat. His forehead gleamed with sweat.

'Let me just –' Ezra looked back into the house where, thankfully, Yonatan appeared from around the corner.

'*Shalom*, Choni. Are you after my father?'

'*Shalom*, Yonatan. Yes, thank you. I need to speak with him.'

Yonatan nodded. 'He's in his study. You know the way.' He stepped aside to let the man in.

'Thank you. Thank you.' Choni entered and walked stiffly to Reb Kaplan's study as though he was going to burst into a run the moment he was out of sight.

'What was that about?' Ezra asked.

Yonatan shrugged. 'People come here all the time, seeking my dad's advice.'

It must have been more than an hour later when Ezra went to the kitchen for a glass of water and saw Choni exiting Reb Kaplan's study. Chest out, shoulders back, he stood tall and confident, and on seeing Ezra he smiled – big and happy. '*Kol tuv*,' he said, waving as he left.

At that age, the wise and righteous Reb Kaplan practically held mythological status in Ezra's mind and following that event he was more convinced than ever that the receipt of advice from Yonatan's father was akin to the performance of a miracle.

Ezra chose a park bench to wait for Yonatan, fifty metres or so from the playground and basketball court. Close enough to hear the bouncing of the ball and the shouts of those playing but not enough to make out their words. Ezra took out his phone, checked his Facebook messages again. It wasn't like Yonatan to be late, either when they were kids or for any of their recent get-togethers. He assumed Yonatan would be coming from the Rathdowne Street side of the park and turned to study people on the western path – joggers, elderly tourists, a homeless man, high schoolers taking selfies, but no Yonatan.

He made the mistake of lingering too long on the homeless man who was now headed in his direction. Shit. Ezra patted his pockets for change, found a dollar and held it out. But instead of taking the coin the man laughed. 'Look at you, performing *mitzvot* without my help.'

'What the . . . Yoni?' His *peyot* were gone, his beard had been cut short and it was uneven and patchy. He wasn't wearing his fedora or even a *kippah*, and what remained of his frizzy red hair stuck out like loose electrical wires. 'What happened?'

Yonatan sat down heavily beside him. '*Oy*. It's a long story.'

Fucking hell. Just when he needed him, the rabbi had to have his own crisis. But then Ezra took another look at Yonatan's bedraggled state and immediately chastised himself. You selfish dickhead. Maybe try asking your friend about himself for once. 'It's all right. I've got time.'

Yonatan shook his head. 'I don't want to talk about it just yet.'

'Okay.'

'So, how about you? Why am I here? What did you want to talk about?'

Yonatan's trousers and suit jacket were wrinkled, and a dark stain, which might have been wine, marked the collar of his shirt. He looked even worse close up and carried a sour stench. Was this really the man he wanted to confide in, be guided by?

Yonatan waited. His patient blue eyes were brightened by the dark circles around them. Curious, intelligent, warm eyes with a glint of something more – knowledge, wisdom, the learnings of countless generations of scholars and intellectuals like his father?

'Tegan and I broke up.'

Yonatan raised himself from his elbows, his mouth open with what looked like genuine surprise. 'What, why? What reason did she give?'

Ezra shook his head. 'It was me. I broke it off.'

'What?'

'I know. Why would a *schmuck* like me break up with someone like her?'

'No. Sorry. That's not what I meant. I just thought that –'

'It's okay, really. There are some things you don't know about, and I haven't been feeling right because of them.' Ezra paused. He might have stopped there if Yonatan had asked him to elaborate, but of course he didn't – he was good at his job. 'I couldn't focus at work, couldn't sleep. I knew I was preventing her from finding someone she deserved – that every additional second I spent with her was one she wouldn't get back.' Ezra closed his eyes, took a deep breath and then opened them.

'The thing is . . . I don't think I ever loved her. Not really. I tried, or at least I think I did. I don't know why I couldn't – she's beautiful and kind and thoughtful. I've never known anyone with more empathy. When the Liberals won the election and her work's funding was cut, she cried for a week over the thought of the women and children who'd suffer, and then she spent all her spare time writing furiously to every MP and philanthropic NGO she could until she secured another year's worth of funding.' Ezra squeezed his hands into fists. 'What kind of person wouldn't love a woman like that? What kind of person would hurt somebody like that?'

'*Oy*.' Yonatan shook his head. 'I don't know what to tell you. These things happen. You cannot blame yourself.'

'There's more. You don't understand, Yoni. I cheated on her.'

'You cheated – with another woman?'

Ezra nodded. 'More than once.'

Yonatan turned away from him, went rigid and stared straight ahead. Ezra was sure he was about to stand up and leave.

'I know – I'm a piece of shit,' Ezra said. 'All she did was love me and that's how I repaid her trust and loyalty.' He shook his head. 'Do you know what she said to me, while I was breaking up with her? She said, "What am I going to think about now? I think about you all of the time." Me! She thinks about me.

And while she's doing that, what am I thinking about? My god damned dick – getting off with a stranger. I don't deserve someone like her, and I've come to terms with that, but I've been thinking lately – if I can't love someone like her, maybe I'm just not cut out to . . . what if there's something wrong with me?'

They sat in silence for a bit then. Two women pushing prams passed on the path. A young girl struggled to keep her golden retriever in check. Voices chattered around them. The basketball bounced. Bird calls whistled and squeaked – *chip, chip, youhoo, chip, chip, youhoo.*

'I'm sorry, Ezra,' Yonatan said. 'I'm sorry you're going through this, but I don't see how I can help.'

'You don't?'

'I'm sorry.'

'I just . . . I don't know . . . I have this memory of when we were kids. There was this guy, seeking your dad's advice. Choni, I think. When he arrived, he looked like he was standing at a precipice, ready to fling himself off, but then your dad spoke to him and he was reborn – there was a light in his eyes, hope, more than that even, and I don't know . . . I guess I was after some of that.'

'Choni? You mean Choni Goldberg?'

'If he came to your house when we were about ten, then yeah.'

'Do you know what happened to Choni Goldberg?'

Ezra shook his head.

'Choni was a homosexual.'

'Really?'

Yonatan nodded. 'And do you know what the Torah says about homosexuals?'

'An abomination.'

Yonatan nodded again. '"Thou shalt not lie with mankind, as with womankind: it is abomination." That's probably why he was there.'

'What did your dad tell him?'

'I don't know. But the direction is often that marriage may solve the problem, and that's what ended up happening to Choni – he married, had children even, three of them. Evidence that he was over the problem, *nu*?'

'What? Of course not.'

'For the community it is. Study Talmud, follow the *mitzvot*, be a *mensch*. Anything else – ignore it, forget about it, repress it. But it didn't work for Choni – his wife found him in bed with another man – a *goy*. Soon after, Choni disappeared. No *get* for his wife, no goodbye for his children. Nothing. You want the Talmud, you want the wisdom of the sages, the advice of a rabbi – you want to end up like Choni?' Yonatan practically spat out the question.

Jesus. What on Earth could have shaken Yonatan's faith like that? 'Did you want to . . . Yoni, what happened? Can you tell me now?' And then a thought struck Ezra. 'Hey, if I've in any way influenced you to change your beliefs . . . Yoni, I didn't intend –'

Yonatan turned to Ezra, looked at him carefully for a moment and then laughed – a loud, chest-shaking laugh that burst through his wall of quiet consternation. 'Sorry, my friend. There is much to envy of what you've shown me of secular life but not quite enough to risk what has been promised to me in the world to come.'

Ezra smiled. 'Oh, right. I didn't really think so, it's just . . . you know.'

Yonatan sighed. 'I'm sorry, Ezra. I wish I could help you, but I'm not in a position to provide moral guidance, for you or anyone. I'm *farblunget*, lost, untethered from the only world I've ever known. How can I give you advice when there is no ground beneath my feet?'

He shook his head and laughed again, but small this time, sardonic. 'It's a funny thing, to be *frum*. Reb Morris Kolovitz is a surgeon, Mendel Lewis an investment banker, Zalmy Gutman a professor of mathematics. Intelligent men, clever by any measure, and yet still their faith in the Torah remains uncompromised. I'm no dolt myself. The universe created in six days, a flood for the Earth, ten plagues and the parting of the Red Sea. I think a part of myself has always known that there's no sense in reading such things as truth. But, as you know, better than most, a Torah scroll laid out before you is a path. Not towards righteousness or heaven or the *Moshiach*, but to known and achievable goals – security, companionship, community – and I think that despite what I felt in my secret heart, I knew that would be enough.

'A full life. Could anyone ask for more? And I was given that. A devoted wife, a good job, the warmth and support of innumerable community, a place in the world. And so I gave back. I *davened* each day, as *Hashem* asked, with the *kavanah* of the most devout men. I studied Talmud and received *smicha* and wept for the destruction of the Temple, begged forgiveness for the sinful doubts that I kept buried, and I sang with unbridled jubilation in celebration of my people's freedom, for their chosenness. But now – now I wake and when my lips instinctively form the words for *Modeh Ani*, I feel sick.' Yonatan paused, took a deep breath.

Why? Ezra wanted to ask, but he stayed silent.

'How can I recite the same words as those who excuse the abusers of children, who protect those abusers and punish their victims? And for what? The appearance of piety, tradition. Is that worth the life of a child?'

Rabbi Hirsch. Ezra lost all feeling in his hands. He twisted the skin on the back of his right – nothing. He had to know. 'I . . . never asked, Yoni. You were in Hirsch's class. Did he ever –'

Yonatan shook his head. 'No. I was spared. And you?'

The back of Ezra's hand throbbed. 'No. I was lucky too.'

Yonatan nodded as though he already knew that.

'Did you hear that his trial date has been set?' Ezra asked. 'It's in a month.'

Yonatan shook his head. 'I had not.'

'Do you reckon you'll go?'

'I don't know if I can –' Yonatan sighed. 'There's a video where a man, who attended Yahel as a boy . . . he speaks of what Rabbi Hirsch did to him. He was just a child, Ezra. Innocent and trusting.' Yonatan paused. 'I know there is evil in this world, the Torah tells us as much, but it's also from the Torah that we derive *pikuach nefesh* – the obligation to save a life above all else, even if it means a breach of *halacha*. And yet the most pious members of our community worked explicitly to protect that man's abuser. His eyes, Ezra. Such extraordinary suffering. I can't express how –' Yonatan shook his head. 'And how do the men who I have embraced as brothers respond? They ignore, they pretend, they make excuses, and when there is evidence beyond doubt, they blame the child, announce a *cherem*, threaten their supporters with the same.

'I cannot do it anymore, Ezra. I cannot repeat the same words as the men who would deny a child's suffering. I cannot teach at a school that refuses to acknowledge such abhorrent sins. How can I be a member of a community that preaches being just and compassionate, but would rather vilify the innocent than admit its own faults? I can no longer wade in the waters of their hypocrisy.

I just –' Yonatan lowered his head, wiped at the corners of his eyes. 'I was drowning.'

Shit. All of this since they attended the rally at Parliament House. How did Ezra miss it? He'd been so wrapped up in his own bullshit. 'I'm so sorry, Yoni. I had no idea. I . . . I don't know what to say. Have you spoken to Rivka? She'd understand, right? If you explained why you're feeling this way. I mean you're about to start a family. Surely you can –'

Yonatan shook his head. 'No, we are not.'

'What? Did something happen? Yoni, I'm so –'

Yonatan raised his hand. 'No, nothing happened. Don't worry. But we're not starting a family. The child isn't mine.'

'What? You're kidding, right? There's no way . . . I mean, Rivka would've had to –'

'She did.'

'You're having me on. She wouldn't have –' The *peyot*, the beard, his clothes. He was telling the truth. 'But . . . she's *frum*. I mean adultery is one of the big ones, isn't it? Why would she –'

'I cannot have children, Ezra.'

'You can't? Are you sure?'

'Six years of marriage without children. I suspected there was an issue with one of us, but only once Rivka fell pregnant, did I work up the courage to investigate.'

'So, it's definitely not yours?'

Yonatan nodded.

'Do you know who the father is?'

'I do. But he doesn't matter.'

'Does she know that you know?'

'Yes.'

'Jesus. How did that go?'

'She wants me to raise the child. She said she did it for me – so we could have a family, complete more *mitzvot* in the name of God.'

'Fuck. And what do you want to do?'

Yonatan shook his head. 'I don't know.'

'Are you going to stay? Are you going to get a divorce?'

Yonatan sighed. 'I honestly don't know. The community has already ousted me as an apostate. And . . . there was an incident in which I confirmed their suspicions. I've since left Yahel as well. Rivka is the only remaining link to my old life, but only if I can find the means to forgive her.' Yonatan paused and wiped his eyes. 'I'm at a loss, my friend. My days, once filled with prayer and blessings, the study of Talmud and the love of my wife, now lie empty before me like a hollow grave. There's so much time, so much nothingness – and to be honest with you, I'm terrified of it.'

Jesus Christ. 'Yoni, I . . .' Ezra shook his head. What could he possibly say?

Yonatan slid forward, resting the back of his head against the wooden bench.

God damn it. Ezra knew he had to do something – be selfless for once in his life. When you had nothing and no-one, he called you friend, held you up and told you that you had worth and were deserving of friendship, happiness, love.

Yonatan closed his eyes.

Go on – tell him.

Tell him he made you feel like living when nothing else did.

Tell him, however you can.

Do something!

Chapter 20

Yonatan

At Yahel Academy's affiliated kindergarten, at the age of three, Yonatan was taught the Hebrew alphabet. For his final exams in the *Derech HaYashar* program, Yonatan had to memorise fifty *blatt* of Talmud. To receive *smicha*, he had to master much of the *Shulchan Aruch*, be versed in the *Beit Yosef* and recite by heart many of the countless opinions of the *Rishonim* and *Acharonim*. All his life, Yonatan had been learning. He knew how to learn, and so, having been thrust into the unfamiliar *goyishe* world, he did what he was best at. He learnt that he wore a size thirty-four in jeans and a large sized t-shirt, that two scoopfuls of detergent would leave white lumps on his clothes, and that he needn't rinse the dishes for them to come out sparkling from the dishwasher. As he once used the Mishneh Torah as a guide to *halacha*, he now used the Internet as his guide to apostate living.

How to iron a shirt.

Best way to cook bacon.

Pizza delivery near me.

He went to a *goy* barbershop in St Kilda and discovered that, clean shaven, he looked five years younger but was also gifted a double chin. After thorough internal debate, he concluded that chicken tikka masala was his favourite microwavable meal from the *treif* supermarket. From the array of secular novels Ezra lent him, Philip Roth was the author he liked best. Perhaps a little too much sex, but he was clever and easy to relate to, as a fellow lapsed *Yehudi*. To counter his otherwise somewhat sedentary lifestyle, he walked to Caulfield Park each afternoon, basketball in hand, and made up drills for himself till the grey asphalt was dotted dark with his sweat.

When he was young, his *bubbe* and *zeyde* had often warned against assimilation, citing their experiences in Europe. 'Never forget,' they said. 'You'll always be *juden* first.' But as Yonatan walked the streets of Melbourne, and for the first time in his life no-one gave him unsavoury looks, gawked, pointed or shouted at him, he was awash with a sense of ease, calm and relief.

Weeks passed. Yonatan lived off the money he'd been putting away since Rivka told him of her pregnancy. Along with a new wardrobe, he bought himself a television, a mobile phone and a laptop computer. He took to going out to dinner with Ezra every Shabbat, eating at a new *treif* restaurant each time, grinning as Ezra glanced at him sideways while he ordered pork tenderloin with green apple gremolata, lobster thermidor, a medium rare porterhouse steak with blue cheese sauce.

But despite the spark of satisfaction that flickered within him with each task completed, each skill learned, each new taste and experience, Yonatan felt an absence, like an ache, when the dishes were done, and he was faced with the prospect of another evening of unnerving quiet. That was the worst of it – the hole once filled by the sounds of another. Creaking bed springs and wrestled-with sheets, hummed melodies that seemed to hang in the air, the shuffling of her small feet.

Another concern that Yonatan had been keeping at bay rose to the forefront of his mind after he completed a budget. At the rate he was going, his savings would only last another two months. What could he possibly do to make money? He didn't have any applicable skills in the *goyishe* world. Maybe there was a chance they would take him back at Yahel? He could agree to teach at the primary school, say it was all an unfortunate lapse in character and swear it wouldn't happen again. He'd also have to grow out his beard and *peyot*. But what about Rivka and the child? *Oy*, it wasn't possible. At their next dinner, he voiced his concerns to Ezra, who suggested he look into teaching Hebrew to the students of Melbourne's Modern Orthodox and Reform schools, where his off-the-*derech* reputation wouldn't precede him.

The next day, he called King David, Bialik and Yavneh, but, being the middle of the school year, none had teaching positions available, and all suggested he try again in the summer. Mount Scopus was his last hope. Unfortunately, the administrator he spoke to answered in kind. Yonatan sighed heavily, thanked her and was about to hang up when she spoke again, saying that a number of students' parents were looking for a Hebrew tutor if Yonatan was interested.

Yonatan's first student was Emile Goldman, Year Ten, sixteen, studying Hebrew and Judaic Studies. Without his beard and *peyot*, Yonatan felt as though he needed to make an effort and retrieved his suit and fedora from the back of his bedroom closet.

Emile lived in Toorak. A mansion of irregularly shaped squares and rectangles painted bone white and encircled by a three-metre-high stone wall. Yonatan rang the doorbell, by an impenetrably thick steel gate, and waited. A moment later, a woman's voice emanated from the intercom, but Yonatan couldn't make out what she was saying for the high-pitched yipping of a dog in the background.

'Ah, it's Yonatan Kaplan,' he said, leaning into the speaker. 'I'm here to tutor Hebrew.'

The woman spoke again – still incomprehensible, but the gate buzzed, and Yonatan was able to open it. Leading to the front door was a tiled path that cut through an impeccably trimmed garden, adorned with stone angels – strange decorations for a Jewish home.

At the large, frosted-glass front door, Yonatan could see the fuzzy outline of a woman.

The door opened. The woman, presumably Emile's mother, had dark curly hair and stringy bronze arms that tapered into thin wrists laden with clinky golden bracelets. 'Hello, Rabbi, sorry about –'

A grey blur shot out from under her legs.

'Milo!' the woman shouted.

A small grey dog with a large white moustache and flared leg hair sniffed Yonatan's dress shoes and growled innocuously. The woman reached out, grabbed the dog's collar and pulled it back inside.

'I'm so sorry about Milo. Please come in, Rabbi.'

A silver *mezuzah* with a gilded *shin* in its centre was affixed to the doorpost. For the sake of appearances, Yonatan touched the *mezuzah* as he passed and then kissed his fingers.

Inside, the aesthetic was again white – a marble tile floor, eggshell walls and a crystal chandelier above a split staircase. The woman let go of the dog, who bounded up the staircase and continued to growl at Yonatan through the balustrades. She held out her hand. 'Rachel Goldman.'

Without hesitation, Yonatan took her hand. Her bracelets jangled as they shook.

'Emile's just in the study.'

Yonatan followed Mrs Goldman around the corner, past a large black piano and a red-cloth pool table, to a room covered in contrasting dark wood. The study was lined with floor-to-ceiling bookcases filled with leather-bound books that Yonatan was sure had never been opened. At the end of the study, sitting on one of two chairs by a long desk, was a pale-faced boy with short brown hair that stood up like a freshly mown lawn.

'Emile, honey,' Mrs Goldman said. 'Rabbi Kaplan is here.'

Emile looked up. 'Hey,' he said before dropping his gaze to a phone in his lap.

'Put that away now, sweetheart,' Mrs Goldman said.

Emile sighed audibly and shoved the phone into his jeans pocket.

'Great. I'll leave you to it,' Mrs Goldman said to Yonatan. 'I'll be back in an hour.'

'Okay, Emile,' Yonatan said, sitting in the chair next to him, 'why don't we start with what you're studying in class.'

Emile picked up a thick textbook from the desk titled *Hebrew Units 1 & 2*, and let it drop with a thud in front of Yonatan. Its spine was uncracked, corners pristinely pointed.

Oy, what had he gotten himself into? Yonatan picked up the book and opened it.

Emile told Yonatan his class had already started unit two, which, according to the textbook, meant Emile would be assessed on his ability to make plans in Hebrew and provide written responses to a text.

'All right then,' Yonatan said, closing the book. 'Let's try to have a conversation and then I'll write a paragraph for you to respond to.'

As the lesson progressed, it became clear that Yonatan's initial concerns were well justified. Orally, Emile appeared to have a limited vocabulary, but he was clever, warding off Yonatan's questions with simple one-word responses or repeating memorised phrases that had near universal application.

Emile's writing was another matter entirely. He could read well enough, with and without vowels, and he appeared to guess the basic meaning of most sentences, but his knowledge of verb conjugation was practically nonexistent and he kept incorrectly guessing a noun's gender.

With five minutes to go in their lesson, Yonatan asked Emile to stop writing. He read over Emile's work, and then turned to him and asked why he wanted to study Hebrew.

'Want to? I don't want to,' Emile said. 'But Mum says it gets marked up really high, and I'll need it for VCE.'

Yonatan nodded – grades. This wall-haired *apikoros* was studying Hebrew for grades. Hebrew, *lashon hakodesh*. Sacred language of the Torah that many in his community refused to speak outside of religious ceremony. He remembered a conversation with Aron Belovski once when he referred to secular *Yehudim* as 'wasted Jewish stock', and then he recalled the memory of his former students singing *Shalom Aleichem* on Erev Shabbat – a choir of nasal, out-of-tune voices resonating with earnest pride and devotion, with all their heart, so that *Hashem* might hear them. Would he ever witness such a thing again? Before the thought could settle, the door to the study opened and Mrs Goldman entered.

'I believe that's it for today.' Yonatan stood up and held out his hand to Emile. '*Lehitraot*, Emile.'

'See ya.' Emile limply shook his hand and practically ran past his mother and out the door.

'I hope he wasn't too much trouble,' Mrs Goldman said. She took two fifty-dollar bills from her jeans pocket and handed them to Yonatan.

'He wasn't,' Yonatan replied, 'but –'

'But what?'

He rubbed the bills between his fingers, tucked them into his inside jacket pocket. 'Honestly – I'm not sure Hebrew is the subject for him.'

Mrs Goldman frowned. 'I know he's behind. But he's a quick learner, I promise. How about twice a week, hour-and-a-half lessons?'

Yonatan felt the slight bulge of the bills in his pocket. 'Let me think about it.'

'All right,' Mrs Goldman reached into her jeans again, 'let me give you my card – it has my work number as well.'

'RACHEL GOLDMAN – YOUR PATH INC – BOARD MEMBER.'

'Your Path?' Yonatan said.

Mrs Goldman smiled. 'You haven't heard of us?' Yonatan shook his head.

'Oh, I would've thought – anyway we're a not-for-profit. We give support to people who are in, or have recently left, self-contained religious communities, mostly ultra-Orthodox Jews, but we're happy to help anyone.'

'What kind of support?'

'Oh, you know – advocacy and resources, counselling. That kind of thing. Those communities . . .' Mrs Goldman shook her head. 'It's fine when you do what they say, but if you don't play along . . . some of our clients, you wouldn't believe what –' She stopped herself.

His face must have given him away.

'Sorry, Rabbi. I don't mean to offend if –'

Yonatan shook his head and smiled. 'No, no you haven't. I just –' He held up her card. 'I will think about your offer.'

'Please do.'

That evening, Yonatan went online and searched for Your Path Inc. The website background was white, lavender and sky blue – soft, welcoming colours. The banner beside the website name showed a woman at sunset, arms outstretched into the distance where birds flew. A little heavy handed.

Yonatan clicked on 'PROGRAMS'. In addition to counselling, legal advice and career guidance, they offered social events to museums, academic talks and even singles' nights. He tried 'TESTIMONIALS' next.

'I was on the brink, alone, with no-one to turn to before I found Your Path. Your Path gave me the confidence to trust my instincts and pursue the life I wanted' – Dina Raichik of Sydney.

'I thought I'd have to live on the street when I left my community, but with the help of Your Path, I have been able to find more than a new home, I've found a family' – Leibel Hurwitz of Melbourne.

Curious to read more about Mrs Goldman, Yonatan selected 'WHO WE ARE' and was surprised to see a familiar face listed as CEO – Avraham Kliger. Yonatan shook his head in disbelief. It was as though he were being steered again and again towards that man. The organisation's address was in the city. Considering the way he was being directed, did he have any choice? He would visit first thing in the morning.

*

Your Path's office was in a building on Lonsdale Street, a block from Melbourne Central station. The elevator was small. A label reading 'YOUR PATH INC.' had been stuck next to the button for the third floor, below the words 'SPIRIT YOGA AND PILATES'. Yonatan pressed the number three, and the doors shuddered as they closed.

Loud, fast-paced music, like Yonatan had never heard, reverberated through the glass doors of the Pilates studio, where men and women in tight fluorescent clothing lay on the ground and kicked about as though they were cycling in the air. Yonatan followed a corridor around the studio for what felt like minutes, until he came to a grey door with 'YOUR PATH INC.' written on a small silver sign. The music was still slightly audible. Yonatan turned the handle.

Inside, there was no reception, only a small clump of three desks, empty but for a middle-aged woman with short greying hair and large thick-lensed glasses.

'Oh, hello,' she said, turning on her office chair, 'can I help you?'

'I . . . I wanted to –' Yonatan realised only then that he had no idea what he wanted to say, or why he was there. 'I saw your website online and I –'

'Are you here looking for help?'

'I . . . I think so.'

The woman smiled sympathetically. 'My name's Shifra. My husband's just in the bathroom. Please take a seat, and he'll be back in a minute.'

Yonatan sat in one of the empty chairs.

'Can I get you a drink? Some water or tea perhaps?'

'Water would be great, thank you.'

Shifra stood and left. The desk in front of Yonatan was littered with pamphlets titled *Your Life. Your Experience. Your Path.*

Beside the desk was a filing cabinet with upside-down placards leaning against it – possibly from the rally at Parliament House.

Half a minute later, Yonatan heard the squeak of the front door, but it wasn't Shifra with the water, rather Avraham Kliger, head down, tucking his shirt tails into his slacks. 'You know, I was thinking –' Avraham's crow's feet stretched taut, and he stood with his mouth open, hands still in his waistband, staring at Yonatan.

Shifra appeared from behind Avraham then, holding a glass of water. 'Here you go,' she said, handing Yonatan the glass.

'Thank you.'

'Avi, this is –'

'Yonatan,' Yonatan said. 'Yonatan Kaplan.'

'Yonatan,' Shifra said, 'would like to talk to you.' Her eyes darted to Avraham's crotch.

Avraham quickly retrieved his hands from his pants. 'Of course.' He walked into the room and sat at the desk opposite Yonatan.

Shifra left the room.

Avraham leaned back in the office chair, appearing to take stock of Yonatan. Yonatan hadn't noticed it at first, but the fringes of a *tzitzit* draped over Avraham's trouser pockets and the puff of a navy-blue *kippah* rose from his crown. Did he still adhere to *halacha*, after everything his family had been through? No doubt, Avraham had noticed the absence of both on him.

'What brings you here?' Avraham asked.

'I . . . Mrs Goldman gave me her card and I thought that maybe –'

'Ah – how is she? I haven't seen Mrs Goldman in some time.' Avraham smiled. 'Some of our board members seem to enjoy handing out business cards more than they do attending meet–' He stopped and stared intently at Yonatan. 'Tell me – do I know you?'

Yonatan shook his head. 'No, but it's possible you've seen me before – I was at Parliament House in March. I saw you speak.'

Avraham nodded and closed his eyes briefly. 'So Hirsch then. For the trial tomorrow we're meeting at –'

Yonatan shook his head again. 'No. I'm not – I did attend Yahel at that time, but I wasn't . . . I'm not here for Hirsch. I was a teacher there myself, until recently.' He lifted a hand to fiddle with one of his absent *peyot*.

Avraham's eyes flicked to Yonatan's raised hand. 'I see. How long ago did you leave?'

'A month or so.'

'And that's why you're here?'

'Yes.'

Yonatan went on to tell Avraham about his festering doubt before he attended the rally at Parliament House, and how his attendance did not go unnoticed. He voiced his disgust with the *cherem* on Avraham's family and of how the community continued to treat Hirsch's victims. He mentioned his reunion with an old, secular friend, how he was shunned for his suspect behaviour and pushed to his breaking point after which he made the decision to leave Yahel and pursue a new life.

Avraham crossed one leg over the other as Yonatan spoke, and though he never broke eye contact, Yonatan couldn't help but feel as though his was a practised concern. But who could blame him? How many stories like Yonatan's had he heard over the years? And what was his tale of slight compared to what Avraham's family had been forced to endure?

'And what of your family?' Avraham asked. 'Do you have a wife, children?'

'My wife, Rivka, she . . .' Yonatan thought it best to leave out her pregnancy and its origins. 'She does not support my decision.'

Avraham uncrossed his legs and leaned forward in his chair. 'You have come at an opportune time. Some of our members have been reluctant to participate in events regarding Rabbi Hirsch. As a former student and teacher at Yahel Academy, your presence and voice will be encouraging.'

Yonatan recalled the bustle of bodies at Parliament House. The aggressive energy of the crowd on the steps. 'Thank you for the offer, but it may be a bit much at this time.'

'A bit much? To stand against a man who abused children? Your classmates? Tell me, did you know my brother at school?'

'Not well, but yes. We had classes together.'

'Before Hirsch, there was a light in Moishe's eyes. He may have been simple, but he was also blessed to be able to experience joy in such an uninhibited manner, as many of us are incapable. Pure and beautiful was his smile. But after Hirsch . . .' Avraham shook his head. 'Hirsch brought darkness and pain like you cannot imagine, and you sit here and tell me that seeing him brought to justice is a bit much?'

Yonatan considered the tired man before him with his *kippah* and *tzitzit*. What *chutzpah*, to try and guilt him into support when he still wore the trappings of a faith that had betrayed them both. He didn't respond to Avraham's rebuke but his expression must have given away his distaste.

Avraham sighed, sank back into his chair and shook his head. 'Forgive me. I'm exhausted and stressed. I know you've been through a lot and you came here looking for help.' He sat back up and met Yonatan's scrutinous gaze. 'Listen, I know how you feel. I know how incredibly isolating it can be. But I promise that we offer more than pamphlets and false hope. We have established a new community here. You don't have to come to the trial tomorrow, but please know you also don't have to do this alone.'

On the train ride home, Yonatan continued to contemplate the meaning behind Avraham's dumbfounding adherence to *halacha*. His suffering and that of his family far outweighed Yonatan's, so why did he insist on clinging to such a hypocritical faith? Was it weakness to hold on to the source of meaning faith provided? Was it strength to see beyond the obvious discrimination and subjugation of women and gentiles inked into the pages of the Torah, and focus on the moral groundwork it lay, the humanity and instruction towards compassion, the good it had brought to Avraham's life? Was it wilful ignorance? The issue weighed so heavily on his mind that Yonatan actually considered seeking counsel from the Talmud and its commentaries. He couldn't quite remember, but he thought Rashi may have said something perceptive about a similar situation.

But on arriving home, Yonatan had barely closed his front door when a furious rapping on the flywire jolted his heart. Half-convinced the clamour had come from his troubled thoughts, Yonatan paused in his hallway, until the rapping came again, faster and thunderous, so that Yonatan was forced to confront its existence with an equal burst of movement and throw open his front door while exclaiming, 'What?!'

It was Menachem, hat askew, cheeks flushed and eyes wild, fist still raised to the now-open door. Lips pursed, he stood for a moment – possibly taking in the sight of Yonatan, looking as *goyishe* as a *yid* could – before he spoke. 'It's Rivka. She's having the baby.'

Chapter 21

Ezra

On the Monday after he met Yonatan in the park, Ezra walked into Steven's office and asked if he had a minute. Steven motioned for him to shut the door and sit down. Ezra closed his eyes, took a deep breath and pretended that he was alone, saying the words to himself out loud. 'I've been having some trouble lately.' He opened his eyes.

Steven didn't say anything, only nodded for Ezra to continue.

'My relationship ended recently, and I haven't been . . .' he took another breath, 'feeling quite right. I'm sorry if it's affected my work, or the team. I figured you have a right to know, and I thought maybe it'd be best if I took some leave.'

'Mate, mate.' Steven shook his head. 'You have nothing to apologise for. You're a human being, not a robot. I get it.'

Ezra exhaled. What had he been afraid of? Steven was a good guy. He should've done this ages ago.

'I'm meant to manage more than just your workload,' Steven said. 'Take time, whatever you need. Your job will be waiting for you when you get back.'

'Thanks, mate. Means a lot I –' Ezra stopped himself and took another breath. He thought he might cry, not out of happiness or anything else – he'd been crying a lot lately and had come to recognise when that distinct heaviness was building.

Steven stood. 'These things happen. Look after yourself and think about the Employee Assistance Program. I've used it myself; they have some good people there.'

Ezra nodded. 'I will.' He stood. 'Thanks again.'

The counsellor Ezra was assigned through the Employee Assistance Program was Charlotte. She was in her mid-forties with long black hair and blue eyes that seemed to shimmer with empathy when Ezra felt his own welling with tears. He wasn't sure whether that kind of response was an industry trick, or simply one of the many things that made Charlotte good at her job.

Charlotte's office was situated in a single-storey Victorian building that reminded Ezra of one of his first share houses. It even had the same kind of lacework off the verandah and a rusting corrugated iron roof. The couch in Charlotte's office was not a chaise longue, but a comfortable blue velvet two-seater, opposite a similar lounge chair. At his first appointment, Ezra struggled to let his guard down, to restrain himself from trying to appear affable and charming as he would in any new social situation. He smiled often, asked Charlotte questions about herself and peppered his responses with self-deprecating humour.

But Charlotte was onto him quickly. 'You don't need me to like you,' she said. 'If I'm going to help, I need to know you, the real you. Tell me why you're here.'

'Okay.' Ezra tried again, told Charlotte about Tegan – the two years they'd been together, clichéd excitement petering out into domestic ease and comfort. How, over time, he was unsure he could reciprocate her feelings and felt himself pushing her away, the cheating and the inevitable break-up that he initiated over his guilt. It was stock standard stuff – sitcom-level honesty. An average middle-class white male protagonist showing just enough emotion and self-awareness to convince an undiscerning audience that he was, in fact, worthy of the out-of-his-league romantic interest.

Charlotte didn't say anything, but she looked down her nose at Ezra – unflinching, sceptical and patient as if to say 'I've got all day'.

Okay. No more bullshit. Ezra closed his eyes, exhaled slowly and edged open the splintered gates of his mind.

You didn't deserve Tegan.

She didn't love you, not the real you – you kept that hidden.

Something's wrong with you, everyone knows it – they've always known.

It's not only Tegan that would be better off – you'd be doing the world a favour if you just –

Ezra opened his eyes but couldn't bear to look at Charlotte and spoke instead to the grey office carpet. 'I guess it's more than the break-up. I think what I want to talk about . . .' His hands were shaking, his voice breaking. He took slow, measured breaths. 'Is that for as long as I can remember, I've felt this kind of pervasive sadness underlying everything. It's there all of the time, like a second skin. And I'm just so damn tired of carrying it around, of being sad all of the time. Most nights I find myself going to bed and hoping to wake up as someone else, or not at all. And I want to change that. I don't want to feel that way anymore.'

'Thank you, Ezra,' Charlotte said. Her eyes glistening. 'That's a good start.'

Their second and third sessions were filled mostly by Ezra talking, giving Charlotte as much background as he could about his childhood and upbringing, and everything else that led him to where he was. He told her about going to Yahel and his best friend, Yonatan, Rabbi Hirsch, and his parents pulling him out of the school. He continued on to his time at Glen Eira High School and university after that, how he moulded himself into someone he thought people would like, but never managed to shake off the feeling that he didn't quite belong. He went into detail about meeting Tegan, how their relationship started off physical and grew into something else. How she was good to him, loved him with everything she had, and how, inexplicably, sometimes that made him feel physically ill.

After nearly a month of seeing her, at their fourth session, Charlotte asked Ezra to dig deeper, tell her about a specific incident from his youth. 'Something that encapsulates how you felt back then. Can you do that? It'll help me gain an understanding of where you're coming from.'

'Okay,' Ezra said. 'I'll try.' He cast his mind back, reviewing the annals of painful memories that had been too stubborn to stay buried, until he found one that felt right. 'The days I hated most were those when Yonatan was sick. Because of recess and lunch. When he was around, Yonatan and I were always together, shooting hoops at the basketball rings or dipping in and out of larger groups of boys who played foursquare or hung out at the edge of the school's quadrangle.

'I told myself those boys were my friends too, but I think a part of me knew they only put up with me because of Yonatan. He was precocious and clever and easygoing. Everyone loved Yonatan. But when he was away, I was at a loss. I'd walk around the school grounds, thinking about which of the groups of boys

I could while away the time with. Head down, hands in my pockets, I'd stumble into one of those groups, raise my head and say, "Oh, hey," as though I'd just bumped into them on the way to somewhere else. I'd ask innocuous questions about homework or upcoming tests, make jokes about our teachers, and then head off again, assuring myself that the faint laughter at my back wasn't directed at me.

'I thought I was good at pretending, but I probably wasn't fooling anyone. I still remember feeling my eyes water as I did laps of the school grounds, how I'd repeat to myself again and again that it was "just the wind" and practise saying it, in case someone asked me what was wrong.

'Once, after the bell rang for lunchtime, I remained by my locker, dreading the empty hour that lay ahead, when I remembered a book by Ellie Weisel that Yonatan had been reading.

'The librarian was Mrs Richardson. She was a very large woman who wore ankle-length, shapeless black dresses, and a poorly fitted brown wig. A bulb of skin beneath her chin shook when she spoke. The children called her *livyatan* – leviathan, the Hebrew word for whale. Needless to say, I was terrified of her, and the moment I opened the library door she flew into my path like no whale you'd ever seen.

'"*Mah atah rotzeh?*" she said. *What do you want?*

'"Just to read," I said.

'"Read what?"

'I shrugged. "A book."

'Mrs Richardson narrowed her eyes. "What book?"

'A torrent of panic swept into my chest, taking the author's name with it. I shook my head. "I don't . . . I just –"

'"What's your name?" she asked.

'I opened my mouth, but no sound came out.

'"I knew it," she said. "Filthy *mamzer*. Leave."

'It turned out that some older boys had been going into the library at lunch and looking at a particular biology textbook with drawings of naked women in it. As a result, some staff were calling for the removal of all secular material from the library. I didn't know that at the time, though, and I'd felt exposed by Mrs Richardson. "*Mamzer*," she'd said. *Bastard. Outcast*.

'Her rejection only confirmed what I already knew, how all the boys treated me. So I turned, went back to the playground and walked my laps, eyes streaming, wishing I could find a safe, quiet place, make myself as small as possible and wait for the bell. God, how I prayed for that bell.'

Charlotte's eyes were dewy. Ezra raised a hand to his own cheeks and, feeling them wet, wiped away the moisture. He sat up, embarrassed, and suddenly irritated that she was making him relive all of that. 'I don't see how any of this is relevant,' he said. 'I'm not a kid anymore.'

Charlotte maintained her steady gaze. 'There's a lot to unpack here, Ezra. It's not going to be easy. Sometimes it's going to feel downright horrible, but it's the only way I see us moving forward.'

Ezra sat back on the couch.

'From what you've told me so far, it seems to me that there's been a lack of intimacy in your life since childhood. You've rarely had strong relationships, someone to open up to and let yourself be vulnerable with. Particularly after you were separated from your best and only friend.'

'That's not true,' Ezra said. 'What about Tegan? We had moments – there were things that I've never told anybody else. That's vulnerability, isn't it? And I still pushed her away.'

'Yes, but . . .' Charlotte leaned forward in her seat. 'I want to explore something with you but with the caveat that there are no easy answers. This is just one of many factors that may have led you to where you are today, okay?'

'Okay.'

'Have you heard of the term "attunement" in a psychological context?'

'No.'

'Effectively it's how well a person is able to sense another's emotional needs and respond appropriately. The loneliness you felt as a child, the pervasive sadness you speak of now . . . I think you've become so used to being alone, not having anyone attuned to giving you what you needed, that when they finally do – when they offer affection and attention and love – you're so unaccustomed to it that you have a reaction, you're repulsed by it. Maybe not consciously, but it's there and that's part of the reason you push them away.'

'Are you saying that's why . . . why I hurt Tegan, why I cheated on her time and again?'

Charlotte shook her head. 'I'm not going to justify your actions for you, Ezra, or admonish you. Your promiscuity may be explained, in part, by your search for intimacy – physical intimacy being the only kind you know. But I also think you have a strong moral grounding – the internal conflict and subsequent anxiety you've spoken about tells me that.'

She was right; he knew what he was doing. He was a piece of shit who hurt people, did awful things and had despicable thoughts. Elbows on his knees, Ezra sank his eyes into the heels of his hands.

'Ezra – what is it?'

Ezra shook his head. 'I'm a bad person. I've done bad things. Tegan had no business loving me, and you know what, I won't put anyone through that again. I'm better off alone.'

'Ezra . . . Ezra, look at me. Nothing is black and white. You seem to have this perception of yourself based on a hyperbolic moral code where things are classed as either good or bad. But life isn't that simple, you know this. Being a human being is complicated. The application of such an extreme moral code doesn't allow for learning, for redemption and rehabilitation.

'Relationships don't always work. You're not broken because you didn't love someone who loved you. Better communication might have helped, or it might have led to the resolution of your relationship sooner. What's important, right now, is that we figure out what lies beneath your "bad" behaviour, and then, with a greater understanding of why you feel the way you do, you might be able to mediate yourself accordingly in the future.'

'I don't get it,' Ezra said. 'What's there to understand?'

'I think your brain needs practice producing serotonin. Low levels of serotonin have been associated with depression, and I think the isolation and bullying you experienced in your youth, along with the loss of your only confidant, reduced your serotonin levels to practically nil, and your brain hasn't been able to produce any since.'

'But . . . does that mean . . . would I have been able to love Tegan, if I had serotonin?'

'That's not for me to say. Your experience of love is subjective, of course, and influenced by various factors, of which serotonin would only be one. But I'm sure there were moments when that underlying sadness you've spoken of dulled or possibly prevented your ability to experience joy or happiness when you otherwise would have.'

That couldn't be right. There must have been times – he knew what happiness was, didn't he?

Ezra tried to pinpoint a recent memory to prove it to Charlotte and found himself thinking of a barbecue the previous December with Tegan's cousin, Val.

*

Ezra liked Val. She was direct, unapologetic and savvy. The invitation was last minute, as was Val's way. Tegan accepted, even though she was exhausted from tying up loose ends at work before the Christmas break. Ezra suspected it was for his benefit – she knew he always had a good time with her cousin and her husband Leon, whose cantaloupe-sized biceps were matched only by his affection for his wife and their Rottweiler, Kiki.

Val and Leon's place was in Aspendale Gardens, a good hour's drive down the Nepean Highway. Tegan drove, and the early afternoon sun of a thirty-two-degree day beat through the windscreen onto Ezra's face as they passed Elsternwick and Brighton. Billboards for upcoming films, cars and plastic surgeons dominated the view, and Ezra had to sit up and focus on a point in the distance to dispel the warm, sickly feeling budding in his mouth.

Val greeted them at the side gate of their house with a big smile and a beer in hand. She led Ezra and Tegan round back to the garden where the radio played Triple J and an inflatable pool, filled with water, covered most of the grass.

'Hon, they're here,' Val called over to Leon, who stood at the other end of the garden, over a smoking grill.

A slight gust blew ripples across the surface of the pool. Ezra watched them ebb towards the reflection of the white sun in the middle of the water.

'Nice, ain't it?' Leon said. 'Been a lifesaver in this heat.'

Ezra looked down at the pool again and, though he wasn't sure why, he had to repress a shudder.

'You guys want some beers?' Leon asked.

'I'll get them, hon,' Val said, 'you focus on feeding me.'

'Aye, aye,' Leon replied, turning back to the grill.

Val ducked inside by the back door and returned a minute later, two beers in hand.

'Where's Kiki?' Ezra asked.

'She's inside,' Val said, pointing to the back door with her bottle. 'Can't let her get near the pool in case she gets her stitches wet.'

'Stitches?'

'She had a lump removed from her back last week.'

'Oh, shit,' Tegan said.

'It's okay,' Val said. 'It was benign.'

'Did they put one of those cones on her?' Tegan asked.

Val smiled wide. 'We just took it off, but she looked so cute. Let me show you some photos.'

Ezra went back over to Leon, sipping his beer, and tried to make small talk. 'How are the snags looking?'

'Nearly done, I reckon,' Leon said. He picked one up with his tongs, brown with black grill marks, inspected it and placed it back on the barbecue. 'How ya been, mate?'

A sudden weight overtook Ezra, and he felt as though it would take all the effort in the world for him to reply, so he didn't.

'Mate?'

'Sorry.' Ezra took a deep breath. 'What was that?'

'How ya been, I said.'

'Not bad.' He knew he should reciprocate the question; it was rude not to, but instead Ezra took another sip of his beer and stared into the rising smoke. It didn't make any sense – he had beer and sun, good company and nowhere else to be, but for some reason Ezra couldn't shake a growing sensation of dread.

'You all right, mate?' Leon asked, breaking the silence.

'I'm just . . . need to take a piss. Sorry, mate.'

'No worries. You know where it is,' Leon said, pointing to the back door with his tongs.

Ezra wasn't two steps inside when Kiki perked her head up from her nearby bed and, on seeing him, let out a short whine. Normally, Kiki would have run to him the moment he opened the door, jumping up with her forelegs and claiming his face with her tongue. But instead, as he approached, all she could manage was a weak thumping of her tail against her bed.

'Poor thing,' Ezra said, crouching to his knees.

She licked his arm as he patted the top of her head, scratched the back of her ears. 'Not feeling great, girl, huh?' He sat down on the floor next to her and hugged her gently. He knew he should get up, splash some water on his face, go back outside, make an effort. But instead, he stayed next to Kiki, on the floor, wrapped his arms around her side, buried his face in her soft, black fur and cried.

*

'There's medication you could take,' Charlotte said. 'SSRIs, SNRIs, a whole range. Effectiveness can differ from person to person, but we'll find the most suitable one for you. And we'll continue to put in the time with our sessions as well, help you boost those serotonin levels.' She smiled. 'It's like strengthening a muscle, but as I've said before it's not going to be easy. What do you think, Ezra, are you willing to work with me on this?'

Chapter 22

Yonatan

'Where are you going?' Yonatan asked Menachem, who was indicating to turn onto Dandenong Road. 'The birthing centre is back that way.'

'Rivka is not at the birthing centre,' Menachem said. 'She's at The Royal Women's Hospital.'

'The hospital . . . why is she at the –' But Yonatan knew why. Again he'd proven Rivka correct – left her to suffer the consequences of his selfishness. It was possible a *cherem* had been declared against him as well. Against his name, against his wife, and as far as the community was concerned, *his* unborn child. 'And the doula, Liat Berkowitz?'

Menachem frowned and shook his head.

'*Ben zona!*' Yonatan smacked the dashboard.

Menachem turned to Yonatan, fire in his eyes, but not for the swearing. 'You brought this upon her,' his stare said, 'you brought shame upon your family, my family!'

That was fair, Yonatan deserved that, but did Menachem

know the child wasn't his? As strict in his beliefs as he was, could Menachem forgive his sister for that sin?

'Thank you for coming to get me, Menachem.'

Menachem stared straight ahead, giving no indication of having heard him.

On passing Crown Casino and the aquarium, traffic into the city slowed to a crawl. Red veins like bursts of lightning marked Menachem's weary eyes. If there were a *cherem* against Yonatan, he had broken it by picking him up. Wasn't that how everything started for Yonatan, with the breach of a *cherem*? What if this event derailed Menachem from the *derech* in the same way? His steely gaze was fixed on the cars in front of them, urging them to move. No, Menachem's faith was stronger, absent the fault-lines in Yonatan's that had needed only the slightest pressure to crack.

The hospital came into view – two white buildings with the sterile look of an office, ten storeys or so tearing into the grey sky. It was no hearth for the welcoming of new life. A strange choice for a place of healing and to prepare for *olam ha-ba*. In his limited time among them, the *goys* still confounded Yonatan.

Menachem drove straight up to a sign that said 'MAIN ENTRY' and pulled the handbrake. 'It's the fourth floor,' he said. 'Maternity ward. I'll park the car and meet you there.'

He needn't have done that, but he needn't have picked him up at all. 'Thank you.' Yonatan opened the car door and walked into the hospital.

On the fourth floor, Yonatan approached a desk labelled 'MATERNITY RECEPTION' and told the nurse sitting there that he would like to see Rivka . . . Kaplan. He hesitated before saying his surname, wondering if Rivka would have been loath to register under it.

'Ah, Mrs Kaplan. She was admitted only a few hours ago. Are you a relation?'

'I'm her husband,' Yonatan said. Not the child's father, her *husband*.

'She's in room 407 down the hall.'

'Thank you.'

Outside of room 407, Yonatan stood and listened for the sound of Rivka's screams, for a loud, encouraging 'Push, push!' But there was nothing. Maybe the nurse had given him the wrong room number. Gently, he edged open the door and peered through the gap.

Rivka lay on her back. A brown kerchief was tied around her head, and her white hospital gown was tented by her distended belly. Her eyes were closed, pallor sickly, cheeks glistening with perspiration. A restless, uncomfortable sleep. Desperately, Yonatan wanted to sweep the loose strands of hair from her brow, press a cool cloth against her forehead, squeeze in beside her and bury his face in the nape of her neck. But no, Rivka wasn't asleep. It was almost imperceptible, but he saw it now – slight contortions of her mouth.

He didn't need to know how to read lips – Rivka was praying. Despite everything, her faith held steadfast. How then would she respond to his being there – a faithless *apikoros*? Perhaps he should leave, lest she fear his presence would provoke *Hashem*'s wrath on her child? He was not beyond that, as the Egyptians knew well.

'Yoni?' Rivka's eyes were open, staring straight at him.

He stepped into the room.

'Yoni, Yoni, you came.' Rivka's chapped lips split into a broad smile, and Yonatan hurried to her side.

'Of course.' He picked up her hand and squeezed it.

‘I’m so glad you’re back, Yoni. You have to know that –’ She froze, mouth open, eyes wide. Rivka arched her back and tore into Yonatan’s palm.

Yonatan gritted his teeth until Rivka lessened her grip. ‘Are you okay? Should I get a doctor?’

Rivka shook her head and pressed a button on the remote attached to her bed. ‘They’ll be here soon.’

‘What can I . . . do you want me to –’

‘You have to go, Yoni.’ Her breathing intensified. ‘I could be *niddah* any moment.’ He didn’t want to leave her side, but a few moments later a midwife entered and, after examining Rivka, she told him there was a while to go yet.

In the waiting area, Yonatan found Menachem standing in the aisle of a row of plastic chairs, eyes closed, shuckling and deep in prayer, likely reciting from the book of *Tehillim*. Then, as though sensing him there, Menachem stopped and turned to Yonatan. ‘How is she?’

‘She’s doing well. The midwife said it may be some time yet.’

Menachem nodded, reached into his pocket, pulled out a small black *kippah* and held it out to Yonatan.

Yonatan took the *kippah*, traced the stitching with his fingertip to its centre. He knew the requisite chapters of *Tehillim* off by heart:

‘Praiseworthy are those whose way is perfect, who walk with the law of the Lord.’

‘Praiseworthy are those who keep His testimonies; who seek Him wholeheartedly.’

‘You shall rebuke cursed wilful sinners who stray from Your commandments.’

He shook his head. No, he couldn’t do it, but when he turned to Menachem to tell him as much, he had stepped away, resuming his prayers in the aisle, so Yonatan buried the *kippah* in his pocket and sat down on one of the uncomfortable plastic chairs.

Hours passed. Yonatan's skin felt too tight, his scalp itched like mad. How long did it take to give birth? Was something wrong? He paced back and forth along the short corridor from the waiting area to Rivka's room, stopping on occasion to listen at the door. The nurse at reception assured him that the amount of time was perfectly normal. Menachem urged him to sit down, but how was he meant to sit there, idle, while his wife suffered?

What had Rivka been about to tell him? That she still loved him, and she would do whatever it took for them to be together – on the *derech* or off? That she would accept whatever involvement he wanted to have with the child, being together was all that mattered? No, she'd asked him to leave for fear of bleeding during birth and being *niddah*.

'I'm so glad you're back,' she'd said. Not *here*, but *back*. She wanted her husband back – the revered Reb Kaplan, teacher at Yahel Academy, stalwart of their community. Could he give her that – go back, despite everything? The betrayal of the community. The inconsistencies and hypocrisy of their faith. *Their* faith? *His* faith? What was it that he actually believed in now? Was it anything? And what about the child? Even if they were not his, they would be part Rivka, and wasn't even the smallest part of her more than worthy of love?

He paused by the door again, waited, and turned to resume his pacing, when a scream of abject pain flayed his skin. There was no choice to be made, no thought to be given to *niddah* or Menachem's certain disapproving glare down the hall. Yonatan twisted the handle and dove in.

Oy, the smell – a wall of sweet and sour, chemicals and tang, bitterness and wet meat. So thick in his mouth he could chew on it.

Rivka was on her back, propped up, legs elevated and spread. Her hands clenching the bed rails. Sitting on a stool by Rivka's exposed crotch, in full scrubs and face mask, was the midwife Yonatan had spoken to earlier.

A nurse with a hand under the back of Rivka's head turned to the open door. 'Excuse me. You can't –'

'I'm her husband,' Yonatan said and rushed to Rivka's side.

Rivka's eyes bulged at the sight of him, and Yonatan almost recoiled, expecting her to curse him out of the room, but instead she let go of the bed rail, picked up his loose hand and squeezed.

'You're doing good, Rivka. We're nearly there,' the midwife said. 'I can see the head.'

Curious, Yonatan stepped towards the midwife, looked over her shoulder and immediately regretted it.

A lump with a swirl of black hair had split Rivka apart like rotten fruit.

Lights danced before Yonatan's eyes, his legs buckled, but the nurse already had her arm on him, holding him up.

'Are you okay, sir?' the nurse asked.

Yonatan moved back to Rivka's side, and focused on the feeling of her fingers beneath his until the lights dissipated and the room was again clear. 'I'll be okay, thank you.'

'Okay. This is it, Rivka,' the midwife said. 'One last, big push. Come on, breathe in and . . .'

Rivka shut her eyes, leant forward and strained. Her body shook with the effort, a cord of muscle bulged at her neck, a blue vein throbbed on her brow. Yonatan couldn't feel his hand in hers, couldn't feel anything for the thrumming in his chest; building, he was sure, to match the pressure within his wife, because they had shared a home and a bed and a life together for the past seven years. Her pain was his, his joy was hers, and together they were strong. Rivka screamed.

The baby screamed. Purple skin, cone-shaped head, a coat of a greasy, cheese-like substance. 'Congratulations. She's a girl,' the midwife said, picking her up and handing her to Rivka.

'A girl, Yoni,' Rivka said. Her face shining with sweat and tears as she cradled her child. 'A beautiful baby girl.'

'*Mazel tov*,' Yonatan said, approaching Menachem in the waiting area. 'You have a niece.' He looked worn. Yonatan half-expected him to ignore what he'd said and chastise him for entering the room while Rivka was *niddah*, but he didn't, only closed his eyes and exhaled.

'A girl then.' Menachem smiled. '*Mazel tov*, Yonatan.' He held out his hand.

'Thank you, *achi*,' Yonatan said, shaking Menachem's hand. 'The nurses have taken her to be cleaned up and to do all of the normal tests. But I'm sure you can see her and Rivka when they return.'

Menachem nodded. 'Thank you, Yoni, but I'm tired, and I'm sure Rivka needs her rest. I'll come back tomorrow.'

Back in her room, Rivka lay asleep on her bed, mouth open, snoring gently. Careful not to wake her, Yonatan took a seat in the corner. Keeping his eyes open took Olympian effort. His own exhaustion had been mounting and with the adrenaline from the birth waning he could feel his grip on consciousness slipping. He let go, and there was nothing. No whiteness, not even darkness – only peace and quiet.

'Would you like to hold your –'

Yonatan's chin snapped up from his chest. The nurse stood before him, holding the child swaddled in a blanket.

'Sorry. Didn't realise you were both asleep. We can come back if –'

Yonatan wiped away a sliver of drool from his chin. 'No. It's fine.'

'She's all cleaned up. Ten fingers, ten toes. Completely healthy. Would you like to hold your daughter?'

'My –' The child, of course. 'Okay, yes.'

'Here you go. Here's Daddy.' The nurse handed her to Yonatan, showed him how to keep her head supported, and left the room.

She was so small and pink. Innocent.

Without thought, he cradled her and spoke. '*Baruch atah Adonai Elohaynu melech ha-olam shehecheyanu vekiymanu vehigi'anu lazman hazeh.*'

Blessed are You, Lord our God, King of the Universe, who has granted us life, sustained us and enabled us to reach this occasion.

'*Amen*,' Rivka said, eyes open, watching Yonatan with her daughter. She smiled, and Yonatan couldn't help but smile back.

Chapter 23

Ezra

During his leave from work, Ezra followed the proceedings against Rabbi Hirsch closely. He and Tegan arranged a time for him to collect the rest of his things and move them into his new place in Princes Hill. Other than that, they hadn't had any contact, but he liked knowing she was probably following the case as well, and imagined her reactions to each of the developments.

'Good to see the DPP is taking it straight to the County Court, no more bullshit.'

'He pleaded not guilty, can you believe that? The fucking arrogance of it. I can't wait till he gets what's coming.'

'Jury trial is a good thing, I reckon. Yahel Academy or someone will have bankrolled Hirsch one of the best barristers out there, but your everyday mum and dad aren't likely to think fondly of any alleged paedophile.'

The trial verdict made the news. 'Emotions running high today,' the reporter narrated over shots of protesters – similar to those at Parliament House the day Ezra ran into Yonatan – cheering boisterously, embracing each other, tears visible on their cheeks. 'As Rabbi Joel Hirsch, a former teacher at an ultra-Orthodox Jewish school in Melbourne's south-east, was found guilty on multiple counts of child sexual abuse.'

Outside the County Court, microphones were shoved under Avraham Kliger's haggard face. 'It has been an incredibly long journey for my brother, myself and my family,' he said. 'But today, justice was finally served, and a message was sent to our detractors in the Jewish community, "We will not tolerate abuse of our children – perpetrators will be brought to justice."' He raised his eyes and looked directly down the camera. 'For any other victims out there, it is my hope that what happened here today has given you the strength, and courage, to come forward – you are not alone in this fight.'

The celebration felt premature to Ezra – guilty, yes, the verdict was in, but the sentencing hearing wasn't for another week, and from what Ezra had gleaned from Tegan in the past, that was where the system let victims down.

The following week, Ezra went to the County Court alone. He hadn't heard from Yonatan in a while, having sent him a message the night of the verdict that, according to Facebook, he still hadn't seen.

The court was on the corner of William and Lonsdale. Ezra must have walked past the building hundreds of times and never given it a second glance. The outside was sleek grey with sharp angles, more tech start-up than courthouse. A sculpture of Lady Justice stood by the revolving-door entrance. Adorned in flowing robes, she held her scales high in one hand and brandished steel in the other.

The need for closure brought Ezra there, or so he told himself. A desire to see Hirsch being led away in handcuffs, covering his face with his jacket. Stupid, he thought as he approached the court entrance, who was he kidding? He wanted to see Tegan, and that's all there was to it.

Inside, Ezra crossed the lobby's shining marble floor to the reception desk, where a man looked briefly over the top of his computer screen, took in the sight of Ezra, and spoke before he could open his mouth.

'Through security to your right. There's a court registry inside.'

Security was the same as at the airport – empty your pockets into a tray and walk through a metal detector. As ever, Ezra felt unnecessarily nervous as he slowly stepped through the gate.

On the other side, a tall, broad-shouldered woman with high, curly hair held a scanner and asked if Ezra would kindly stretch out his arms and legs. 'Jury duty?' she asked, passing across his chest.

'Sorry – ah no.'

'Get into some trouble then, did ya?'

'What? No, I –'

She laughed and stepped away. 'I'm just teasing, mate. You can lower your arms now.'

He collected his wallet, keys and phone.

'Don't forget to bow to the judge,' she said with a smile.

Bow? Was that right, or was she still taking the piss? He couldn't remember anything about court procedure from law school.

Maybe this was a mistake. He was so damn jumpy already, and there was no guarantee that Tegan would even be there. But if he left now, he'd have to pass that security guard again, listen to some other smart-arse comment – better if he pressed on.

At the registry, he was told the sentencing hearing was taking place in Court 7-2, Judge William O'Connor presiding.

Outside the courtroom, on the seventh floor, were rows of plastic chairs, the kind you'd find at the airport or a doctor's waiting area. The door to the courtroom was plain, light-brown wood with a slit of window – pragmatic. He'd been picturing ornate, golden-handled double doors, glistening with varnish.

He walked up to the door, thinking he'd peer through the glass and assess the situation without committing to go in. But when he did, Ezra saw that the judge was already seated and then he swore that he'd caught his eye, so Ezra opened the door, and not knowing if he was making an arse of himself or not, bowed like he was in *The Karate Kid*.

The judge's bench was an elevated slab of long panelled wood. A young woman wearing a black robe sat at a smaller bench in front of the judge, and in front of her was a ground-level desk where another robed woman and a man sat flanked by suited men. Ezra had expected the room to be bursting with the university students he'd seen on TV, calls of 'Order in the court' by the judge as he pounded his gavel, but instead a dozen casually dressed people peppered grey plastic chairs in what must have been the public gallery.

The judge wasn't wearing a wig – he was bald. But he did have on a black gown, lined with purple. It had a thick white collar, the ends of which hung down to his chest like exaggerated cartoon rabbit teeth. If he wasn't before, the judge was definitely looking at Ezra now, as he finished bowing and stood idle by the door.

Shit. Should he not have bowed? Was he even in the right place? He couldn't see Tegan anywhere. Maybe he had it wrong. Maybe he didn't know her as well as he thought. There was an apology on his lips, and he'd half-turned back to the door, when he spotted her on the far side of the public gallery. Her suit had sharp shoulders and pinstripes – was that new? Her hair was tied back, no more fringe, and she was wearing glasses with bold red rims. She smiled and waved to him.

Ezra made his way over to her. 'It's good to see –'

'Shhh.' Tegan pointed up at the judge.

The rebuke made him want to cower in his seat, but then Tegan reached over and squeezed his hand.

The judge picked up a stack of papers and leant towards a microphone in front of him. 'Mr Hirsch, please remain seated until I ask you to stand.'

Ezra hadn't recognised Rabbi Hirsch, standing next to the man in robes at the long table. The picture news reports had been using showed Hirsch with a full brown beard, and his large frame straining against a black kaftan. But this grey bearded, listless-eyed man looked shrunken in a suit at least two sizes too large for him.

'Mr Joel Hirsch, on 15 July 2019, a jury of your peers found you guilty of three charges of sexual penetration of a child. Each of the charges carries a maximum penalty of fifteen years' imprisonment. You pleaded not guilty, and you have a right to do so, but subsequently you will not be afforded the benefits from an indication of remorse that a guilty plea would have demonstrated. On the evidence and consistent with the jury's finding of guilty I am satisfied that the offences were committed in the following circumstances:

'At the time of your offending in the year 1999, Mr Hirsch, you were aged forty, two of the victims were aged twelve and one thirteen. You knew each of the victims as a result of your teaching position at the Yahel Academy where you taught for nearly a decade. Each of the victims portrayed a lack of social skills and a predilection towards isolation that limited their interaction with fellow students and increased their dependence on and, without doubt, their vulnerability to yourself as their teacher. In each circumstance, you used your position to garner their trust and take advantage of them sexually.

'Each of the victims were led by you to a concealed location where you penetrated them until ejaculation. Regarding the sexual assault of Moishe Kliger, a child with established learning difficulties, you invited him to your home under the pretence of providing additional teaching support. When alone, however, you proceeded to . . .'

God – Ezra felt sick. How could someone do those things to a child? It was all too much. He tried to focus on something else, the lines of his palms, the whorls of his fingertips, a mole on his arm that might have changed shape, anything but the words of the judge echoing throughout the courtroom.

'. . . the long-term consequences of these offences, for each of the victims and their families, have been more than significant. On the whole, I have taken into account the sentencing practices at the time of your offending, your psychiatric history, the counselling you have received in the past and the major depressive disorder with which you have been diagnosed. I have further noted the attention your prosecution has garnered in the public and media and the subsequent impact this has had on your reputation, both inside and out of your community. Against these matters, I have balanced the severity of your offences, and the importance of general deterrence in cases of sexual offending against children.

'Mr Hirsch, if you would now please stand.' Hirsch stood uneasily from his seat. 'On Charge One, sexual penetration of a child, you will be convicted and sentenced to four-and-a-half years' imprisonment. On Charge Two, sexual penetration of a child, you will be convicted and sentenced to three-and-a-half years' imprisonment. On Charge Three, sexual penetration of a child, you will be convicted and sentenced to four years' imprisonment.

'In accordance with the principle of totality, I must have regard to your period of home detention in Israel where you were remanded for a period of five years. and I find that I am obliged to moderate to some extent this sentence to meet the totality principle. Taking that into account, you are sentenced to serve a total effective period of seven years. I direct a minimum term of three years and two months to be served before eligibility for parole.'

The formalities followed – copy of the order, sex offenders register, signature – a blur of administration, and then the judge stood and bowed. 'Adjourn the court.'

Everyone stood. Beside Ezra, Tegan leant over the gallery divider, her head bobbing back and forth, looking for someone. Avraham Kliger, most likely. She probably wanted to see his reaction, tell him his fury was justified, that he had an ally in her and countless others who believed in his cause – but if Avraham was there to hear the sentence, he had already disappeared.

Tegan turned to Ezra. 'Can you believe that shit? How many lives did that man ruin? How many years did he take from those boys, and he gets three bloody years!'

Ezra didn't know what to say. Three years. None of it made any sense.

'Come on,' Tegan said. 'Let's get out of here, before I get myself into trouble with that judge.'

Wordlessly, they exited the County Court and, without consultation, walked in the direction of Flagstaff Gardens visible a block away. Tegan's fingers tapped restlessly on her legs as they walked.

'It's just so fucking ridiculous,' Tegan said. 'We have all these laws and committees and inquiries – standards we say we're going to uphold. We say we're going to be progressive and equitable, but the inherent structure of our society was developed by the powerful, the abusers, to protect themselves. This shit . . .' She gestured back to the court. 'It's embedded, and I just . . .' Tegan sighed. 'I don't know. Sometimes I feel like we just need to start over.'

Ezra had heard that kind of resignation from Tegan before but despite her lapses into pessimism, he knew she wasn't capable of giving up. Deep down, she believed in people, even if they didn't deserve it. After all, she'd believed in him.

'Every time I expect the worst,' Tegan said, 'and yet every time I'm still surprised when my expectations are met. You'd think I'd learn.' She shook her head and let out a short, frustrated laugh.

'I'd say that just means you're an eternal optimist,' Ezra said.

They entered the gardens. 'Forever destined for disappointment,' Tegan said, shielding her eyes from the low-lying sun.

Disappointment? Was that a reference to him, everything he'd put her through? Not knowing how to respond, Ezra stayed quiet, in step with Tegan, who veered from the path to a spot where the grass was split into shadow and sunlight. Tegan plonked herself down, half-shaded, half-bright.

Ezra sat beside her. He felt a need to break the silence between them, but wasn't quite sure how – where to begin?

'I wasn't sure you'd come,' Tegan said. 'I'm glad you did, though.' She smiled.

Ezra smiled back and looked at Tegan's hand splayed in the sunlight. He had an urge to cover it with his own, but he didn't. 'I like your hair,' he said.

'Thanks.' She placed her hand on her forehead. 'Thought I'd show off my five-head.'

Ezra laughed. It was time – while the moment was amiable and the verdict wasn't at the forefront of her mind. Why else had he come? 'So, how's it going? How have you been?'

'Oh you know, grant applications, Senate inquiries, stakeholder conferences, hardly a moment to myself – the usual.'

Ezra nodded. 'But other than work – how are things?'

'Oh –' Tegan gave him a weak smile and pulled at the grass by her feet. 'I'm getting there. It hasn't been the easiest since . . . but I'm going to be all right . . . really.' She smiled again, one she was able to hold up. 'How about you?'

'I'm good.' He paused for a moment to consider what he'd just said – he meant it, possibly for the first time. 'I took some time off work. Thought I should try and figure things out. I've been talking to someone, professionally, and it's helped a lot. I'm probably the best I've been in a long time.'

'Oh – glad to hear it,' Tegan said. She ducked her head and tore at some more strands of grass.

Right, of course – he'd basically just said he was better off without her. He'd left too much unsaid, and he owed her a lot more than that. 'Hey, listen, I wanted to . . .' Tegan turned to him, eyes light and warm, kind and gentle. 'I'm learning more about myself every day. And while I still get anxious and sad and scared, I think I'm beginning to understand why, but that's no excuse for how I was when we . . .'

He shook his head. 'I should've done a better job of letting you know how I was feeling while we were together. I let everything build up to the point of bursting, and even when it started to bubble over, I kept you at bay. And I know it must have hurt to be shut out like that when all you wanted was to help, and I knew it then too. It wasn't right, and you didn't deserve to be treated like that. No-one deserves to be treated like that.'

Tegan spun from him. Her shoulders shook. 'Tegan, are you –'

'I'm fine.' She turned back to him, wiped her cheek. 'Really, Ez.' She reached over and took hold of his hand. 'But thanks, means a lot.'

They stayed like that for a minute or so, holding hands on the damp grass and looking into the distance, and for Ezra it was nice to be touched again, and it was comfortable and familiar and warm, but he'd stopped wishing things could be different, so he let go of Tegan's hand and sat up. 'So, what's next?' he asked.

'What do you mean?'

'You know. Where to from here?'

'Oh, you know. There's been rumours about a federal Royal Commission into family violence. If we could convince them of the need to amend the Family Law Act – I mean, there's a real chance we can . . . what? Why are you smirking like that?'

'See,' Ezra said. 'Eternal optimist.'

Tegan laughed. 'Maybe you're right. I'm doomed, aren't I?'

'Absolutely.'

'How about you?' Tegan said. 'What's next?'

'Not completely sure, to be honest.' Ezra's eyes trailed a kelpie running beside its owner, off-lead. 'I've been thinking some space might do me some good. My department has some regional offices. Maybe Geelong or Bendigo, somewhere green. Get a dog, maybe grow something.'

'Oh, Ez,' Tegan said with a wide smile. 'That sounds like a great plan.'

They stayed in the gardens, for Ezra couldn't say how long. He caught Tegan up on Baz's antics, and she on her office gossip – Lydia was pregnant. Tegan told him she'd finally convinced their old landlord to replace the split-system air conditioner, and they reminisced about the carefully worded emails they'd drafted together, fuelled by wine and a lack of feeling in their toes. It was good and it was easy between them, as it had been in the beginning, though this time there was the warmth of shared nostalgia and the slight marring of a delicate sadness. Ezra didn't notice the encroaching shadow until the spot they were sitting in was dark, and Tegan was rubbing her arms and checking her phone for the time.

'I'd better get going,' she said. 'It was good to see you, Ez.'

So that was it. It felt sudden, but that was how things always felt when you didn't want them to end, wasn't it? 'It was good to see you too.'

Together, they stood. Ezra held out his arms, and Tegan stepped into them, fitting into the hollow of him perfectly. They pulled apart, and Ezra watched Tegan walk away until she faded into the dying light of the day, and then he gathered his bearings and also walked, taking the nearest path towards home.

Acknowledgements

This book is a work of fiction but along with countless books, articles and other texts, the materials made available by the 2013 Royal Commission into Institutional Responses to Child Sexual Abuse were an invaluable resource in its development.

I'd like to thank everyone at Penguin Random House that helped make this dream a reality, with special thanks to Patrick Mangan for his editing prowess and Justin Ractliffe for believing in this book from day one. I'd also like to thank Akin Akinwumi for placing my words in Justin's capable hands.

Thank you as well to Kill Your Darlings for shortlisting the book for their unpublished manuscript award, and to the Copyright Agency and Varuna for the digital residency which encouraged me to refine the manuscript. I'd also like to give a special mention to Rebecca Starford for her kind words and thoughtful assessment of an early version of this book.

Some early chapters of this book were drafted with the benefit of a fellowship from the Katharine Susannah Prichard Writers' Centre for which I'll forever be grateful.

Thank you to Irma Gold and Patrick Mullins who encouraged me throughout my time at the University of Canberra even though I was often obnoxious and stubborn and incorrigible.

Special thanks to John Safran and James Bradley for reading advance copies and being so generous with their words.

Thank you to Imogen Oakes for reading early chapters with the kind, generous and brilliant eye she applies to everything.

To my former Bath Spa coursemates, Gemma Reeves and James Farrell, for applying their keen literary minds to those early chapters as well. And again, to you both, for your friendship during my year abroad – I miss those days and think of them often.

To my supervisor at Bath Spa, Maggie Gee. Endless thank yous, Maggie. Your belief lifted me up and this book is the result.

To my friends, Vlad, Nat, Guy and Bobby – apologies for what I put you through while writing this book and apologies in advance for all of the books to come.

And to Candice for everything, all of the time, words aren't enough.